MR MOONLIGHT

Ben Cheetham

Cover designed by thecovercollection.com

This book is a work of fiction. Names, characters, places, and incidents either are products of the author's imagination or are used fictitiously. Any resemblance to actual persons, living or dead, events, or locales is entirely coincidental.

Visit my website at www.bencheetham.com

Printed in the United Kingdom

First Printing: December 2019

ISBN-13 978-1-6739551-4-9

PROLOGUE

2005

When Christine and Julian arrived at the house, the dining-room had been made ready for communing with the dead. Thick curtains shut out the early evening light. Six candles encircled a bowl of steaming soup in the centre of the oval dining-table. There were three chairs – two on one side of the table, one on the other. In front of each chair, a little mound of salt dotted the table's dark, polished surface. The house was bathed in the mouth-watering aroma of freshly baked bread. Alice was busy in the kitchen, removing a loaf from the oven and drumming her slender fingers against its golden brown underside.

"What are you doing, Grandma?" asked Julian.

Alice smiled down at him, her heavily made-up face wrinkling like an overripe peach. "Checking to see if it's cooked through, darling. If it's done, it'll make a sound like tapping on an empty box." A mischievous gleam flickered in her luminous blue eyes. "Or like the echo of a spirit's voice."

"Mum," Christine said in a rebuking tone.

"What? Well, it's true." Satisfied by what she heard, Alice took the bread into the dining-room and put it beside the soup.

"What's the food for?" asked Julian.

"It's to help attract the spirit we want to contact. You see, darling, the spirits of the dead get hungry just like we do."

"Mum," Christine snapped again. "How many times do I have to tell you? I don't want you talking about this stuff to him."

1

"Oh for goodness sake, Christine, he's ten-years-old. You knew everything there is to know about my business by the time you were his age and it didn't do you any harm."

"I had nightmares for years."

Alice wafted her hand dismissively. "You shouldn't coddle the child, Christine. There's nothing worse than an over-coddled child."

Lips compressing into a tight line, Christine grabbed Julian's hand and pulled him towards the front door. "Where are you going?" asked Alice.

"Home. If you'd told us you were holding a séance today, we wouldn't have come in the first place."

"Oh come now, Christine, there's no need for that." Alice's voice was suddenly contrite. "Please, I've been looking forward to your visit all week. I hardly ever get to see you and Julian anymore."

Puckers of uncertainty formed around Christine's eyes. "OK, Mum," she sighed. "But you've got to promise me you won't go filling Julian's head with your mumbo-jumbo."

A twitch of irritation passed over Alice's face at the word *mumbo-jumbo*, then her smile slid back into place. "Whatever you say, darling." She made a mouth-zipped gesture.

Christine closed her eyes, massaging her forehead. "Are you getting one of your headaches?" asked Alice.

"I'm fine."

"You don't look it. You look wiped out. Why don't you go and lie down? I'll keep an eye on Julian." As the lines of uncertainty found their way back onto Christine's face, Alice added, "Don't worry, I'll send him up to you as soon as things get under way."

"Aw, do I have to go upstairs?" Julian groaned. "There's no telly up there."

"You'll do as you're told, young man, or your father will hear about it," Christine warned him. "Do you understand?"

2

Julian nodded sullenly.

"Don't worry, darling, the séance shouldn't last more than an hour," said Alice. "Then you can watch whatever you want all evening."

Christine wearily plodded upstairs. Near the top, she turned to call down to Julian, "Stay out of the dining-room. I don't want you messing around in there."

Alice put her arm around his shoulder. "You can help me in the kitchen. I'm making your favourite – chocolate cake."

His face brightening, Julian followed her back into the kitchen. She handed him a whisk and a bowl of cake mixture. "Give that a good whisk."

He did so until his wrist ached, while Alice lined two cake tins with well-buttered paper. "That looks just about perfect," she said, taking the bowl back and spooning its contents into the tins. She gave him the spoon to lick clean, which he did with relish.

Julian watched with big curious eyes as Alice buzzed around the kitchen, humming to herself. Once or twice he opened his mouth, but snapped it shut again with a click. "Grandma," he began sheepishly at last, then fell silent, chewing his lip, as if he'd been about to say something he shouldn't.

She gave him a knowing, amused glance. "Yes, darling, what is it?"

"I was wondering…" Julian chewed his lip a little more, working up the nerve to continue, "Whose ghost are you going to speak to today?"

"We say spirit, not ghost," Alice corrected. "And we're not supposed to talk about this, Julian."

"I won't get scared."

"I know you won't, but I promised your mum." Smiling, Alice reached to stroke Julian's freckled cheek. "Someday, darling, you'll find out that there's a great big world beyond this town, but not today. Now go on, go watch television."

Julian mooched into the living-room and switched on the cartoons. A short time later, there was a knock at the front door. Alice poked her head into the room. "They're here, you'd better go upstairs."

Julian gave out a groan, but did as he was told. His mum was asleep in the back bedroom. In the grey light filtering through the curtains, she looked washed-out, faded, like an old photograph of herself. Lately she always seemed to be tired, and she was losing weight too. Julian had asked her if she was ill. She'd assured him she wasn't, but looking at the dark smudges under her eyes and the shadows under her cheekbones, he found himself wondering if she'd lied. He couldn't believe she'd do that. She'd always told him, *Lying is the worst thing in the world, Julian. I can forgive almost anything, but not a lie.*

He lay down beside his mum. After a while, he noticed a murmur of voices from the room below. He heard his grandma's voice and a man's voice, but they were too indistinct to make out what was being said. His grandma sounded strange, a little shrill and strained, almost scared. The man's voice came in jerky spurts, as if he were being forced to speak. There was a burst of laughter. It wasn't pleasant to hear. It was a discordant, harsh sound that sent a crawling feeling across Julian's shoulders.

His mum stirred, but didn't wake. He lay perfectly still, barely breathing, listening. A powerful urge, almost a compulsion, was growing in him. He had to know what that awful voice was saying, and more than that, he had to see who it belonged to.

As quietly as possible, Julian rose and padded from the room. His heart beating so hard he felt every pulse, he crept downstairs to the dining-room door. His grandma's voice was clearly audible now. "Give them the closure they seek, give them peace," she said.

There was a brief pause, then the other voice snarled with such acid fury that Julian flinched, "What's peace? There is no peace. No fucking peace!"

"Tell them where to find Susan."

Another pause, then, "Fuck you! Fucking bitch. Slut. Dried up old cunt..."

As the voice ranted off a string of insults the likes of which Julian had never heard before, he reached for the door-handle. It felt greasy and cold in his hand as he slowly depressed it. He opened the door a crack, squinting through. In the flickering candlelight he saw a sandy-blonde haired man and a redheaded woman sat with their backs to him, hands resting palm down on the oval table. The man's head was stooped as if a heavy hand was pressing on the back of it. The woman was trembling right through her body.

Then Julian saw his grandma. Only it wasn't his grandma. The corners of her lips were drawn up into a sneering grin. Her mouth jerked open and closed. And from it, like a ventriloquist's trick, came the voice. Saliva stretched from her lips to the table top. Her nostrils were flared like those of an enraged bull. Her eyes were unrecognisable, the pupils dilated and bulging. They seemed to spit hate. They shrivelled Julian's insides with fear. He wanted to look away, but stood transfixed.

Suddenly, the eyes turned their glare on him and he fell backwards as if he'd been punched in the chest. Scrambling to his feet, he ran upstairs, no longer caring how much noise he made. He dived under the duvet and hugged his mum tightly, eyes squeezed shut, breath coming in shallow gasps. Without waking, she put out an arm to hug him back.

Julian's breathing gradually slowed and he slid into a troubled dream. He was lying in a tree-fringed grassy clearing. A naked man was looming over him. The man was skinny-limbed and chicken-chested, but with a hairy belly that sagged over his crotch. His bloodshot eyes were as huge as the full moon that haloed his bald round head. As he bent towards Julian, his lips peeled back from crooked teeth.

Julian tried to squirm away from him, but his body was heavy and immobile. His stomach lurched queasily. The man's breath stank like rotten meat. He sniffed at Julian as if trying to identify his scent. A grotesquely long tongue unfurled from the man's mouth and slithered across Julian's cheek. Julian squirmed and whimpered at the rough, wet feel of it.

The man's hands clamped onto Julian's throat, digging deep into his flesh. Tears sprang into Julian's eyes. He tried to scream, but all that came out was a thin squeal. His head felt like a balloon inflated to bursting-point. The man's face began to blur and melt into darkness. Julian felt himself stop breathing. He felt himself die. Then he awoke, screaming and screaming and screaming.

Christine's eyes snapped open. "What's going on?" she gasped. "What's the matter? Julian, calm down and tell me–" She broke off as the door swung open and Alice staggered into view.

Alice was pale and sweaty. Her make-up had run in ghoulish streaks. Her eyes were her own again, but clouded and distant, as if seeing through a veil of pain and fear. "Mr Moonlight knows Julian's here," she cried, clinging to the door as if she would fall over otherwise.

"What are you talking–" Christine started to say, then her features hardened into a frown of realisation. "What have you done, Mum? Tell me," she demanded.

"There's no time. You must leave right away. Go. Get out!"

Putting her arm around Julian and pressing his face into her shoulder, Christine shepherded him from the room. She paused by her mum, glaring at her with something close to detestation. "I don't know what's gone on here. But I do know one thing – if you've done any lasting harm to Julian, I'll never forgive you. I'll cut you out of our life forever. Do you hear? Am I coming through the ether loud and clear, you selfish old witch?" Without waiting for a response, she hurried Julian downstairs and out of the house.

CHAPTER 1

2019

Julian stared down at his hands. They were trembling ever so slightly. He lifted his eyes to a slim, fifty-something woman sitting opposite him in an armchair. A pen and notepad rested on her lap. Shoulder-length silver hair framed her calm features. A certificate on the wall identified her as 'Gail Weeks. Chartered Psychologist'.

Gail returned Julian's gaze as if waiting for him to speak. He ran his tongue uncertainly over his lips. "I…" he began, but fell silent, closing his eyes. They snapped back open as if he didn't like what he saw in the darkness behind his eyelids.

"It's OK, Julian," Gail reassured him. "This is a safe space. There's no judgement. Whatever you say here, will remain here."

He shook his head as if to say, *No it's not OK*. Drawing in a deep breath, he tried again. "The dream has changed. I'm in the forest and it's a full moon as usual, but now I'm not lying on the ground. I'm standing over a woman. She's about my age. Blonde, pretty. Or at least she would be pretty if her face wasn't all twisted with fear. I recognise her. She's Susan Simmons."

"The girl whose parents took part in the séance?"

Julian nodded, grimacing faintly at the mention of *that* night. "She's staring up at me with these big, terrified eyes. I want to tell her she has nothing to be afraid of, but I know that's not true. She does have something to be afraid of." He touched his chest. "Me. Because there's this feeling inside me. It's hard to describe, it's like I've been taken over by…" he strove to find the word, "*something*. And before I know it, my hands are on her throat. I'm strangling her and she's making this awful rasping sound and her eyes look like they're going to pop out of their sockets..."

He trailed off into silence, blinking away from his therapist's gaze, his eyes tortured by the memory of the dream.

"Would you like a glass of water?" asked Gail.

Julian shook his head. "There's more." His voice was quiet with shame. "As Susan's dying, I feel her strength leaving her and coming into me. But it's not enough. I want more. I want everything she's got. So I tear open her throat with my teeth. Hot blood gushes out. I rub it all over myself, then look up at the moon and howl like a wild animal. I don't care if anyone hears. I'm Mr Moonlight. I'm invincible."

A moment of silence passed. Julian's gaze returned to Gail's. "What's wrong with me?"

"Post-Traumatic Stress Disorder," she stated. "You display many of the classic symptoms – nightmares, avoidant behaviour, overwhelming feelings of guilt and shame."

Julian's features twitched with doubt. "Sometimes I feel like there really is something out there trying to..." He faded off as if wary of saying what was in his mind.

"Trying to what? To hurt you? To get inside you and make you do terrible things?"

Julian made no reply, but his haunted eyes confirmed that the psychologist's words had hit the mark on both counts.

"OK, Julian," continued Gail. "Let's look at this logically. Since witnessing the séance, you've had a recurring dream that you're being strangled to death by Mr Moonlight. Now the dream has changed. There's nothing unusual in that. In fact, it would be more unusual if the dream always remained the same. Yes, this new dream is even more disturbing to you, but it's simply another expression of your worries and fears. In a way, you're right, something has taken control of you. How long has it been since you saw your mother? I mean in the flesh, not on FaceTime."

Another grimace pulled at Julian's lips. "Four years ago when she came to my graduation. That was the last time she was well enough to travel. I spoke to her last Monday. She sounded..." a hitch came into his voice, "worse."

Gail spread her hands as if to say, *Well there you go.* "Really it's no wonder you feel as if you've lost control of your life. Your mother is seriously ill, but your PTSD prevents you from seeing her, which leads to frustration and anger, which in turn leads to more nightmares. It's a vicious cycle."

"So how do I break the cycle?"

"I think you know the answer to that question, Julian. It's natural to avoid things that frighten us, but sometimes this does more harm than good. The more you run away from what happened at your grandma's, the deeper you sink into PTSD. You have to find the courage to face your fears."

Julian's lips compressed into pale lines. He could feel cold sweat prickling his palms at the mere thought of returning to his hometown.

"I'm not suggesting you leave here and go charging straight to your grandma's house," said Gail. "We need to come up with a plan to manage your fears. And when you're ready, we'll put the plan into action. OK?"

Blowing out his cheeks, Julian nodded.

Gail smiled. "I can imagine how upsetting this new dream is, but I think it's a positive development. Things are finally moving forwards. You're confronting the trauma and it hurts. But that's OK. Sometimes we have to be willing to hurt in order to heal."

"Hurt in order to heal," Julian parroted with as much determination as he could muster.

Gail glanced at her wristwatch. "We'll have to leave it there. I'll see you same time next week."

Thanking the psychologist, Julian rose to leave. Gail's office was on the ground floor of a house set back from a busy road. Julian got into a VW parked in the driveway and edged into the traffic. As he crawled along congested streets, he wound down his window and listened to the sounds of the city, letting them soothe away the chattering of his mind.

He parked in a gloomy subterranean car park and caught a lift to the twelfth floor of the tower block where he lived. He stood at his floor-to-ceiling living-room window, staring out at London's anonymous sprawl. Here his past didn't matter. Here people didn't look at him and see the grandson of that crazy witch Alice Stearne.

His grandma's fear-filled voice echoed back to him through the years – *Mr Moonlight knows Julian's here!* He touched a hand to his throat at a familiar tightening sensation. Not for the first time since the new dream had assaulted him, he found himself wondering, *Could you ever do that to someone?* He shook his head hard. Of course not. It was like Gail had said – the dream had changed because he was facing his fears.

But Grandma Alice's voice continued to reverberate in his mind – *Mr Moonlight knows Julian's here. He wants to hurt him.*

He shook his head again. His mind was embellishing. Grandma Alice had never said that last part.

He wants to make him hurt others.

"She never said that either," Julian retorted like a challenge. "Anyway, whatever she said has no power over me. She's just an old fraud."

He went through to a bedroom whose blank walls and bland furniture were as devoid of personality as the living-room. Without bothering to undress, he flopped onto the bed. Talking to Gail always left him mentally and physically drained. Sleep tugged at him. He resisted it for a while, but the tugging became too insistent. Closing his eyes, he meditated as Gail had taught him, emptying his mind, transforming it into a blank space.

The dream came anyway.

Susan's baby-blue eyes were swollen and wet. He inhaled her scent – floral perfume and something else far sweeter. His blood quickened, pulsing in his temples. Horrified at what he was doing, he licked her face, tasting her. She shuddered and struggled, but his hands were on her throat like steel pincers. Then he was frenziedly tearing at her throat with his teeth, seeking out its veins and arteries. Oh the blood! He bathed in it like a pig in muck. The pulsing intensified to a thundering, so powerful it shook his body. Chest heaving, he rose and stared down at Susan's mutilated corpse. It was as if he was seeing her from a great height. She was an ant and he was a giant. A god!

He awoke soaked in sweat, his head reeling as if he'd downed a bottle of whisky. He made it to the toilet just in time to vomit. When the retching finally subsided, he rinsed out his mouth and returned to bed. He couldn't bring himself to close his eyes. The thought of the dream sent shivers of revulsion through him. When he couldn't bear to lie there with his thoughts any longer, he got up and made a cup of tea. He drank it on the sofa, numbing himself with the visual Valium of television.

He was still sitting there when the first pink fingers of dawn slid through the blinds. He showered, shaved and put on a suit and tie. He made his way to the front door, but stopped short of it, his stomach gurgling ominously. The prospect of spending the next eight or nine hours at his desk was almost enough to send him running for the toilet again. He scrolled through his phone's contacts to 'Angus'. He let out a little breath of relief when the call went through to voicemail. "Hi Angus. It's Julian. I'm afraid I won't be coming into the office today. Stomach upset. Sorry. Bye."

He hung up and switched off his phone in case Angus called him back. Pulling off his tie, he returned to the sofa and resumed mindlessly channel-surfing. His finger stopped suddenly over the remote controller. He leant forward with a deep cleft between his eyebrows.

'GIRL MISSING IN THE TOWN OF GODTHORNE' ran the headline at the bottom of the screen. A female reporter was standing in front of a sign that read 'GODTHORNE HIGH SCHOOL'. Julian recognised the boxy brick building in the background only too well. He'd spent seven years of his life cooped up inside it.

"Police are gravely concerned by the disappearance of Chloe Crawley," the reporter was saying. "The fifteen-year-old was last seen leaving school at approximately 3:30 p.m. on Tuesday the 23rd of July. This afternoon, Chief Inspector Tom Henson appealed for help."

The camera cut to a stocky, middle-aged man with short dark hair and a handsome face running to fat. "Chloe, if you're watching this, you're not in trouble," he began in a matter-of-fact voice. "Please contact the police or your parents as soon as you can. Your parents are extremely concerned and want to make sure you're safe. I would also like to appeal for members of the public who have any information whatsoever regarding Chloe's disappearance to contact the police."

A photo appeared on-screen of a young girl with reddish-purple bangs hanging into her smoky grey eyes. A silver chain with black beads looped from her right earlobe to her corresponding nostril. A silver stud in her lower lip accentuated an anaemic emo-kid pout. "This is the most recent photo of Chloe we have," said the reporter. "However, she is known to have dyed her hair blonde just days before she went missing."

A phone number flashed up. "And you can contact the police on this number," continued the reporter. Her faux-grave face returned to the screen. "Perhaps inevitably, Chloe's disappearance has stirred up memories of the shocking events that occurred here in Godthorne some fifteen years ago. Back then the town was subjected to a reign of terror by Kenneth Whitcher, the brutal killer dubbed Mr Moonlight. Whitcher murdered five teenage girls and young women from Godthorne and the surrounding area before his capture in July 2005. He committed suicide in Belmarsh Prison five months later. The fear here is that Chloe's disappearance could mark a return to those dark days."

Julian switched the television off in disgust. Drawing a spurious connection between the murders and Chloe Crawley's disappearance was the worst kind of sensationalism.

But what if the connection isn't spurious? piped up a voice at the back of his mind.

"Whitcher hanged himself in his cell," Julian replied out loud. "He's been dead nearly fourteen years."

But the questioning voice refused to be silenced. *What about your dream? Only days after the dream changes, a girl goes missing.*

"So what? What could one thing possibly have to do with the other? It's just coincidence."

But what if it's not? What if it's not?

Julian pressed his hands to his ears as if to block out the nagging voice. It was ridiculous, totally absurd. Whitcher was long dead. "He can't hurt you or anyone else," he told himself. "The dreams are nothing but PTSD. You and only you have the power to take control of your life."

So do it. Take control.

"I will!"

With a sudden decisive movement, Julian rose and went into the bedroom. He flung some clothes and toiletries into a bag, then left the flat and caught the lift down to his car. He started the engine, but hesitated to accelerate away as his grandma's voice filled his mind again.

Mr Moonlight knows Julian's here!

"I'm done listening to you, Grandma. I refuse to be afraid anymore," he shot back, but his palms were slippery on the steering-wheel as he pulled out of the car park.

CHAPTER 2

Julian headed south-east out of the city, following signs for the M3. Housing estates gave way to light industrial estates, then flat fields. A leaden sky made the scenery look lifelessly drab. The further he got from London, the more the traffic eased off. The motorway curved south, passing the outskirts of Farnborough, Basingstoke and Winchester. The Sat Nav informed him it was thirty minutes to his destination. He took a deep breath and tried to exhale away the knot of tension in his stomach.

He left behind the motorway for an A-road overhung by oak, ash, beech and elm trees. He passed a sign with 'New Forest' on it. Stretches of dense woodland were interspersed with fields grazed by sturdy chestnut and grey ponies. The sun broke through, dappling the road. Julian's heart lifted. He lowered the window and inhaled the cool green scent of the forest.

He loved the forest. He loved its sights, sounds and smells. But most of all he loved its secrecy. His mind drifted back to the countless hours he and his childhood friends had spent hacking their way through its thick undergrowth of bracken and bramble, exploring its darkest recesses. They'd pretended to be outlaws, building secret hideouts, starting fires, setting rabbit snares. And as teenagers, they'd got drunk, stoned and – if they hit jackpot – popped their cherries in its furtive gloom.

Mile after mile of forest did more than any amount of therapy to soothe away Julian's tension. In places the wide-spreading branches formed a tunnel that enclosed the road. He emerged from one such tunnel at a green Forestry Commission sign for 'FOXWOOD'.

Julian's stomach tied itself into knots again. A single-lane gravel track curved away from the main road into the trees. A police car blocked the turn off. A constable was waving on rubbernecking drivers.

Did it have something to do with Chloe Crawley? What else could it be? Perhaps they'd found her. Foxwood had always been a favourite partying spot for local teens. The knot cinched tighter as an image rose into his mind of Chloe lying bloody and mutilated amidst the trees.

"Only you have the power to take control of your life," he told himself. "There's nothing to be afraid of. You have to hurt to heal. Hurt to heal. Hurt to heal…" The image faded as he focussed on the mantra.

A mile or so further along the road, he came to a sign that proclaimed 'Welcome to Godthorne'. Beyond it, the forest suddenly opened up.

To the left of the road, the manicured fairways of 'The Forest Golf Club' butted up against the trees. A faint frown touched Julian's face. He'd spent many reluctant Saturdays caddying the course for his dad in return for a few quid of pocket money. *You have to work for everything in this life, Julian.* That had been – and still was – his dad's mantra. Julian had begrudgingly taken the words on board, along with an abiding hatred of golf.

To the right, beyond a sign for 'Hope Road', was an estate of maisonettes with communal lawns. The maisonettes had the cheerless look of council properties. The line between Julian's eyes deepened as he recalled how he and his mates had used to sneer at kids from the estate, calling them No-Hopers. He gave a shake of his head. Christ, what a stuck-up little prick he'd been.

A group of people at the roadside were handing out fliers to passing motorists. Julian braked, lowering his window to take one from a pale, skinny girl with a swirl of black hair hanging down almost over her eyes.

Looking at him with a searching intensity that made him want to blink, she asked, "Have you seen this girl?"

Chloe's pouting face stared out of the flier. 'MISSING' was printed beneath it in blood-red lettering. And beneath that was a brief paragraph – 'Chloe Crawley has been missing since the 23rd of July 2019. Her parents and the police are concerned for her safety. If you've seen her or have any information regarding her, please contact us on the number below.'

"No. Sorry," said Julian.

He drove on, passing a sign for 'Hampshire Constabulary. Godthorne Police Station'. A broad driveway approached a rectangular, two-storey brick building whose couple of dozen windows looked watchfully towards the council estate. The station's carpark was crammed with vehicles. Amongst them were TV news vans with satellite dishes perched on their roofs. Reporters were milling around at the station's entrance. Was there going to be a press-conference? Did they have something to announce?

The stomach-churning image of Chloe threatened to force its way back into Julian's mind. As if trying to outrun it, he put his foot down on the accelerator, passing a motley collection of thatched Tudor cottages, Georgian and Victorian townhouses and post-WW2 semis. He slowed down at a street of three-storey terraced houses that branched off the main road.

Fresh sweat popped out on his palms as his gaze slid slowly along the street. Grandma Alice's house was at its far end. Flinching as a car behind him beeped, he accelerated towards the town centre. He wasn't ready to set eyes on his grandma's house. Not yet.

He turned onto a high-street of local shops, restaurants, cafés, pubs, banks and the like. Many of the buildings were painted white with black doors and window frames. Some were crisscrossed with uneven Tudor beams. A stone church steeple towered over the high-street. Union Jack bunting was strung above the road as if there was something to celebrate, but the people on the high-street didn't look as if they had much to be happy about. Most were going about their daily business with downcast eyes. Others were chatting in little groups. Their grim expressions made it clear what the topic of conversation was.

Julian recognised several faces. His gaze lingered on a lad in paint-splotched overalls repainting a shop's exterior. They'd been in the same school year, but they hadn't been friends. After sixth-form, most of Julian's friends had headed off to university. And after graduating, they'd gone where the jobs were, which mostly meant London. Not that they would have moved back to Godthorne even if they had they chance. After all, they'd spent their teenage years moaning about what a dead-end place it was.

He headed south out of the town centre into a leafy, affluent suburb. At the far edge of town, he turned onto a street of houses whose back gardens ended at the forest. The houses were set well back from the road behind tall hedges and fences. Pulling up to a sleek, solid wooden gate, he reached out of the window to punch a code into a keypad. The gate slid open. He drove along a tarmac driveway flanked by immaculate lawns and yews clipped into abstract shapes.

As usual, a feeling of ambivalence arose in him at the sight of the single-story, ultra-modern house of concrete, steel and glass. On the one hand, he loved the way the house's glass walls allowed the forest to penetrate to the heart of its interior. On the other, he hated it for the same reason. He could never quite get used to its openness. It made him feel exposed and vulnerable, especially on nights when a full moon shimmered over the forest where Mr Moonlight had taken his victims. As a child, he'd lain awake under his duvet on such nights, too afraid to close his eyes, but equally fearful of what he might see if he looked out of the windows.

He parked up and sat gathering himself. It wasn't simply his memories that held him in place, it was the thought of his mum. What would it be like seeing her without the filter of an iPhone screen between himself and the ravages of her illness?

After an extended moment, he got out and climbed a gentle ramp to a front door that slid, rather than swung, open. As he entered a cool, air-conditioned hallway, a black Labrador ran up to him, tail wagging.

"Hello boy. Hello Henry," said Julian, smiling as he ruffled the dog's glossy fur.

Henry trailed after him along the minimally but tastefully decorated hallway to a gleaming kitchen of stainless steel and granite. The kitchen had low work surfaces and no high cupboards. A short, thickset brunette of about fifty was chopping vegetables. She turned with a start. Her eyes widened. "Julian! You gave me a fright."

"Hello Lily."

"What are you doing here?" she asked in a rolling Hampshire burr, putting down her knife and moving to envelop him in a hug.

"I decided to pay a surprise visit."

"I'll say it's a flippin' surprise. How long's it been?"

"Too long."

Lily nodded agreement. "Let me get a proper look at you." She drew back to give him an appraising once-over. Her gaze lingered on the dark smudges under his eyes. "Why didn't you call?"

Julian blinked awkwardly, unsure how best to answer her question.

Lily's broad features softened into an understanding smile. "Well, whatever brought you home, I'm glad you're here."

A nervous edge came into Julian's voice. "Where is she?

"Where do you think?" Lily motioned with her chin towards the garden.

"How is she?" he asked hesitantly, as if afraid what the answer might be.

"She had a bad night. I told her to take it easy. Christine, I said, the garden will still be there tomorrow, but you might not be if you don't rest up. But would she listen? Would she hell. You know how she is about her precious roses. They won't prune themselves, she says. Mind you, what do I know – or the doctors, for that matter? They said she wouldn't last six months, and that was almost fourteen years ago." Lily shook her head in awe. "She's an amazing woman, your mother. A lesson to us all. How long will you be staying?"

That was another question Julian had no answer to. "I'm not sure."

"Well, don't you dare leave without us having a proper chat. I want to know all about what you've been up to in London."

Julian smiled somewhat uneasily. Lily had originally been brought in as a childminder when his mum returned to work six months after giving birth. She knew as well as anyone why there were bags under his eyes. As much as he wanted to catch up with her, he didn't relish the thought of dancing around her questions.

"I'd better go see Mum."

With Henry at his heels, Julian headed out of the back door. A series of flat, smooth paths wound their way amongst the lawns, flowerbeds, rockeries, ponds and ornamental trees. He followed one to a rose garden alive with pollen-gathering bees. Some roses were coming into bloom, others were turning brown. They exuded a sweet fragrance of life and death in the afternoon sun.

Christine was bent forward in her wheelchair, her silver bob hanging over her face. She was pinching the deadheads off with clippers clasped in her right hand. Her other hand rested in her lap, clenched like an unopened flower. Her wrists were as thin as Lily's were thick.

"I see you're still not listening to Lily," said Julian.

Stiffly, Christine straightened to look at her son. The right side of her mouth lifted into a smile, the left remained immobile, a sliver of drool sliding from it onto her chin. She reached out with her good hand to touch his arm as if to make sure he was real. Tears came into her hazel eyes as he stooped to kiss her right cheek – he could hardly bear to look at the drooping left side of her face, never mind touch it.

He took her hand in his. "Hello Mum."

"Hello you," she replied, slurring slightly.

"You look well."

"I look bloody awful," Christine said with her usual frankness. "And so do you." She studied her son's face as if examining it for symptoms of some disease. "You've lost weight."

"I've been missing Lily's cooking."

"What about your sleep?"

Christine's eyes probed Julian like fingers. He knew there was no point trying to evade her questions. The massive stroke that had consigned her to a wheelchair hadn't dulled her mind. If anything, enforced inactivity had sharpened her intellect. "I haven't been sleeping well," he said, lowering his voice as if he was admitting to something shameful. "That's partly why I'm here. My therapist thinks the best way to beat the dreams is to confront my fears."

"I think she's right."

"And I wanted to see you."

Christine nodded as if to say, *I know*. She gently squeezed Julian's hand. "I can't tell you how happy I am that you're here, Julian. Your father and I have been so worried about you."

He couldn't help but raise an eyebrow at the mention of his dad.

"What's that look about?" asked his mum. "Your father loves you very much. You know that, don't you?"

"How is he?" Julian asked evasively.

"He's been working too hard."

A sardonic smile crossed Julian's face. "I don't remember a time when he wasn't."

Christine's voice took on a faintly remonstrative edge. "I know you think your father should spend more time with me."

"He should spend *all* his time with you. It's not as if he can't afford to retire."

"Your father's never been any good around sickness. Being with me twenty-four-hours a day would kill him a hell of a lot faster than this

sodding disease is killing me. Like it or not, that's just the way it is."
Christine's lopsided smile reappeared. "Give me a hug, will you?"

Julian bent to do as his mum asked. Tears rose into his own eyes at the feel of her. She was little more than skin and bone. She held onto him as tight as her wasted muscles would permit. When she finally let go, she said with a sigh, "I needed that."

Not wanting her to see his tears, Julian turned to survey the garden. "The place looks amazing."

"It keeps me going. I don't know what I'd do without my garden." Christine inhaled the delicately perfumed air and sighed with pleasure again. "Have you had lunch?"

"No."

"Come on then. Let's get you fed."

Christine pushed the joystick on her wheelchair and the motor kicked in. Julian followed her back into the kitchen where Lily was already making him a sandwich. As he ate, Lily bombarded him with questions. How was life in London? Was he enjoying his job? And, of course, the all-important – had he found himself a girlfriend?

He answered as succinctly as possible. London was… well, it was London – hectic, noisy, expensive. The job was OK. He spent most of his time with his head buried in spreadsheets. The answer to the final question was a simple no.

Lily clicked her tongue in disapproval. "How's that possible? A handsome young bloke like you with thousands of beautiful girls to choose from? Tell you what, I'll ask my Rosie if any of her friends are single and looking for love? We'll have you set up in no time."

"Leave the poor boy alone," Christine put in with a chuckle. "I don't want you scaring him off now he's finally home."

The kitchen television was on but turned down low. Julian's eyes were drawn to the screen by a middle-aged woman as gaunt and glassy-eyed as a heroin addict. She was sitting hunched over a microphone on a long table. She was clutching a threadbare teddy bear with a heart on its stomach that read 'This is all I have to give'. At her side was the broad-shouldered, suited figure of Chief Inspector Tom Henson.

Julian reached for the controller and turned up the volume. "If there's somebody who has taken Chloe, please contact the police," pleaded the woman, her voice weak and tearful, pitiful to hear. "The family don't feel safe anymore, it's broken us apart. It makes you think you can't trust anyone, not even the people closest to you. If you have Chloe, please let her go."

"Turn it off," said Christine. When Julian did so, she added, "Sorry, but I just can't bear it."

"I take it that was Chloe Crawley's mother," said Julian.

Lily nodded. "Tracey. She looks in a right old state. Mind, it's only to be expected, poor thing."

"You know the Crawleys." It wasn't a question. Julian would have been amazed if Lily didn't know them. She was a local local – someone whose family went back generations in Godthorne. Apart from the seasonal influx of second-home owners – who were generally viewed with derision by local locals – she knew pretty much everyone in town.

"Not all that well, but well enough." Lily's tone suggested the Crawleys were not a family she saw fit to associate with.

"Do they live on the Hope Estate?"

"That's right. Why do you ask?"

Julian told her about the people handing out fliers, adding, "There were police at Foxwood. I thought they might have found a body or something."

"Found a body?" Lily echoed in horror. "Thank god they haven't. Besides, if you ask me, Chloe's not dead. She's run away somewhere. Chloe Crawley is a troubled girl."

"Do you mind if we talk about something else?" sighed Christine. Her slur was more pronounced. The left side of her lips was sagging lower, dragging her face further out of shape.

Julian and Lily exchanged a knowing glance. "It's time for your afternoon nap," said Lily. "Let's get you to bed."

Christine cast a hopeful look at Julian. "Will you be here when I wake up?"

Smiling, he nodded. His gaze followed her and Lily from the kitchen. When he was alone, he heaved a sigh. As if sensing his sadness, Henry ambled over to nuzzle and lick his hand. The tension faded from Julian's face as he scratched behind the Labrador's ears. With Henry padding at his heels, he made his way along a sterile-smelling glass corridor. His heart gave a squeeze as he entered his bedroom. Nothing had changed. The same band and movie posters papered the walls. The same trashy novels and junky trinkets occupied the bookshelves. The bed was made up as if in anticipation of his visit.

He dropped onto it. Henry curled up at his feet. Sunlight slanted hazily through a glass wall. Julian's body felt heavy and ready for sleep. He had no intention of sleeping, though.

He Googled Chloe Crawley. She had Instagram and Facebook profiles that were set to private. He scrolled down her Facebook friends list. He didn't recognise any of the names, but a photo caught his eye. It was of a girl – maybe eighteen-years-old in a sleeveless black mini-dress draped with silver bondage-style buckles. Tears of mascara streaked from her lost-looking eyes. Her tongue was stuck out, revealing a silver stud embedded in its centre. There was a matching stud in her nose and several hooped earrings in either lobe. A red rose tattoo, its thorns dripping blood, wound its way around one of her pale, slim thighs. Dozens of tiny cuts like tribal markings were visible on her inner wrists. As the cuts ran down towards her hands, they crisscrossed to form the contradictory words 'FUCK YOU' on one wrist and 'HELP' on the other.

The girl was instantly familiar, but it took Julian a few seconds to work out where he recognised her from – she'd handed him the missing person flier. Her name was listed as 'Dolor'. Her profile was also set to private. He Googled 'Dolor' and found that it was Latin for 'pain'. He lay staring at her photo. Something about it – something he couldn't quite define – held him strangely fascinated. Was she in pain because Chloe was missing? Or did she herself need help?

He sent her a friend request. Then he scrolled through his phone's contacts list to 'Kyle' and pressed dial. A surprised voice answered, "Julian, long time no hear. What has it been? Three, four years?"

"Six."

"Six!" Kyle whistled. "Shit. I can't believe it's been that long. So how's it going?"

"It's going…" Julian blew a breath between his lips. "You know."

"Yeah, I know." Kyle's tone indicated that he understood only too well where Julian was coming from.

"The reason I'm calling is I'm back in town for a few days."

"You're shitting me! I thought you were gone for good."

"I was starting to think the same thing myself. Do you still live around here?"

"Yeah, still living with my parents," Kyle admitted with a sheepish chuckle.

"Fancy meeting up for a beer?"

"Sure, it's my night off. When and where?"

"Nineish at The White Rabbit."

"I'll be there. Listen, Julian, I'd better get off the phone. I'm working."

Now it was Julian's turn to sound surprised. "Working?"

Kyle laughed again. "Yeah. Who'd have thought it, eh? So anyway, I'll see you later."

"Yeah, later."

CHAPTER 3

Julian frittered away the hours browsing the internet. The sun dipped behind the trees, dousing the room in shadow. Hearing the burr of his mum's wheelchair motor in the hallway, he rose to open the door. Sleep had restored a little colour to her cheeks. The droop of her lips wasn't quite so pronounced. He caught a flicker of relief in her eyes at the sight of him.

"I thought perhaps I'd dreamt you coming home," she said.

He smiled. "No, I'm really here."

"How long will you be staying?"

"Maybe a couple of days. If that's OK."

"Of course it's OK, darling. You're welcome to stay for as long as you want."

The smell of cooking drew Julian and Christine to the kitchen. Lily was preparing a meal. "Won't be long," she told them. "Robert phoned. He's working late."

Julian resisted the impulse to comment sarcastically, *Surprise, surprise.*

True to her word, within minutes Lily was serving up plates of steamed vegetables and fish. Julian and Lily sat facing each other with Christine at the head of the kitchen table.

Christine used a fork with a sharpened edge for cutting. She mashed her food up and ate slowly, swallowing with obvious discomfort.

"How are things at the factory?" asked Julian.

"I wouldn't know." Christine's abrupt reply suggested the question had touched a nerve. "Your father doesn't talk to me about the business. He thinks he's got to wrap me up in cotton-wool. I keep telling him, I worry more not knowing what's going on."

Julian frowned. "You make it sound as if the factory's struggling."

"Like I said, I wouldn't know."

Julian spotted Lily looking at him with wide eyes and compressed lips. Taking the hint, he changed the subject. They chatted about lighter topics – Christine's gardening projects, the mixed bag of summer weather, the cost of living in London.

Out of nowhere, Christine asked Julian, "Will you be visiting your grandma while you're here?"

He was silent for a moment, before replying, "I don't know."

"I think you should. I'll come with you, if you want."

Julian's eyebrows lifted. For months after the séance, Grandma Alice had phoned and come knocking, pleading for forgiveness. She'd met with a wall of silence. Gradually, the phone calls and knocks at the door had become less frequent, until one day they stopped altogether. He couldn't remember the last time his mum had even mentioned Grandma Alice, let alone suggested going to see her. He thought about the way he'd felt simply driving past his grandma's street. How would he react when he actually saw her house? What if he fell apart, had a panic attack? He didn't want his mum to see him like that. "Thanks, but if I go, I'll go alone."

With a nod of understanding, Christine reached to give Julian's hand an encouraging squeeze.

He helped Lily clear the table and load the dishwasher. Then Lily gave Christine her daily massage. Julian watched as she worked scented oils into his mum's back and limbs. The paralysed limbs looked like wilted vines. It was clear, though, from the way Christine grimaced as Lily pushed her hands over their slack, veiny flesh, that there was still some life in them.

Afterwards, Christine apologetically said to him, "I need to lie down for a while."

"That's OK. I've arranged to meet up with Kyle for a drink."

"Kyle?"

"He was in my school year."

"He means Kyle Hughes," put in Lily. "He works at The Swan."

"Oh yes, I remember Kyle. Polite boy."

A smile tugged at one side of Julian's mouth. 'Polite' was hardly the word he would have used to describe Kyle. Dropout, layabout or stoner would have been more apt, unless Kyle had changed drastically in the past six years.

"Don't stay out too late, Julian," said Christine. "You need a good night's sleep."

A telltale tightness seeped into Julian's expression at the mere mention of sleep. He gave his mum a quick kiss on the cheek and headed for the front door.

CHAPTER 4

The road arrowed between ranks of trees. A cloudless sky was softening into darkness. The moon would be out tonight.

A mile or so beyond the outskirts of Godthorne, Julian pulled up outside a dingy-looking pub. Rows of powerful motorbikes were parked in a cracked concrete carpark. The faded sign above the door depicted a white rabbit springing down a burrow. A sign in the window stated 'No Drugs or Nuclear Weapons allowed inside'.

As Julian opened the door, he was assaulted by ear-splitting heavy metal music. The gloomy barroom was packed with leather-clad bikers chucking back pints and shouting to make themselves heard. On a small stage, a band caked in tattoos and sweat were grinding their guitars and belting out angry lyrics. A twenty-something man with long brown hair, a devilish goatee and a faceful of piercings waved to Julian from the bar-counter.

"Shit, dude, you cut off your hair," observed Kyle, leaning in close. "You said you'd never cut it."

"Yeah well my boss told me it's the job or the hair. The job won."

Kyle shook his head sadly. "Conform or die. They should carve that above the door of every office."

Julian smiled. "You haven't changed."

"You know this town. Nothing much changes." Kyle handed Julian a bottle of beer.

Julian took a swig. "Yeah, it looks as if this dive hasn't been cleaned since the last time I was here."

"Hey, don't go slagging it off just cos you're a city boy now. For some of us, this is all we've got."

"So why don't you leave? You always used to bang on about travelling the world."

"I *did* travel the world. Europe, North America, Australia. Got together with this gorgeous Aussie in Sydney." Kyle cupped his hands in front of his chest. "Tits like rugby balls."

"Sounds amazing. Why did you come back?"

Kyle shrugged. "I just woke up one morning and thought, *It's time to go home*. That's the thing about the forest. Everyone who leaves seems to end up back here eventually. Even you."

"I'm not back for long."

"In that case we'd better hurry up and get more beers in. I'm in the mood for getting properly shit-faced."

"I'm driving."

Kyle's face creased in disgust. "Aw, what the fuck?"

"I thought maybe we could score some weed, drive out to Foxwood for a smoke. Like old times."

"Sounds good. Only we can't go to Foxwood. Haven't you heard? The coppers are there looking for that little bit of jailbait."

Julian had hoped for some such reply. His suggestion had been more about fishing for information than wishing to revisit their childhood haunt. Back at school, Kyle had been the only one of his friends who hung around with the No-Hoper kids – primarily because they'd provided him with a steady supply of weed. He had an ear to what was going down on both sides of town.

"You mean the girl who's missing," said Julian. "Do you know her?"

"Not really. I've spoken to her once or twice. She's serious trouble. She's fucked her way through half the scuzzballs in town."

"You're kidding?"

"Nope. And that's not even the worst of it. I heard she was selling it."

Julian's eyebrows pinched together doubtfully. "Bullshit. Where did you hear that?"

"Anyone who knows anything around here knows it for a fact. If you don't believe me, just ask around." Kyle chuckled. "Although I doubt you'll find many dudes willing to admit to shagging an underage prossie. I'll tell you what *is* bullshit – the way her mum keeps banging on about her being abducted. My money's on one of her customers having done her in and dumped her in a ditch."

As Kyle finished speaking, a quartet of goth-punk types, all black leather, torn drainpipe jeans, fishnet stockings, tattoos, jet black hair and heavy makeup, entered the bar. There were two late-twenties-looking men, a similar-aged woman, and the girl who Julian knew only as Dolor.

The girl looked drunk or stoned, her eyes glassy and vacant, a vacuous half-smile, half-sneer playing on her lips. She and the woman made their way around the room, passing out fliers with Chloe's face on them, while the men headed for the bar.

Julian's gaze followed the girl. Kyle nudged him. "Don't even think about going there. That's Phoebe Bradshaw. Dylan Bradshaw's twin sister."

"Who's Dylan Bradshaw?"

"A total headcase, that's who. The coppers are after him for all kinds of shit. There's a rumour going around that he's hiding out in the forest. Like we used to. Only for real."

"Do you reckon Chloe could be with him?"

"She could be, but then why would Phoebe be handing out those fliers?"

"So Phoebe and Chloe are good friends?"

"Best-buds. I used to see them around town dressed in matching Goth gear, wearing the same makeup. Twins of evil, that's what I call them. I know this guy who went with Phoebe for a while. He said she's proper crazy, said she wanted him to do all sorts of weird shit to her."

"Like what?"

"Pull her hair, slap her around, strangle her. He couldn't handle it so he dumped her."

Strangle her. Julian felt a stirring of the same nausea that had overwhelmed him after his dream. It started in his stomach and crawled, cold and slimy as a slug, up his throat. He pushed it back down with a swallow of beer.

Phoebe and the woman seated themselves at a table by the stage. They were joined by their male companions with a tray of Aftershocks. Julian watched Phoebe down two shots in quick succession. She seemed oblivious or indifferent to him staring at her, but one of the men was treating him to a none-too-friendly look.

"Come on, let's go for that smoke," suggested Kyle. "I know where we can get our hands on some primo skunk." He tugged at Julian's sleeve as the man started to stand. Julian allowed himself to be drawn away from the bar. A mocking peal of laughter followed them to the door. The sound sent a shiver through him, like he was coming down with something nasty. Glancing back, he saw that it came from Phoebe.

"Are you trying to get the shit kicked out of us?" asked Kyle.

"Who was that bloke?"

"Just some scumbag. Why are you so interested in a pair of no-marks like Chloe Crawley and Phoebe Bradshaw?"

"I'm not particularly. Doesn't it freak you out though? I mean, if what you've told me is true then... Well you expect that kind of thing to go on in a city, but not around here."

"You crack me up, Julian," laughed Kyle, shaking his head. "You really don't know diddly about this town, do you?"

CHAPTER 5

Julian closed the front door quietly and crept to the kitchen to make a sandwich. Henry pattered across the tiled floor to snuffle at his hand. Julian broke off a chunk of cheese for the Labrador, then headed for his bedroom.

"Well, well, the prodigal son returns."

The gravelly voice pulled him up abruptly at the living-room door. He turned towards a figure reclining in a leather-and-chrome armchair. The only light in the room came from the pale rays shimmering through the black glass. The figure's face was lost in shadow, but Julian knew only too well who was sat there cradling a tumbler of whisky.

"Hello Dad."

"I heard you were home, but I wouldn't have believed it without seeing it. Where've you been?"

"I met up with Kyle for a drink."

Robert leant forwards, moonlight highlighting the streaks of grey in his swept back brown hair and the craggy lines at the corners of his eyes. "Kyle Hughes? The dropout?"

Julian found himself caught between irritation and amusement. Trust his dad to say it as he saw it. The irritation won out. "He's not a dropout. He works at The Swan."

Robert shrugged as if to say, *Same difference.* "That boy could be anything he wants to be. I'll bet his parents feel sick to their stomachs."

Maybe they're just happy to see him happy, Julian resisted the temptation to reply. "How come you're still up?"

Robert raised his glass. "Just winding down after a hard day's work. That OK with you?"

There was a defensive edge to the question. Robert was well aware of Julian's opinions on him working late. A silent moment passed. Julian let slip a sigh. This was the way it always was between them. They'd exchange a few words about this and that, but they never *really* talked. Not when it was just the two of them. There was a distance there, a deadness. Christine was their conduit, the only person who could make them connect. The current of her emotion conducted life between them. In her presence they chatted, laughed, argued and cried, they were father and son. Without her, they were like two halves of a severed wire.

Robert motioned to the sofa. "Sit down. Eat your sandwich."

The weed had given Julian the munchies, but the conversation had killed his appetite. He found himself looking into the darkness beyond the windows, wondering if Dylan Bradshaw was really hiding in the forest. He imagined himself in Dylan's situation, sleeping under the stars, moving camp every few days to avoid detection. The idea appealed to something within him that longed for a secret place away from the reality of daily life, away from the pressures of family and work.

"No thanks. I think I'm just going to go..." Julian trailed off. The plan had been to get stoned enough to pass out the instant his head hit the pillow, but a tingle of tension had replaced the pleasant heaviness in his limbs. To get the heaviness back would require the spliff in his pocket. "I'm going out for a walk."

"A walk?" Robert's tone was tinged with disapproval. "It's past midnight. You'll get yourself into trouble going out walking at this time. Look at this Crawley girl business."

"Lily reckons she's just run away."

"Let's hope Lily's right, but until we know for certain it's best to err on the side of caution."

"Even if she's wrong, I'm pretty sure whoever took Chloe won't be out looking for twenty-four-year-old men to abduct."

Robert swiped his hand towards the door. "Oh do what you bloody want, Julian. You always do anyway."

Julian continued to look at his dad for a moment. *Do you know what it's taken for me to come back here?* he felt like retorting, but he would only be wasting his breath. His dad was a self-made man. He'd built his business out of nothing. He had no time for mental frailty. Julian sometimes got the impression that his dad wondered how he'd managed to sire such a pathetic, over-sensitive creature.

He returned to the kitchen, picking up a torch and a key on his way out the back door. Henry raced ahead as Julian made his way to a locked gate in a tall hawthorn hedge at the rear of the garden. Beyond the gate, a path wound its way up a wooded slope. Anaemic moonlight seeped through the trees. He didn't switch on the torch. He knew the path off by heart, and his feet led him forwards, anticipating every dip, rise, twist and turn. He couldn't see Henry, but he could hear him charging through the undergrowth.

At the top of the slope, beyond a bracken-infested clearing, the path forked into three. Henry was waiting for him there, panting. Julian paused to light the spliff, before taking the fork's central prong. The path descended into a shallow valley where it merged with an old cart track.

Julian coughed out a lungful of hot, sweet smoke. It had been years since he'd smoked weed. The joint was doing its job, soothing away the lingering irritation he felt from his encounter with his dad. He glanced at the moon, which was a crescent amidst countless stars. The full moon – Kenneth Whitcher's killing moon – was a good few nights away.

A face materialised in his mind – full lips, slightly too long nose, pale blue eyes, sandy blonde hair tied into a ponytail. *Susan Simmons.* As a teenager, he'd read everything he could get his hands on about the Mr Moonlight murders. He could still recite the names of the victims in the order they'd been killed – *Sophia Philips, Charlotte King, Daisy Russell, Zoe Aslett.* Susan was the last victim. Police had recovered the other four victims' bodies from locations spread around the forest, but Susan was still out here somewhere.

Grandma's Alice's voice suddenly filled his mind – *Give them the closure they seek, give them peace.*

An all too familiar thought followed – *If the police had found Susan, her parents wouldn't have been at Grandma Alice's and I wouldn't have had to go through all this shit.* He shut down the thought with a shake of his head. He knew it only led to anger and despondency.

He stiffened at a snuffling from nearby. He clicked on the torch and shone it into the trees, his mind awhirl with lurid images of a blood-masked, wild-eyed Kenneth Whitcher.

The light landed on Henry, nose pressed to the ground, hot on the trail of a rabbit or some such thing. Julian frowned at the half-smoked spliff. "This crap's making you paranoid," he muttered, dropping it and grinding the glowing tip under his heel.

Henry began to bark. Julian swept the trees with the torch again, but the dog was nowhere to be seen. Something seemed to have spooked Henry. Julian looked uneasily at the track ahead, which curved around a tree-lined corner. Shortly beyond the bend, he knew, was a derelict sawmill. The mill was a magnet for teenagers, occasional tramps and other undesirables. Locals had long been petitioning the council to tear it down. Had Henry picked up some untoward sound from the mill?

"Henry," he called in a hushed voice. "Here boy."

The barking stopped, but Henry remained lost to sight. Julian stepped off the path, his feet sinking into a thick layer of fallen leaves. Stooping to avoid low-hanging branches, he followed what looked to be a faint animal track. Now it was his turn to sniff the air. An unpleasant smell tickled his nostrils. With every step, it grew stronger. It was like dustbins on a hot day, only much, much worse. He could taste it in his mouth, as if he was eating rancid bacon. It gripped his lungs, dragging him on.

A low growling came from up ahead. "Henry," he hissed. The growling intensified. His torch found a flash of black fur. Henry was jerking his head from side-to-side, tearing at something. Julian's heart stuttered as he made out a leg, a black boot. He rushed forwards to kick Henry. The dog yelped, skittering away. Julian looked down. He clapped a hand to his mouth as his throat contracted into a choking retch.

Chloe didn't look like her photo. Her face was bloated and blistered. Maggots were squirming in her eye sockets. Her lips were drawn back in a grotesque parody of a smile. Something that might have been dried vomit or blood crusted her chin. Watery pus oozed from teeth marks that Henry had inflicted on her throat and face – at least, Julian assumed Henry had inflicted them. Her blonde hair lay so lankly against her skull that it looked painted on. If it hadn't been for the ear-to-nose chain of black beads and the silver stud in her lower lip, he wouldn't have been able to identify her with any certainty. She was wearing a black leather jacket, red plaid miniskirt and military boots. Her skin showed green with a marbling of purple-black veins through ripped fishnets. There were things crawling all over her – fat blood-sucking flies, beetles and mites. They moved like groping fingers under her clothes.

Julian stood staring at the corpse as if it was mesmerizingly beautiful. A dribble of vomit escaped his lips. He swiped it away with his sleeve. A gnawing sound seeped into his shocked senses. Henry was hunkered down chewing on something that was maybe just a stick, or maybe something ripped from the corpse. More vomit came up. Julian spat it out and snapped, "Drop that. Drop it!"

Henry jumped up and retreated, the brown thing dangling from his mouth like a withered tongue. "Stay," commanded Julian, approaching the dog. Henry turned tail and ran in the direction from which they'd come. Julian gave chase, but quickly lost sight of Henry. He didn't slow down, though. He sprinted all the way back to the house as if he was being chased by Mr Moonlight.

Robert was dozing in the armchair. He jerked awake as Julian burst into the living-room.

"What's wrong? What's happened?" asked Robert, looking in alarm at his son's pale, sweaty face.

"I… found… her," Julian panted, struggling for breath to speak.

"Found who?"

"Chloe."

Robert's forehead furrowed. "Chloe Crawley?"

"Yes."

"Is she…" Robert's voice became uncharacteristically hesitant. "Is she dead?"

Julian nodded.

"Are you sure?"

Another, more vehement, nod. "She's over by the sawmill."

"The sawmill," Robert exclaimed as if that explained the matter. "Did you know used hypodermics were found there a few months ago? I bet she overdosed. I've lost count of how many times I've told the council they need to do something about that bloody place. Perhaps now they'll listen." He reached for the phone.

"Who are you calling?"

"Who do you think? The police."

Julian dropped onto the sofa, burying his face in his hands. Robert's eyes glimmered with what might have been concern, but he offered no words of comfort.

After a short time, several police cars and a 'SCIENTIFIC SUPPORT' van arrived at the front gate, lights flashing. Robert buzzed them in. "They'd better not wake your mum," he said with a frowning glance at Julian, as if it would be his fault if they did.

Julian knew his dad was fretting needlessly. His mum took a nightly cocktail of painkillers and sedatives that would have knocked out an elephant. A stocky man in a suit got out of the lead car. Julian recognised Chief Inspector Tom Henson from the TV.

Robert shook the chief inspector's hand. "Hello, Tom." He motioned to Julian. "This is my son, Julian."

Tom treated Julian to what seemed like a knowing look. Wondering if his pupils were still dilated from the weed, Julian strove to stop himself from fidgeting under the policeman's steady gaze.

"We've met before, although you probably don't remember," said Tom. "The last time I saw you, Julian, you were about yea high," he hovered his hand at chest height, "and hauling your dad's clubs around the golf course."

"Best caddy I ever had," Robert remarked.

First I've heard of it, Julian thought dryly.

"So let's get down to business," said Tom, rubbing his hands together as if in anticipation of a treat. "Show me where you found her."

Julian led the chief inspector and several other officers to the body. Although it was a sultry night, he couldn't help but shiver as they neared the spot. The stink of decomposing flesh seemed even more intense. It hit him in the gut so hard that he doubled over, heaving. He couldn't bring himself to go within sight of the body again.

It was getting light by the time Julian finished giving his statement. "How long will you be in town?" asked Tom.

"A few days."

"Good. I'll most likely need to talk to you again."

While Robert showed Tom out, Julian went to the bathroom. He stood under the shower for a long time, scrubbing his skin as if it was polluted. Before leaving the bathroom, he listened at the door. He didn't want to bump into his dad and have to see the *I told you so* look on his face.

Henry was asleep on Julian's bed. There was no sign of the withered-looking thing the dog had been chewing. Aching with tiredness, Julian lay down and tentatively closed his eyes. He knew he'd see Chloe's corpse in his mind's eye. But even worse, he seemed to smell it too. He futilely tried to meditate into a blank state. With a resigned sigh, he got up, flung open a window and sucked in great lungfuls of the morning.

CHAPTER 6

When Julian dragged himself, gritty-eyed and rumple-faced, to breakfast, Christine said in a concerned tone, "You look as if you haven't slept a wink. Bad dreams?"

It was apparent from the question that she was unaware of the previous night's events. Julian noticed his dad peering at him over his morning newspaper. Robert gave a tiny shake of his head.

"I'm fine," said Julian.

Cocking an unconvinced eyebrow, Christine reached for his hand. "You know I'm proud of you for being here." She glanced at Robert. "We both are, aren't we?"

Robert put on his best sincere smile. "Yes, we are. Very proud."

Christine smiled too, a wobble of emotion entering her voice. "I was starting to think I'd never be sat between my two favourite boys again."

Robert lifted her paralysed hand and kissed it.

After breakfast, Julian followed him from the kitchen and asked, "Why haven't you told her?"

"I don't want her worrying about that nonsense."

"She'll find out sooner or later."

"I'm well aware of that," muttered Robert, sorting through his briefcase, clearly not wanting to hear what Julian was saying.

"She worries more not knowing what's going on." Getting no reply, Julian persisted, "If you don't tell her, I will."

Irritation flared in Robert's expression. "No, you bloody well won't." He lowered his voice. "Look, I'll tell her this evening when there's time to do it properly. Just do me a favour and keep shtum until then, will you?"

They both turned at the whirr of Christine's wheelchair. "What are you two talking about?" she asked.

"I was just telling Julian to relax and enjoy himself today."

Robert bent to kiss his wife. He kissed her twice – once on the lips and, with an almost fearful tenderness, once on the drooping side of her face. "Don't overdo it in the garden today," he softly cautioned. With a furtive half-warning, half-pleading glance at Julian, he left the house. Julian watched him get into his Audi and accelerate out of the driveway.

"It's going to be a lovely day," observed Christine, glancing at the cloudless sky. "Fancy helping me in the garden?"

What Julian really wanted was a long, dreamless sleep, but he found a smile for his mum and nodded.

Christine set him to work weeding the flowerbeds. She stayed nearby, chatting on about this and that. Her words occasionally became almost too slurred to understand, but there was a spark of vitality in her eyes that Julian hadn't seen in a long time.

He stared at the forest, wondering if his dad was right about the way Chloe had died. Or was there something more sinister to it? He thought about Chloe's mum, the teddy-bear clutched to her chest, her eyes glazed and pleading. She would know by now that her daughter was dead. Phoebe Bradshaw might know too. And there'd be others – grandparents, aunties, uncles, cousins. All of them united in grief, anger and incomprehension. He heaved a sigh.

Lily called from the house, "Julian, Mike Davis is on the phone for you."

His heart accelerated a few beats. As well as being a golf buddy of his dad's, Mike was the owner of the local newspaper The Godthorne Guardian. Surely there could only be one reason for him phoning.

"What does he want?" wondered Christine.

With a shrug, Julian hurried to the house. From the way Lily looked askance as she passed him the phone, he guessed Mike hadn't let the cat out of the bag. He went to his bedroom, away from prying ears. "Hi Mr Davis."

"Hello Julian. I hope you don't mind me phoning, but I heard what happened."

"How?"

"C'mon now, Julian, this town's too small for something as big as this to be kept under wraps. How are you bearing up?"

"I'm OK. A bit shook up."

"I can imagine. It must have been a huge shock finding her like that. I was wondering if you could come over to the house this morning for a proper chat. I won't keep you long." Like a salesman sweetening a deal, Mike added, "Eleanor's home. She'd love to see you."

She said that? Julian felt like asking, thinking back to the tears in Eleanor's eyes on the day he left for university. He remembered holding her hands and telling her he wanted to break up. He'd trotted out all the usual clichés to justify ending their seven-month relationship – it wasn't her fault, it was his; he wanted to be free to experience university life to the full; he didn't want to have to lie to her about what he was getting up to. She'd said she understood. Said she wanted them to remain friends. He'd often wondered since then whether he'd made a mistake. None of the girls he'd met at university had come close to her. They all seemed to be trying on modified personas. He'd never known Eleanor try to be anything but what she was – a kind, down-to-earth girl.

"OK, Mr Davis. I'll see you soon." Julian hung up and went back outside. "I have to go out," he called to his mum. By way of explanation, he added, "Eleanor's home."

Before she could ask any awkward questions, he turned on his heel and headed for his car.

CHAPTER 7

Julian had always liked the Davis's house. It was old and comfortably cluttered with books and knick-knacks. Its lattice windows gave light and privacy. There were plenty of corners and nooks to hide in. Mike greeted him at the front door. He looked the same as ever – hazel-brown eyes with a keen glint, wispy hair combed over his bald crown, cigarette planted in the corner of his mouth. He gave Julian an appraising look. "I see someone's been burning the candle at both ends and the middle," he said through his cigarette.

"I didn't get much sleep."

"I'll bet."

As Mike ushered Julian inside, Eleanor came down the stairs a little hesitantly. A tingle ran through Julian at the sight of her. It was almost two years since they'd last spoken. They'd bumped into each other on Oxford Street. Both of them had been in a rush. They'd exchanged mobile numbers and promised to catch up, but it never happened.

Her hair was shorter, darker, more styled. She was slimmer, too, more angular, less cute. As she drew nearer, he saw the smiling light in her eyes and realised with relief that the change was only surface. Like his mum, like everything real and good, she was unchanged through change.

"Hi, Julian," she said.

"Hi."

Mike beckoned for Julian to follow him. "You two can catch up when we're done."

They went into a study hazy with cigarette smoke, its walls lined with shelves bowed beneath the weight of books and newspapers. Mike seated himself behind a desk strewn with papers. He motioned Julian to a chair. "So tell me all about it," he said, pen and notepad at the ready.

Julian gave him the gory details, describing how Chloe's corpse had looked, how it had smelt.

Mike's bushy eyebrows pinched together. "Jesus."

"Will you put that in the paper?"

"People don't need to read that. I'd appreciate it if you don't go repeating it to Eleanor, either."

"Don't worry, I won't. Any word on how Chloe died?"

Mike shook his head. "It'll be a few days before the coroner's report comes in."

"I heard some…" Julian sought the right word, "unpleasant things about Chloe."

"You mean like she was prostituting herself?"

"So it's true?"

"I can't say for certain, but I think so."

Julian blew out his cheeks. "What would make her do that?"

"Heroin."

"Seriously? She was an addict?"

"Again, I don't know for sure. I'm merely making an informed guess. You probably don't realise this, Julian, but this town has quite the thriving drug's trade. There's money here, but there's poverty too. A lack of decent local jobs. Sky-high property prices. It's a toxic mix."

"I'm finding out a lot about this town I didn't know."

A knock came at the door. "Are you two almost finished?" enquired Eleanor.

"Be out in a minute, sweetheart," said Mike. Stubbing his cigarette out in an ashtray with a touch more force than was necessary, he added to Julian, "Better not keep her waiting."

Julian was glad to leave the study. Mike understood why he'd split up with Eleanor. In Mike's opinion, it was the best thing that could have happened. Julian knew this because Eleanor had repeated it to him when he phoned one time in a drunken haze of guilt to apologise for the way he'd treated her. He also knew, or rather sensed, that Mike wouldn't be anywhere near as understanding if he hurt his daughter a second time.

Julian felt that tingle again as he met Eleanor's eyes. "Do you want to go for a walk?" he asked.

"Sure."

They strolled along the street, standing close, but not touching. Julian suppressed an impulse to reach for Eleanor's hand. It was turning into a hot day. Eleanor was wearing a vest top. Her arms were smooth and unblemished. He thought about the cuts on Phoebe Bradshaw's arms.

"Dad told me what happened," said Eleanor. "That poor girl."

Julian made no reply. Even if he hadn't promised not to, he wouldn't have repeated what he'd said to Mike. He felt a sudden strong desire to keep Eleanor as far away from that business as possible.

"It makes me feel like crying to think about it," she went on.

"So how are you finding life in London?"

A frown touched Eleanor's forehead at his obvious attempt to change the subject. "You know, Julian, sometimes you remind me of my dad."

"Is that a compliment or a criticism?"

"Both. How long have you been back?"

"Only since yesterday. What about you?"

"Almost a month."

Julian gave Eleanor a surprised look. "What about your job?"

"I was made redundant."

"Shit. What happened?"

"The company needed to make cutbacks. I was one of the newest members of staff so…" Eleanor trailed off into a sigh.

"I'm sorry to hear that."

"What can you do? It happens," Eleanor said equably. "Besides, it's nice to be back here."

"Are you back for good?"

Eleanor replied with a *we'll see* shrug. "Depends on what jobs come up."

They walked on in silence for a while – they'd always been comfortable in each other's silence. Julian had never met another girl he felt that way with. "Listen, Eleanor, I want to apologise for not calling you."

"I didn't call you either."

"True, but I feel like shit about it anyway."

"Well don't."

Eleanor reached to hook her arm through Julian's. His skin prickled with pleasure at her touch. "If you like, we could do something tonight," he suggested. "Get something to eat, go for a drink, whatever."

She smiled. It was a warm, open smile, the only one she had in her facial vocabulary. "That sounds good."

She made to turn into a lane that branched off from the street. Julian hesitated. The lane led beyond the edge of town to a meadow where there was an old hay-barn. As boyfriend and girlfriend, they'd gone there often. In its grass-smelling gloom they'd progressed from eager fumblings to tender explorations of each other's body. Julian resisted a groin-tingling tug. He couldn't allow himself to go back there, not unless he was certain that was what he wanted.

"I have to go," he said.

"Are you sure?"

As Julian looked at Eleanor's soft brown eyes and heart-shaped lips, the tugging intensified. Not wanting to take the chance that he might give into it, he replied, "I should really spend some time with my mum."

Eleanor nodded with sympathetic understanding. "How is she?"

"Not great, but she's getting on with things." Julian heaved a sigh. "I don't know how she does it."

"Say hello to her from me."

"I will do."

They walked back to Julian's car. "What time shall I pick you up?" he asked.

"Seven."

"See you then."

Eleanor raised a flawless arm to wave as he drove away.

"You're a fucking idiot," he told himself, waving back.

His phone rang. It was Kyle. "Fancy meeting up tonight?" he asked Julian.

"Can't. I'm going out with Eleanor."

"What? Like a date?"

"No, not a date. Just two friends catching up."

Kyle sniggered. "Yeah, right. You know she's still hung up on you? Every time I see her she's like, have you spoken to Julian? How's he doing? And I'm like, forget Julian, I'm free and single. But she doesn't even notice me. Not in that way." His tone was jokey, but an edge of seriousness entered his voice as he added, "So go easy on her, cos she's one of the good ones."

A Facebook notification pinged up on the phone – 'Dolor confirmed you as a friend'. "Listen, I'll call you later," said Julian.

He cut off the call and pulled over. He followed the notification link to Phoebe's profile. Underneath her photo it said 'There has to be a reason for all this pain. A purpose...' On her wall, she'd posted 'R.I.P. Chloe. I love you'. There were photos of her and Chloe pouting, sneering and brandishing the cuts on their arms like badges of honour. And there were photos of them with men in their teens and twenties, drinking, smoking and simulating sex. One in particular caught Julian's attention. The girls flanked a bare-chested boy who was maybe eighteen or nineteen-years-old. He had a skinny muscular body, like a junkie boxer. His hair was shaved to the skull. A tattoo of a wolf baring its teeth decorated his chest. Surely he was Dylan Bradshaw – he had the same face as Phoebe, only thinner and more sunken. There was the same sullen pain in his eyes too.

A message from 'Dolor' appeared in Julian's Facebook inbox – 'I'll be in The White Rabbit tonight'.

He stared at the message, a queer sensation in his stomach, like a hunger pang, only deeper and heavier. He wasn't debating what to do. He knew he had to meet Phoebe. The question that bothered him was, to what end? What would come of it? 'See you there' he typed and hit reply.

His gaze strayed out the window. Lines clustered on his forehead. He was only a few streets away from his grandma's house. He sat for a moment, running his tongue nervously over his lips. With a determined nod, he restarted the engine.

CHAPTER 8

Tension seeped through Julian as he drove along the street of redbrick Victorian terraced houses, stiffening his shoulders and tightening his throat.

"Hurt to heal, hurt to heal," he repeated, battling an intense urge to turn the car around and speed away.

His gaze came to land on a house with bay windows veiled by net curtains. Several slates had slipped on the steep roof. The window frames and front door were in dire need of a lick of paint.

Julian's eyebrows squeezed into a single line. Like her daughter, Grandma Alice had always taken pride in her garden. In the summer it had been a riot of climbing roses, jasmine and lilac. One time when he'd been helping her with the gardening, she'd told him, "Did you know that friendly spirits smell like flowers? If you ever smell flowers where there are none, it means a loved one is watching over you from the other side."

There were no roses in the small front garden now. It was choked with weeds. The privet hedge almost blocked the pavement. Was Grandma Alice ill? Or had she simply grown too old for gardening?

He parked up and got out of the car. Flaking paint cracked beneath his fingers as he opened the waist-height garden gate. Slowly, like someone approaching the unknown, he climbed several worn stone steps to the front door. He hadn't seen Grandma Alice since the night of the séance. What would she look like after all these years? He remembered her as a tall woman with eyes that seemed to shine out of her face.

He lifted his hand to knock, but hesitated. His hand dropped to the doorknob. The door clicked open. A stale, unwashed odour wafted out. Scratched varnished floorboards creaked as he stepped into a high-ceilinged hallway. Stairs with a threadbare carpet runner held in place by brass rods rose steeply to his left. There were two panelled wooden doors to his right and a third door at the far end of the hallway.

He poked his head into the front room. It was the same as he remembered it – boxy TV, green velvet three-piece-suite, mahogany sideboard, crimson flock wallpaper, blue glass ornaments, moody landscape paintings – except everything looked shabbier and dustier.

Like a sneak thief, he moved on to the dining room. His hand trembled as he turned the squeaky doorknob. There was no dust in the dining room. The oval table and three chairs sparkled with polish. Six tall candles formed a circular palisade in the table's centre.

Julian's breath caught in his throat. Suddenly he was ten-years-old again and sneaking a peek at the séance. Susan Simmons's parents had their back to him. Grandma Alice was sat opposite them. Her hate-swollen eyes pinned him in place like a butterfly to a board. *There is no peace,* she snarled in a voice that didn't belong to her. *No fucking peace!*

"Julian, is that you?"

The soft, tremulous voice came from away to his right. It reeled him back into the present. He turned to see his grandma standing at the bottom of the stairs. Not his grandma as she'd been in 2005, but his grandma as she was now – as skinny as a scarecrow, face lined by too many wrinkles to count, hair a thin white frizz. She seemed to have shrunk. Or maybe it was simply that he'd grown. A faded floral dress hung sack-like. In contrast to her age-racked body, her eyes were as luminous as ever.

"Hello Grandma," he replied.

"You shouldn't be here. He's still looking for you."

"Who? Mr Moonlight?"

"Shh!" Alice darted a wide-eyed glance around herself. "Don't speak that name. You must leave this house at once."

The fearful urgency in her voice infected Julian. Almost before he realised what he was doing, he was hurrying for the front door. His grandma's voice pursued him down the steps. "Leave this town, Julian. Go far away. Never come back here again. Do you hear? Never come back!"

His heart palpitating, he ducked into the car, started the engine and sped away from Grandma Alice's house. In his mind's eye, all he could see were those hate-filled eyes. *No fucking peace.* Those terrible words seemed to echo over and over in his ears.

He was almost at the north edge of town when another word rang out in his mind – *Stop!*

He hit the brakes, forcing the car behind to swerve sharply around him. *No,* he said to himself, shaking his head. *You're not going to run away again. She's just a crazy old woman.*

"Just a crazy old woman," he repeated out loud. "She can't hurt you."

He took slow, deep breaths and, gradually, his heart stopped pounding against his ribcage. He did a U-turn. When he arrived at his parents' house, his mum and Lily were eating soup in the kitchen. Lily rose to ladle some into a bowl for him. Both women looked at him expectantly, but he ate his lunch without meeting their eyes. Christine and Lily exchanged a glance and held their silence.

When his bowl was empty, he said, "I went to see Grandma Alice."

Christine gave a little nod as if she'd expected to hear some such thing. "What happened?"

"She said..." Julian's voice faltered as an involuntary shudder ran through him.

"She said Mr Moonlight is still looking for you."

Julian's eyebrows lifted. "How did you know that?"

The right side of Christine's mouth twitched into a sardonic smile. "Because I know my mother only too well. Once she gets something in her head, she never lets go of it."

Julian dropped his gaze as if ashamed. "I ran away from her. I was going to leave town."

"But you didn't. You faced her and you're still here. Look at me, Julian." He met his mum's gaze, and she continued, "How do you feel?"

Julian thought about the question. Now that the panic had faded, all that was left was a sense of emptiness. He shrugged.

"You should feel very pleased with yourself," said Christine. "The hardest part is over with."

"Your mum's right," put in Lily. "All that Mr Moonlight stuff, well, it's nothing but a ghost story."

"But Grandma really believes it," said Julian.

"Shall I tell you what I believe, Julian?" said Christine. "I believe in this moment right now. I could easily give in to fear, seek comfort in séances, tarot cards and all the rest of it. But I refuse to waste what little time I have left worrying about what comes next."

Julian's forehead creased. "You've got loads of time left, Mum."

"I hope so, but who knows when their time is up? The point is, I choose not to be afraid." Closing her eyes suddenly, Christine grimaced as if waves of pain were breaking over her.

"Are you OK?" Julian asked worriedly.

Christine nodded. "I'm fine."

"No, you're not. You overdid it in the garden, as usual," chided Lily, rising from the table. "Come on, let's get you to bed."

She wheeled Christine out of the kitchen. Julian headed for his own bed. Tiredness throbbed behind his eyes. He hesitated to close them.

What if the dream comes? he asked himself.

What if it doesn't? countered another part of his brain.

"I choose not to be afraid," he said and closed his eyes.

CHAPTER 9

Julian's eyes snapped open. He jerked upright, lungs heaving as if he'd sprinted up a mountain. Sweat dappled his forehead. His dilated pupils darted around the bedroom as if he didn't recognise his surroundings. After a moment, his eyes came back to themselves. He flopped onto the pillows, relief and dismay mingling in his expression. The dream had been more vivid than ever, only this time his victim hadn't been Susan Simmons, it had been Chloe Crawley.

"I faced my fear, so why am I still having the dream?" he demanded to the empty air. "Why won't it just fuck off?"

He knew what Gail would say – the dream has changed again. That's progress. Right at that moment, though, with his mind full of Chloe's fear-contorted face, it didn't feel that way.

He went through to the kitchen to make a cup of tea. A sedated silence hung over the house. His mum was apparently still in bed. There was no sign of Lily. She was probably grabbing forty winks too. Henry clambered out of his basket, wagging his tail. Julian stroked him, glad of something to take his mind off the dream. It didn't work for long. His thoughts were soon back on Chloe – the way little veins had burst in her eyes as he throttled her, the salty metallic flavour of her blood as he'd ripped out her throat.

He paced back and forth, futilely trying to shake off the images. He took out his phone and dialled Gail. Perhaps speaking to her would help. "Fuck," he muttered upon getting through to an answering service. He ground the heel of his hand against his forehead. He needed to get Chloe's face out of his head. But how? Who else could he speak to? Not his mum. He'd burdened her with enough. And definitely not his dad.

On an impulse, he navigated to Facebook and messaged Phoebe 'Can we meet up right now?' As he waited for her to reply, something like deep hunger pangs squeezed his stomach. He didn't have to wait long. A message pinged up – 'Foxwood. Half an hour. Bring vodka'.

'See you there' he replied, already on his way to his car.

He stopped off at an off-licence in the town centre to buy vodka. *This is a bad idea,* he told himself. *This girl is trouble.* But he didn't turn the car around.

As he passed the police station, he noted that its car park was all but empty. No doubt the TV vans had decamped to the woods behind his house. It wouldn't be long now before news of his discovery came out.

This time there was no police car at the entrance to Foxwood. He turned onto a gravel lane that descended gently between a sea of tree-shaded bracken. After about two hundred metres, the lane ended at a small carpark.

Phoebe was perched on a wooden stile, smoking a cigarette. She was dressed much the same as on the previous day – thick-soled black boots, torn fishnets, black PVC miniskirt, waist-constricting corset, leather jacket. She couldn't have looked more out of place amidst the sun-splashed forest.

Her heavy black eyeliner was streaked as if she'd been crying. She wasn't crying now, though. Her eyes were like cold blue porcelain. They looked on intently as Julian got out of the car.

"I'm Julian," he said, for want of something to say.

Phoebe arched a disdainful eyebrow. "Yeah, I know."

"I just wanted to tell you how sorry I am about your friend."

The blue eyes narrowed almost imperceptibly. "Why should you be sorry?"

"Because... Well, because I am..." Julian trailed off lamely.

Phoebe took a drag on her cigarette and exhaled in his direction. "You got the vodka?"

Julian took out the bottle.

Phoebe eyed it approvingly. "Want to go for a walk?" Without waiting for a reply, she hopped off the stile and set off along a grassy path.

Julian hurried to catch her up. "How did you know Chloe?"

"Why do you give a shit how I knew her?"

"I... I don't suppose I really do." Julian frowned, irritated at his halting tone. Why did this girl make him so nervous?

Phoebe stopped and gave him a sizing-up look, as if trying to decide whether she could take him in a fight. "You're not going to hurt me, are you?"

Julian's stomach gave a little lurch. "What do you mean, hurt you?"

"We're all alone here. You could do whatever you wanted with me – rape me, kill me, bury my body in the forest."

The queasiness flared, pushing up his throat. "What makes you think I'd hurt you?" he asked with a swallow.

"Nothing in particular. You look harmless enough, but if this town's taught me one thing it's that appearances can be deceptive."

"Well I'm not going to hurt you."

Phoebe stared at him a moment longer. Smiling humourlessly, she reached to pluck the vodka bottle from his hand. She unscrewed it, took a swallow, then offered Julian the bottle.

"No thanks."

With a *suit-yourself* shrug, she resumed walking. They turned off the path and waded through the undergrowth to a small grassy clearing. At its centre, stones encircled a heap of ash, blackened logs and crumpled beer cans. She sat down and leant back on her elbows, listlessly staring, trying to appear relaxed, bored even. But there was a tension about her. Julian noticed that her right hand was fidgeting with something in her jacket pocket.

"Tell me what Chloe looked like," she said.

"Are you sure you want to know?" Julian didn't fancy describing the corpse for the second time that day.

Her face as intense as a knife cut, Phoebe leant forwards close enough that he could smell her vodka-laced breath. "I want every detail."

He reached for the vodka, swilled down a mouthful, then told her. She listened, seemingly impassive, but after he was finished she drew in a quivering breath, took back the vodka and drained half the bottle in one.

"Whoa, you'll make yourself sick," said Julian.

"So what if I do?" Phoebe's eyes narrowed to slits of eyeliner. "So do you reckon someone killed her?"

"I don't know."

"You said there were bite marks on her."

"Yeah, but my dog made those. I think. Everyone I've spoken to reckons she overdosed."

Phoebe snorted. "They would."

"You think they're wrong?"

"Fucked if I know. She probably did OD. She always said that was how she'd go out. And if she was right, well, all those fuckers you spoke to can nod and pretend to be sad."

It's not like that, Julian wanted to say. But it was like that, and he knew it. "What was she taking?"

Phoebe shrugged. "Anything she could get her hands on. Speed, acid, E, ketamine."

"Heroin?"

A frown gathered on Phoebe's face. "She said she didn't do junk, but I saw the needle marks on her arms."

"What about you? You ever tried it?"

"Once," Phoebe admitted as if it was something she'd rather forget. She added quickly, "I didn't inject it. There's no way I'd stick that shit in my arm. I didn't want to do it at all, but Chloe kept on and on about it. She had this thing about trying everything once before she croaked. I said yes just to shut her up, but I made her promise we'd only do it once. We had this big fuck-off row when I saw the needle marks. I called her a liar, and she told me to go fuck myself. That was a couple of weeks ago." She chewed her lips, pain shining in her eyes. "We never spoke again."

"Where did you get the heroin?"

Phoebe laughed as if to say, *You've got to be kidding*. She lit a cigarette. "Why are you here, rich boy?"

Julian's forehead twitched with annoyance. "Don't call me that."

"Why not? That's what you are, isn't it? Do you feel sorry for me or something?"

"No."

"Then what's your deal?" Phoebe gave him another of her probing looks, her eyes glazed with alcohol. She threw her head back, bursting into laughter again. "You want to fuck me? Is that what this is?"

"No. Absolutely not," Julian protested perhaps a little too vehemently, a redness creeping up his neck. He rose to his feet as if to leave.

Phoebe motioned for him to sit. "Chill. I'm only winding you up."

He stared at her uncertainly for a few seconds, before sitting back down. She pressed the bottle into his hand and lifted it to his lips. As he gulped down the throat-burning vodka, he fought an urge to choke, determined to show he could match her drink for drink. Only a few centimetres of liquid were left in the bottle when she pulled it away from his lips. He shot her a triumphant grin. His grin faded as she responded with more laughter. He suddenly felt like a fool for wanting to prove himself to her.

"So what's it like being a rich kid?" asked Phoebe.

Julian ignored her.

"Don't be shy," she taunted. "C'mon, what's it like living in a big house, driving a nice car, knowing you only have to put out your hands and everything you ever want will drop into them?"

Julian sighed. "Am I supposed to be ashamed? Have I done something wrong?"

"I dunno. Have you?"

To his irritation, Julian found himself blinking away from Phoebe's gaze. "Must be nice," she said. "Not being stuck in this shitty little town, living a shitty little life."

Now it was Julian's turn to snort. "Who says I'm not stuck?"

"You live in London, don't you?"

"How do you know that?"

Phoebe smiled coyly. "Someone told me."

"Yeah, well, did they tell you I'm doing a job I fucking hate? I spend my days stuck behind a desk, staring out the window and wishing I was somewhere else."

Phoebe was thoughtfully silent, then she said, "I guess we're all trapped in our own little box."

They shared the last of the vodka. His eyelids as heavy as bricks, Julian lay back and watched wisps of cloud scudding across the sky.

"What if someone wanted to disappear?" asked Phoebe. "I mean like really disappear. Do you think that's possible?"

Julian shrugged. "There was this guy at uni who dropped out and went to live on a commune in Wales. They generate their own power, grow their own food."

Phoebe sniffed down her nose. "Sounds boring as fuck."

"Not to me it doesn't. Apparently everyone's welcome and you can stay as long as you like – a day, a year, whatever. No one asks about who you are, where you're from or why you're there. No boxes. You can be whoever you want to be."

Phoebe was silent for another moment, then she shook her head. "That guy was bullshitting you. No place like that really exists. Sometimes I think there's only one way to truly disappear."

"Which is?"

Phoebe made no reply. A distant look came into her eyes. Her hand sliding into her jacket pocket again, she began to rock gently as if listening to music only she could hear. With a quick intake of breath, she snatched her hand out of her pocket. A sliver of blood glistened on her palm.

"What happe–" Julian started to ask, but fell silent as she lifted her hand to lick off the blood. His throat was suddenly so tight he couldn't get the words out.

"It's strange," said Phoebe, watching more blood well up. "When I first saw you yesterday, you seemed so familiar. It was as if I knew your face from somewhere." She turned her intense gaze on him. "You feel the same way, don't you? I can tell by the way you look at me."

Julian replied hesitantly, "I'm not sure how I feel when I look at you."

A silence passed between them. Phoebe suddenly moved to kiss Julian – a kiss as deep and heavy as the ache in his stomach.

Pull her hair, slap her around, strangle her.

As Kyle's words rang out in his mind, Julian pulled away from her.

"What's the matter?" she asked. "Don't you want me?"

Yes, he wanted her, but the blood hammering in his temples told him that giving in to that want would be about a sensible as stepping in front of a runaway train. "It's not that. I just…" He trailed off, unable to put his feelings into words that wouldn't offend.

"I thought we had a connection."

"We do."

"So what is it then?" Phoebe pouted, obviously not used to being turned down. "Maybe you think you're too good for a No-Hoper like me, eh rich boy?"

"Don't be an idiot."

Phoebe's eyes flashed. "I'm not the idiot here." She jumped up and stormed off, flinging over her shoulder, "If you don't want me, I'll just have to find someone else to fuck."

"Wait, Phoebe, don't go."

Julian tried to stand, but whether from the vodka or lack of sleep, his body felt like lead, his limbs like straw. The trees swallowed Phoebe. He lay thinking about the thin line of blood on her palm. She must have had a knife in her pocket – perhaps for self-defence, perhaps for use on herself, perhaps both. He ran his tongue over his lips, tasting her. With a low groan, head spinning, he closed his eyes, surrendering to the tiredness. The instant he did so, the dream attacked him as savagely as a drug-induced hallucination.

When he awoke, the sky was fading into starlit darkness and he was shivering. He sat with his shoulders scrunched forwards, his nose running and his mouth full of bitter saliva. A sort of raw sickness gnawed at his insides. The moon edged out from behind the trees. The sight of it pulled him to his feet and sent him scuttling to his car.

CHAPTER 10

Christine was drinking coffee in the kitchen. Her left eye was almost closed. A landslide of wrinkles clustered under it. Her lips drooped like dead leaves. She looked so fragile that Julian made to put his arms around her.

"Don't," she said with a wince of anticipation. She gave him a faint apologetic smile. "Sometimes, even with all the tablets, everything hurts so much I can't bear to be touched."

"Is there anything I can do?"

"You're already doing it just by being here."

Julian ground his teeth in frustration. "I wish there was something more I could do."

"That makes two of us." With a tremor of effort, Christine lifted her hand to touch Julian's cheek. "You look so tired. Where have you been?"

"I… I went out to meet a friend." It wasn't a lie, but it wasn't exactly the truth either. To distract from the guilty hesitation in his voice, he poured himself a coffee.

"Who? Not Eleanor."

"Eleanor," exclaimed Julian, recalling that he'd arranged to pick her up at seven. He glanced at a clock on the wall. It was almost nine. "Shit."

"You were supposed to be taking her out this evening." At Julian's look of askance, Christine explained, "She called to find out where you were."

"Was she upset?"

"She was more worried than upset, especially after what happened last night."

Julian hesitated to reply. Was she referring to him finding Chloe?

"I've spoken to Mike," Christine continued as if answering the unasked question. "I knew something was up when he called you this morning. It didn't take long to get it out of him." She rested her hand on Julian's wrist. It was so cold he almost shivered. "We don't have to talk about it if you don't want to. But if you do want to talk about it or anything else, then I'm here. I'll always be here for you, Julian."

Tears tickled the back of Julian's throat. He swallowed forcefully, knowing that if he let them go the dream would come out with them. He would offload every vile new detail onto her. He couldn't allow that to happen. He managed a thin smile. "I know." He withdrew his arm from his mum's hand. "I'd better call Eleanor."

"Better still, why don't you go see her? It's not all that late."

"What about you?"

"Lily's on her way over to put me to bed."

"Where's dad?"

"At the factory. He'll be home soon."

Julian frowned, but his mum's eyes warned him to keep his thoughts to himself. "I'll wait around until Lily gets here."

"There's no need. I'll be fine. Go on, or it *will* be too late."

Julian kissed his mum's cheek as lightly as possible, then hurried to his car. Upon arriving at the Davis's house and seeing that Eleanor's bedroom light was on, he threw gravel at the window. Her face appeared between the curtains. She opened the window and peered down at him, waiting for his explanation.

"I'm sorry, Eleanor."

"Is that it? Aren't you even going to bother to make an excuse?"

"I could give you some bullshit, if that's what you want?"

"What I want, Julian, is to know why you stood me up."

He made no reply.

"Fine," said Eleanor. She started to close the window.

"Wait, Eleanor. Truth is, I had too much to drink this afternoon and, well, I suppose I passed out."

"You passed out?" Concern softened Eleanor's voice. "For god's sake, Julian, what are you trying to do to yourself?"

"It was stupid," he said, recalling how he'd let Phoebe hold the bottle to his lips. "I don't know what I was thinking."

"Were you drinking alone?"

Again, Julian said nothing. He'd never flat-out lied to Eleanor and he didn't intend to start now. But neither could he bring himself to tell her the truth.

She heaved a sigh. "Go home, Julian."

Before he could say anything else, she shut the window. He threw more gravel at the glass, but she didn't reappear. He reluctantly returned to his car. He didn't want go home and sit listening to the silence or, even worse, have to attempt conversation with his dad. He drove to The Swan – a pretty pub with white walls and a red-tiled roof on the western edge of town.

The cosy, beam-ceilinged barroom was packed with well-heeled, gingham shirt and chino-wearing clientele. Julian spotted a few familiar faces amongst them. Not wanting to get caught up in conversation, he put his head down and made his way to the bar where Kyle was pulling pints. Kyle's hair was tied back and he had on a white shirt and black tie.

"Look at you," grinned Julian. "I've never seen you looking so respectable."

Fuck you, Kyle mouthed. "What are you doing here?"

Julian shrugged. "I had nothing better to do."

"I thought you were taking Eleanor out."

"I was supposed to be." Julian fell silent, not wanting to talk about it in the crowded barroom.

Kyle took the hint. "Do you want a beer?"

Julian shook his head, which was still pounding from the vodka. "I'll have a lemonade."

Kyle sloshed bubbling liquid into a glass. "It's on me," he said as Julian took out his wallet.

"Cheers, Kyle. What time do you finish work?"

Kyle glanced at his wristwatch. "In about forty minutes. Why?"

"I thought we could go for a..." Julian simulated smoking a joint.

Grinning approvingly, Kyle turned to serve a punter. Julian messaged Eleanor 'Sorry for messing you around. I know I don't deserve it, but will you give me another chance?'

He stared at the screen, hoping for a reply. When one didn't materialise after several minutes, he sighed and pocketed his phone. Kyle was too busy to chat, so Julian took his drink to a quiet corner. His thoughts returned to Phoebe. The sour smell of her breath. The sweet taste of her lipstick. A shudder slid through him.

Gradually, the pub emptied until Julian was the only punter left. Kyle cleared the tables and gave the floor a perfunctory sweep, then he and Julian headed out the door.

Kyle took off his tie, muttering, "I hate these fucking things."

They drove out into the forest, pulling off the main road onto a tree-shrouded track. "I've blown it with Eleanor... Yet again," said Julian, watching Kyle expertly roll a cone-shaped spliff.

"You do surprise me," Kyle replied sarcastically, licking the edge of the Rizla papers. "What did you do this time?"

"I stood her up for Phoebe Bradshaw."

Kyle jerked his head up in astonishment. "You what? Are you insane?"

"It's not what you think. I wanted to talk to Phoebe about..." Julian hesitated.

"Go on, spit it out."

"I shouldn't be telling you this, but I guess you'll find out soon enough anyway. I found Chloe Crawley's body in the woods behind our house last night."

"Ho-o-oly shit," exclaimed Kyle. "I told you she was dead, didn't I? How did she die?"

"How should I know?"

A ghoulish light gleamed in Kyle's eyes. "Had she been, like, mutilated or anything?"

"I didn't get close enough to see." Julian knew better than to mention the bite marks.

"Fuck, this is massive." Kyle pulled out his phone. "I've got to tell everyone about this."

"You can't do that. You'll drop me right in the shit."

Kyle pursed his lips disappointedly. "Can't I tell just a few people? I mean, what difference would it make? Half the town probably knows by now."

"That's not the point. Look, do me a favour and keep this to yourself until it comes out on the news, will you? Then you can blabber on about it as much as you want."

"Aw, where's the fun in that?"

"Where's the fucking fun in talking about it at all?" Julian snapped.

"Alright, chill." Kyle held up a conciliatory hand. "Jesus, you're so uptight these days."

"Yeah, well, I haven't had much sleep."

Kyle sparked up the spliff and passed it to Julian. "Have a toot on that. That'll sort you out."

Julian inhaled the sweet smoke deep into his lungs and heaved it out in a sigh. "Sometimes life can be a real pile of shit."

"Tell me about it. You should try serving pints to a bunch of city-boys turned wannabe lord of the manor night after night."

They passed the spliff back and forth for a while, then Kyle asked, "So what are you going to do about Eleanor?"

Julian shrugged. He didn't know what to do about Eleanor. He didn't know what to do about Phoebe, the dreams, his mum's illness, his dad's absence. His thoughts were as confused as his emotions. A vertigo-like sensation swirled through him. He shoved it away with a long suck of smoke.

"Do you still like her?" asked Kyle. "What I mean is, do you *really* like her? Cos, and don't take this the wrong way, Julian, but if you don't *really* like her, maybe you should keep your distance."

Julian stared out the window. Kyle was right. Eleanor would be better off without him and his problems in her life.

"All I'm saying is she doesn't deserve to be fucked around," went on Kyle.

"I know, I know, but drop it, will you? All I want to do is get stoned and think about nothing."

A warm heavy sensation settled over Julian as they smoked the joint down to its roach. "I could murder a kebab," said Kyle.

They headed back into town and pulled over at a little place with a neon sign in the window that read 'KEBAB & BURGER TAKE AWAY'. They ordered and took their food outside. Apart from an occasional punter heading home from the pubs dotted around town, the streets were deserted. "Still turns into a graveyard after eleven I see," said Julian.

Kyle repeated his favourite mantra. "You know this town. Nothing much changes."

A black car with amateurish red flames spray-painted along its side pulled over, grinding rock music pumping out of its open back window. Phoebe was in the backseat. In the front was the older woman and, behind the steering wheel, one of the men Julian had seen Phoebe with in The White Rabbit.

Poking her head out the window, Phoebe called to Julian, "Hey, rich boy. What you up to?"

He suppressed a niggle of irritation. "Not much."

"We're heading out to Foxwood. You want to come along? Just you." She glanced at Kyle as if he was an annoying insect. "Not him."

Julian struggled to swallow a mouthful of greasy meat. The way Phoebe was looking at him with her piercing blue eyes made his throat thicken. He opened his mouth to speak. *No thanks* was what he intended to say. But to his surprise, he heard himself saying, "OK."

"Oh what the fuck?" exclaimed Kyle.

"I'll call you tomorrow." Julian's tone was apologetic. To Phoebe he added, "I'll follow you."

Dropping his kebab in a bin, Julian headed for his VW. Phoebe flicked Kyle the finger and wound her window up.

"Fuck you too," yelled Kyle as, engine flaring, the flame-licked car sped away.

CHAPTER 11

Julian had difficulty keeping up as they sped out of town. When he arrived at Foxwood car park, Phoebe and her companions had already set off walking. Using his mobile phone to light the way, he hastened after them. The man, whose skull-like face and protuberant eyes were framed by thin shoulder-length hair, had his arms slung around Phoebe and the woman. Phoebe jerked her thumb at him. "That's Gollum."

"Fuck you," he said in a reedy voice.

Phoebe laughed. "Well that's what I call him."

"You can call me Ash, unless you want a slap," the man said to Julian.

Phoebe motioned to the woman. "And that's Gemma."

"Hi," said Julian, ducking his head to see past the mane of raven black hair that shrouded Gemma's pale powdered face.

Her mascara-encrusted eyes didn't deign to acknowledge him.

They followed a path of beaten-down bracken to the clearing. Ash squirted a can of lighter fluid over the remains of the old fire. He lit a match and dropped it. Flames whooshed up, throwing crazily dancing shadows everywhere. He stretched out on the ground beside Gemma, stroking her torn stockings. There was a tattoo of an inverted cross on the back of his hand. Phoebe patted the ground for Julian to sit next to her.

Ash pulled a sheet of semi-translucent yellow paper printed with a grid of cutting lines from his jeans pocket. He tore off two five-mm squares and, as if inserting contact-lenses, placed one under each of his eyelids, before passing the sheet to Gemma.

"What are they?" Julian asked.

"They're Windows," said Phoebe. "They let you look through hidden windows."

"And see what?"

Phoebe shrugged. "Whatever's on the other side. Want one?"

"No thanks. The state my head's in, I'd have a bad trip."

"There are no bad trips on this shit," said Ash. "I'm telling you, mate, until you've fucked on this stuff you haven't fucked."

Gemma handed the Windows to Phoebe. She applied them to her eyes, before looking askance at Julian. He shook his head. He had no wish to see what was on the other side of any hidden windows, be they in his mind or the forest. He'd seen enough already to know it wouldn't be good.

Ash and Gemma moved off into the shadows, hand in hand. Muffled grunts and moans soon drifted back to the clearing. Phoebe and Julian sat listening, not touching, but close.

"So did you find someone else to fuck?" enquired Julian. He didn't want to ask, but somehow he couldn't help himself.

"Why?" Phoebe looked at him sidelong, her eyes gleaming with amusement. "Have you changed your mind?"

"No," Julian said vehemently, as if trying to convince himself he meant it.

Phoebe burst into laughter. She laughed so hard that tears filled her eyes. With disconcerting abruptness, she caught her laughter and asked, "Have the coppers told you anything about Chloe, about how she died?"

"No."

Phoebe gazed at the trees, which seemed to tremble in the firelight. A far-horizon look came into her eyes. "Sometimes I think Chloe's lucky. At least she's out of this shit."

Julian uneasily thought about the lattice of cuts on Phoebe's wrists. "You shouldn't talk like that. Things can't be that bad."

"Can't they?" Phoebe jerked her dilated pupils to him. "What the fuck do you know about my life?"

"Nothing, but..." After an awkward pause, Julian added, "We can talk about it if you want."

Phoebe stared at him for a few seconds, then burst out laughing again. "You're a nice little rich boy. You don't want to know where I've been, where I'm going."

Julian sucked in his irritation, determined not to play her game by getting angry. "I wouldn't have said it if I didn't mean it."

Phoebe gave him another assessing look. "Seriously, you don't want my life in your head."

"Why invite me here if you don't want to talk?"

"Because I like you," Phoebe said with her usual directness. She reached to brush her hand down Julian's face. "Hey, wow, the acid's really kicking in." She jumped up and swirled around the fire. "The visuals are insane." She skipped off into the trees. Afraid she would get lost, Julian hurried after her. Caution slowed his feet as darkness enfolded him. He shone his phone around. He couldn't see Phoebe, but her laughter echoed back to him.

"Phoebe, wait. Phoebe—"

A scream cut him short. Forgetting his caution, he rushed forwards and almost tripped over her prone form. She was stiff and trembling as if in shock. "What happened?" he asked.

"I saw her." Phoebe's voice was tiny and high-pitched, stripped of pretension by fear.

"Saw who?"

"I saw her," she repeated. "I saw her, I saw her, I saw..." She mumbled off into incoherence.

Julian helped her up and, with one arm around her waist, guided her back to the fire. She sat hunched, shoulders shivering, eyes goggling at the flames. He started to move away from her.

"Where are you going?" she asked anxiously.

"To get your friends."

"Don't leave me alone." Her eyes pleaded with Julian. He sat down beside her. "I feel cold inside," she said through chattering teeth. Tentatively, as if she might bite him, he put his arm around her. She squirmed closer, pressing her head against his shoulder. At first deep tremors passed through her body into him every few seconds, but after a while he felt her relax.

"Why I haven't seen you around town before now?" asked Phoebe.

"This is the first time I've been back to Godthorne in years."

"How come?"

Julian said nothing for a long moment, then he began hesitantly, "I've been having these nightmares. I thought if I stayed away from here they'd stop, but they just keep getting worse. My therapist says I need to face my fears. So here I am." He trailed off, his gaze lifting to the moon as it passed behind a cloud.

"What are the nightmares about?"

His voice dropped low as if he was afraid of being overheard. "Mr Moonlight."

Phoebe lifted her head, her eyes shining with curiosity. "The serial killer?"

Julian nodded. "For years I used to dream I was one of his victims, but..." His eyes fell away from Phoebe's as the memory of the most recent dream filled his mind with Chloe's face.

"But what?" she pressed.

"But now I dream that I am Mr Moonlight. Have heard of Susan Simmons?"

"The name sounds kind of familiar."

"She was Mr Moonlight's final victim."

"How many victims were there?"

"Five, all killed on or around a full moon." Like he was reading from a newspaper, Julian reeled out the names and details. "The first was Sophia Philips, a nineteen-year-old photography student at Bournemouth University. She went missing on her way to Bournemouth train station on the 26th of November 2004. The second was Charlotte King, a twenty-five-year-old barmaid from Southampton. She went missing on the 25th of March 2005 while walking home from work. The third was Daisy Russell, a twenty-year-old hairdresser from Godthorne. On the night of May 23rd, she went out for a pint of milk and was never seen again. Then on the 21st of June, Zoe Aslett, an eighteen-year-old A-level-student at Godthorne High School disappeared on her way home from a friend's house. Just two nights later, Susan Simmons..." Julian faltered as if struggling to remember. "She... Well she went missing too." He faded off, unable to bring himself to say any more.

"How come you know so much about this stuff?"

"When I was sixteen, my mum took me to a therapist who thought unravelling the mysteries of the dream would take away its power. So I read all about the murders."

"Do you dream about killing all those girls?"

"No. Only Susan. I see myself doing... terrible things to her." Swallowing the lump of shame in his throat, Julian forced himself to meet Phoebe's gaze. "You must think I'm sick in the head."

"I dunno what you are, but I'm guessing you're no more fucked up than the rest of us."

"Yeah, but not everyone has recurring dreams about murdering people."

"It's only a dream, right? Just because you dream it doesn't mean you actually want to do it. Does it?"

"Fuck no," exclaimed Julian. "It makes me want to puke just thinking about it."

"Well then, there you go." Phoebe went on slightly hesitantly, as if she was saying more than she should, "I've come across some bad people in my time. I'm not talking about dickheads like Ash. I'm talking about the kind of people you never, ever want to meet. Take it from me, Julian, you're not a bad person. You don't even come close."

Julian smiled faintly, touched by Phoebe's words, but clearly unconvinced.

She frowned in thought. "When did you first have this new dream?"

"About a week ago."

Phoebe pressed her fingers to her temples as if struggling to process what she'd just heard. "So let me get this straight. At the same time Chloe went missing you started having this dream, which made you decide to come home for the first time in years, and that same day you found Chloe."

"Like I said, I came back because of my therapist. Me finding Chloe has nothing to do with my dreams."

"You're wrong. Don't you see it? It's like something..." Phoebe sought the right word, "*called* you back here."

Suddenly feeling as if spiders were crawling under his skin, Julian pushed out a grin. "By 'something' you mean the ghost–" *We say spirit, not ghost,* he could almost hear Grandma Alice correcting, "or spirit or whatever of Mr Moonlight?"

"I dunno. Maybe."

Turning to the trees, Julian called, "Hey, Mr Moonlight, are you there?"

Phoebe's huge glassy eyes flew around the clearing. "You can take the piss, but I've seen things out here."

"That's hardly surprising, the amount of stuff you take." Julian heaved a sigh. "I don't even know why I'm talking to you about this crap."

"I do." Phoebe's gaze landed back on him. "You're like me. We're damaged goods."

Julian's silence seemed to confirm her words. He gave a slight flinch as she took hold of his hand. He looked into her eyes. A powerful urge to kiss her swept over him.

"Tell me more about Mr Moonlight," she said.

The request killed the urge. Julian blew out his cheeks. Where to start? "His real name was Kenneth Whitcher. He lived on–"

"Hope Road. Yeah, I know. He lived with his mum four doors down from me, but I don't remember him."

"You'd have only been about four when they caught him."

"I do remember his mum. Her name was Doreen. She was seriously creepy. She looked about a thousand-years-old. Only ever came out of her house at night. Like some sort of vampire."

"More like someone ashamed to show their face."

Phoebe wrinkled her nose disapprovingly at the prosaic explanation. "Maybe that's why Mr Moonlight always killed when he did. Maybe he changed into a vampire on a full moon."

"It's werewolves that change on a full moon."

Phoebe chuckled. "Oh yeah. Whoops."

"Kenneth Whitcher wasn't a vampire or a werewolf. Although, who knows, maybe he thought he was. He never said why he killed on a full moon. It could've just been because he needed the moon to see what he was doing. I'm sure of one thing, he killed because he wanted to, not because of the moon."

"Boooring," declared Phoebe. "I reckon *that's* why he did it, because he was so bored of this town."

A smile passed across Julian's lips. "You might be onto something there."

"Too fucking right I am. God, imagine living here your whole life. If I was Doreen, I wouldn't have hung around this dump, too ashamed to leave my house. I'd have fucked off to somewhere hot and spent my last few years pissed out of my skull. You know she died three or four years back? Lay rotting in her bed. They only found her cos of the smell and all the flies. I heard no one went to her funeral. Not that I suppose she would have given a toss. She'd probably been waiting to die ever since Kenneth was caught."

Julian gave a little nod of agreement. "They only caught him by chance. He used to take stuff from his victims – jewellery, underwear, that type of thing."

"I've heard about how serial killers keep trophies."

"Yeah well Kenneth kept a box of trophies in his bedroom. Only thing is, one night some local scumbag burgled the Whitchers' house. Doreen called the police. When they picked up the burglar, he had jewellery belonging to four of Mr Moonlight's victims. The only victim missing from the list was Susan Simmons. Susan only ever wore one piece of jewellery – a ring engraved with 'You are the joy in our hearts'. It was a present from her parents. It's still missing along with her body."

Phoebe's dilated pupils drifted to the darkness beyond the firelight. "So she's out here somewhere." Her grip tightened on Julian's hand. "Hey, I've got an idea," she exclaimed. "We could do a séance."

"A séance?" Julian repeated as if he doubted his ears.

"Yeah, Chloe and me used to do them all the time for a laugh. We could try to contact Susan. Maybe she knows who killed Chloe."

Julian stared at her, too gobsmacked to reply.

"We did one here a few weeks back," continued Phoebe. "We weren't trying to contact anyone in particular. We just wanted to find out if anyone was," she waggled her fingers at the trees, "out there. So we made a crappy Ouija board out of paper and asked the spirits of the forest to join us. No bullshit, the coin we had our fingers on moved by itself. It spelled out one word three times – *well, well, well*. What do you think it means?"

"How should I know?" Julian shook off Phoebe's hand. "And you're off your rocker if you think I'm messing with that shit." He rose to his feet, suddenly wanting to be anywhere but there.

"What's your problem?" Phoebe called after him as he strode away. "What are you so fucking scared about?"

Julian flipped her the finger without looking back. Turning on his phone's torch, he weaved his way through the trees. He pulled up as a lanky figure stepped in front of him. Ash's pupils seemed to fill his eye sockets. He leaned in close, grinning sleazily. "Get what you came for, did you?" he asked. "I'll bet she can suck it dry, can't she? Just like that little dead slut pal of hers. Now she was a good suck job. First time she did me I was like, oh baby, that was some fucking good suck. Did your daddy teach you that?"

Ash chuckled as if he'd told a joke. Julian drew away from him, nose wrinkling with revulsion. Without replying, he stepped around Ash and continued on his way.

Ash's words kept going around in Julian's head. He pressed a hand to his stomach. There was that cold, slimy feeling again, spreading from the pit of his stomach to his other internal organs, as insidious as cancer. It made him queasy and angry. He dug a business-card out of his pocket and dialled the number on it. Although it was half-one in the morning, Chief Inspector Tom Henson answered in a crisp, professional tone.

"There's this guy you might want to talk to," Julian told him. "His name's Ash. He drives a black car with red flames painted on it."

"Crucifix tattoo on his left hand?"

"That's him."

"Ashley Metcalfe. An unpleasant piece of work. Been in and out of prison since he was a teenager."

Julian repeated what Ash had said about Chloe.

"Well, well, I must have a chat with Mr Young. Thanks for that, Julian. But how do you know him?"

Julian told the policeman about Phoebe. Not everything. Just the bits he needed to hear.

"Now I've got something to tell you," said Tom. "I spoke to the coroner earlier tonight. Chloe Crawley died from a heroin overdose."

Well all those fuckers you spoke to can nod and pretend to be sad. Phoebe's words rang back to Julian. "So she wasn't murdered?"

"Doesn't look like it, which means there's no need for you to remain in town." A cautionary note entered the policeman's voice. "Oh, and if I were you I'd have nothing else to do with Phoebe Bradshaw. You're likely to get yourself in trouble hanging around with *her* kind."

Irritation prickled through Julian. *What do you mean by 'her kind'?* he felt like retorting. *So what if she comes from a bad background? That doesn't make her bad, just unlucky.* Keeping his thoughts to himself, he said curtly, "Thanks," and hung-up.

He stood staring at the green-carpeted forest floor. A brick of sadness had replaced the cold feeling in his stomach. In a way, the cause of death was good news. There was no crazed killer stalking the town. But still, the thought of his dad and Godthorne's other upright citizens doing as Phoebe had predicted made him want to shout at the unfairness of life.

He glanced uncertainly in the direction he'd come from. He knew Tom Henson was right. He should have nothing more to do with Phoebe. He also knew he had to go back and speak to her. It wasn't simply that she had a right to know about Chloe. He'd caught a glimpse of her vulnerability. It made him fear for her, fear that she might destroy herself if her hatred of life grew any deeper.

He returned to the clearing, keeping an eye out for Ash. He didn't want to bump into that prick again. He was relieved to find Phoebe alone. She was lying on her back close to the fire. He thought at first that she was gazing at the stars, but as he got closer he saw that her eyes were closed. A ripple of concern went through him. Her face was as pallid as the moon. He hovered his hand over her mouth. Her breath tickled his palm. She appeared to be either passed out or asleep.

One of her arms was flung out to the side. In her hand was a little black book that looked like a diary. He stared at it uncertainly. The thought of prying into someone else's secret place made him uneasy. And yet, surely it was justified if he found something he could use to pull Phoebe away from the edge he sensed she was swaying on.

He gently removed the book from her hand. A dog-eared photo fell out. A girl of about eighteen or nineteen smiled at him from it. Her mousey blonde hair was tied back. Her face was dusted with cinnamon freckles. Her features were strikingly similar to Phoebe's – same eyes, same nose, but her mouth was fuller and the curve of her jaw was softer. She and Phoebe could have been sisters, or mother and daughter.

Julian's gaze moved to the pages the photo had marked. They were dated 16th July – just a day or so before Phoebe saw Chloe for the last time. 'How much is enough?' was written at the top of the page. Underneath was a horribly lifelike sketch of a jowly, thick-featured face with a snoutish nose. A monobrow snaked over close-set pea eyes. Swollen-looking lips curved up into a smile that seemed to exude a repulsive leering cynicism. The portrait – if that's what it was – was labelled 'Mr Ugly'.

"Hey, what the fuck are you doing?"

With a guilty start, Julian lifted his eyes to Phoebe. She was glaring at him. "Sorry… I just…" he stammered.

"You just wanted to stick your nose where it doesn't belong." Phoebe snatched back the book and shoved it into her pocket, eyeing Julian narrowly. "Why did you come back?"

He took a deep breath and told her how her best friend had died. He saw, perhaps, the faintest quiver in her eyes. But other than that, nothing. "Is that all you have to tell me?" she asked stonily.

Before tonight, Julian might have been tempted to call Phoebe a cold-hearted bitch. But now he knew – or at least, thought he knew – that her hard expression was a mask she wore to protect herself. Somewhat awkwardly, he replied, "I want to help you."

"What makes you think I need help?"

"Your Facebook photo."

Phoebe thought for a moment. Realising what Julian was referring to, she said, "You mean what I wrote on my wrist? That was a joke."

"Well it wasn't very funny. Earlier you mentioned having met some bad people. That drawing in your diary – Mr Ugly – is that who you were talking about?"

"None of your fucking business."

"Is he trying to hurt you somehow?"

Phoebe laughed contemptuously as if to say, *No man could hurt me.* "Who says he's even real? Maybe he's just a ghost. Like Mr Moonlight."

"I don't believe in ghosts."

"Really? Then prove it. Let's do a séance. If you don't believe in ghosts, what is there to be afraid of?"

The taunting words were like a hand reaching out to grab Julian's throat. He wondered if he'd got Phoebe right first time after all, perhaps she was just a cold-hearted bitch. But even as the thought passed through his head, he glimpsed her vulnerability again as she continued, "Even though I know how Chloe died, I still want to talk to her. I…" Her voice faltered. Her eyes fell away from Julian's. "I didn't have chance to say goodbye to her."

A prickle of unease swept through Julian as he found himself actually considering saying OK.

No peace. No fucking peace!

The prickling intensified to a shiver. He hugged his arms across himself. "I'm sorry, I can't."

Phoebe's eyes flared like blue flames. "Then what fucking use are you to me? You say you want to help, but you don't mean it."

"Yes I do, but…" Julian trailed off. He'd been about to launch into an account of what happened at his grandma's on the night of the séance, but it occurred to him that doing so would only reinforce Phoebe's belief that 'something' had called him back to Godthorne. He glanced around frowning as a bark of lewd laughter reached them from beyond the circle of firelight, closely followed by a scream of delight.

"You shouldn't hang around with that guy," said Julian, realising as the words left his mouth how much he sounded like Tom Henson.

"Who? Gollum? He's OK."

"No, he's not. He said some stuff about you and Chloe."

"Like what?"

"I don't want to repeat it, but it wasn't nice."

Phoebe's eyes hardened to slits. "You know something? You almost had me fooled that you were different, but you're just like the rest of them. Who the fuck do you think you are, telling me who I should hang around with?"

"I'm only trying to look out for you."

"Yeah, well, I don't need you to look out for me. I can take care of myself. I've been doing it all my life. So go on, piss off."

Julian stared at Phoebe as if to say, *Is that what you really want?*

She returned his gaze unblinkingly. There were no flames in her eyes now. They were like lightless windows. With a heavy sigh, he rose to leave.

"See you later Mr Moonlight," she said softly, a smile playing around her lips.

A flush of anger coursed through Julian, bringing with it an almost overwhelming urge to slap the smile off Phoebe's face. He pictured himself doing it, then grabbing her throat, squeezing and tearing...

Blood hammering in his ears, he turned to hasten from the clearing. This time, he didn't stop until he reached his car. He sped away from Foxwood, but he couldn't outrun the sickening images. They pursued him all the way home.

CHAPTER 12

As Julian pulled into the driveway, his heart lurched at the sight of an ambulance. A pair of paramedics were climbing into the front seats. The ambulance passed him as he parked up. His dad was standing in the front doorway. Julian sprang out of his car. "What's going on? Is Mum OK?"

"She was having breathing difficulties."

"Are they taking her to hospital?"

"No. They managed to get her breathing under control."

Julian made to move past his dad. Robert put an arm out, blocking his way. "Where are you going?"

"To see her."

"She's sleeping." Robert subjected Julian to a scrutinising look. "We need to talk."

There was a note in his voice that instantly put Julian on his guard. "About what?"

Robert motioned for Julian to follow him. As they headed into the house, Henry emerged from the kitchen to greet Julian with a bark. Robert shushed the Labrador and shooed him back into the kitchen. They went to the living-room. Robert poured himself a large whisky. "Do you want one?"

"No."

Julian sat down on the hard, modern sofa. Robert dropped into his reclining armchair. He sipped his drink, treating Julian to another probing look. Julian returned his dad's stare, waiting for him to speak. He'd learned long ago that the best policy at such times was silence.

"Where have you been?" Robert asked at last.

"Out with..." Julian was about to say friends, but he realised that was hardly an accurate description, "some people I know."

"Some people you know?" echoed Robert. "What does that mean?"

Julian shrugged evasively. "What I said."

"You stink of smoke."

"We went for a drink in the forest."

"A drink?" Robert's voice was laced with scepticism. "Is that why your pupils are like saucers?"

There was another extended silence. It was all Julian could do not to squirm in his seat.

"If you want to do drugs back in London that's your business," continued Robert. "But what you do in this house..." He tailed off, letting his words hang meaningfully between them.

"Is that it?" Julian's voice was flat. Suddenly, he didn't feel nervous. He simply felt irritated. How could his father sit in judgement when he himself spent his evenings knocking back whisky like there was no tomorrow?

"No, Julian, that's not it. Do you know why your mum had an episode tonight? Because she's worried about you." Robert shook his head in exasperation. "These bloody dreams of yours. It's too much for her."

Julian winced at the thought that he might be making her health worse. "I've barely spoken to her about any of that."

"You don't have to. It's written all over your face. Just look at the bags under your eyes."

Julian cocked an eyebrow in sardonic surprise at the fact that his dad had noticed the bags. His voice rose. "Uh-uh, no way, you're not putting it all on me. I'm not–"

"Keep your voice down."

Julian continued in a spiky whisper, "I'm not the only one she's worried about. You're hardly ever here. There's obviously some shit going down at the factory. Either that or you just can't stand to be around mum."

"That's rich coming from someone who hasn't been home in six years." Robert's tone was controlled, but his hands flexed against the armrests as if he was struggling to restrain himself.

Julian shifted uneasily. Not because he was scared, but because the sight reminded him of how Phoebe's Mr Moonlight taunt had made him feel. He'd always considered himself to be more like his mum, but in truth maybe he had more in common with his dad. He dismissed the possibility with a sharp little shake of his head. "Well I'm here now. And I'm not going anywhere."

"What's that supposed to mean?"

Julian didn't have a reply. He'd been as surprised as his dad to hear those words coming from his mouth. He rose to leave the room.

"Don't you walk away when I'm talking to you," snapped Robert.

Ignoring him, Julian made his way along the hallway. He paused by his mum's bedroom door. Very quietly, he depressed the handle and cracked open the door. A sharp antiseptic aroma, mingled with the soft scent of rose massage oil – two odours that always made him think of his mum – emanated from the room. Christine was lying on a hospital-style adjustable bed. An oxygen tube was strapped to her nostrils. The light from the hallway highlighted the hollows of her eye sockets.

Julian's heart squeezed at the sight. He watched her sleeping for a minute, before continuing to his bedroom. As he got undressed, he thought about his parting shot at his dad – *And I'm not going anywhere.* What exactly had he meant by that? Had he merely been trying to rile the hypocritical prick?

He lay down and closed his eyes, knowing the dream would come, but too exhausted to care.

CHAPTER 13

Julian jerked upright, gasping like all the air had been vacuumed out of the room. For an instant, everything reeled in front of his eyes. Then the room swam into focus. He shielded his eyes from the sunlight slanting through the windows.

His eyebrows pulled together in thought. The dream had mutated yet again. He'd reverted to being the victim, but his attacker hadn't been Kenneth Whitcher, it had been Mr Ugly. The sordid, piggish face was still faintly superimposed on his retinas, like a hologram. Who was Mr Ugly? Did he even exist or was he just a product of Phoebe's troubled psyche?

"How much is enough?" he asked himself. "How much is enough for what?"

As the face faded, his thoughts turned to his mum. He quickly dressed and headed to her bedroom. She was still in bed. A smile curled one side of her mouth as he approached. She stretched her good hand towards him. He took hold of it as carefully as if she was made of spun glass. He studied her face. The lines were a fraction more deeply etched, the shadows a shade darker than when he'd first arrived home. There was a hint of blue in her lips.

"How are you feeling?" he asked, smiling though he felt like crying.

"I'm fine," Christine replied in a weak voice that suggested she was anything but. "How did it go with Eleanor?"

Julian shrugged.

"That good, huh?"

"I think she's finally had enough of me."

Christine gave a slight shake of her head. "That girl is head over heels for you, Julian. She always has been."

I don't know why. She could do so much better. Julian kept his thoughts to himself. He didn't want to say anything that might upset his mum. His gaze strayed to the glass external wall. A multi-coloured swathe of roses were unfolding their petals at the sun's touch.

Christine followed his line of sight. "Your father thinks roses are old-fashioned." She drew in a breath of pleasure. "But I love everything about them. The colours, the smells, even the way they look when they're dying. Sometimes I just sit and watch their petals drop off."

Julian spoke through a sting of tears. "You're not dying, Mum."

Christine's bloodshot eyes slid back to him. "We're all dying, Julian."

"You know what I mean."

Christine summoned up another smile. "Do you remember what the doctors said after I had my stroke?"

"They said you'd be dead within six months."

"Yet here I am. And here I'll stay for as long as I can. But you need to be prepared for the possibility that–"

"No," broke in Julian, shaking his head, refusing to hear it. He turned at the sound of someone entering the room. His dad was approaching with a tray of tea and toast. Julian glanced at the alarm clock. It was almost eight. Normally, his dad had been at the factory for a good hour by now.

"Where's Lily?" asked Julian.

"I gave her the day off," said Robert. "I'm staying home to look after your mum."

His tone was casual, but Julian wasn't buying it. His dad was clearly out to prove a point. Robert set the tray down on the bedside table. "You're looking much better this morning, my love," he said, stooping to kiss Christine's forehead. Glancing at Julian, he asked pointedly, "Sleep well?"

Julian pushed out a strained smile. "Fine thanks. How about you?"

"I was too worried to get much sleep."

Julian bit back the temptation to respond sardonically, *Worried about what? Your precious factory?* He released his mum's hand, saying to her, "I'm going for a shower. Afterwards, if you're up to it, we could go into the garden and watch the petals drop." He noted with satisfaction the look of puzzlement that crossed his dad's face at this remark.

"Your mum will be staying in bed today," said Robert.

Julian met his dad's gaze. "That's up to her, isn't it?"

The two of them eyed each other, neither blinking.

"I don't mind where I am so long as I get to spend the day with my boys," Christine put in diplomatically.

Julian broke eye contact to leave the room. Robert followed him and asked in a low voice, "How much longer will you be staying?"

"Why? Would you rather I wasn't here?"

"I just want what's best for your mum."

"So do I." As Julian said it, he realised what he'd meant by, *And I'm not going anywhere.* "That's why I'm not going back to London. I want to be with mum. Not just a day here or there, but every day."

Robert frowned. "What about your job?"

"I'll hand in my notice."

The lines on Robert's forehead sharpened. "You can't do that."

"Why not?"

"Four years of bloody university. That's why not. Do you know how much it cost me to put you through university?"

Julian heaved a sigh. "I never asked for your money."

"Only because you never had to. You've never had to ask for anything in your entire life." Robert nodded with a twist of his mouth, as if he'd hit upon some minor revelation. "Maybe that's the problem. Maybe if I'd stuck to my guns and we hadn't simply given you everything you wanted, you wouldn't think this kind of brattish behaviour was acceptable."

"I want to help look after Mum. How is that brattish behaviour?" Julian fired back.

"Your mum doesn't need you here." Robert stabbed a finger at the world beyond the windows. "What she needs is for you to get out there and make a success of yourself."

"And what constitutes success? Being miserable in London?"

"Working hard, playing hard, finding yourself a girlfriend, living life to the full. That's what constitutes success. Not dossing around this town, getting stoned with your mates."

"You've lived here all your life. It's always been good enough for you."

"I didn't have the chances you have. When I was your age I was working three jobs. If there's one thing growing up without money taught me, it's that the world doesn't owe anyone a–"

Rolling his eyes, Julian interrupted, "Here we go again. How many more times do I have to hear the tale of how you worked yourself up from poverty to the business colossus you are now?"

Red splotches stained Robert's cheeks at the barbed retort. "You'll hear it as many times as you bloody well need to hear it. And hear this too, if you think you can live here rent free, you've got another thing coming."

"I'm happy to pay board. Or if you don't want me here, I'll find somewhere to rent."

"And how are you going to pay for that? Do you have any idea how expensive rents are around here?"

"I'll get a job."

"Where?"

Julian looked at his dad silently.

Robert's eyes widened in realisation. "The factory?" He let out a harsh, almost mocking laugh. "You expect *me* to give you a job?"

"You always said you want to keep the business in the family."

"Yes, but I was thinking of further down the line, when you have a family of your own to support. Besides, what makes you think I'd employ someone who's willing to walk away from a job at the drop of a hat?" When Julian made no reply, Robert spread his hands as if to say, *Point proved.* "This is what I was talking about, Julian, you've had it so easy you don't think you have to work for anything."

"I am willing to work for it," protested Julian. "I'll work on the production line, sweep the floors, make cups of tea, whatever."

Robert wrinkled his nose as if he'd sniffed something rotten. "Do you think I've worked fifteen hours a day all these years so I can watch my son struggle like I had to?"

"But you just said I've had it too easy."

"Don't twist my words to your ends, Julian."

"I'm not. I'm just asking for the chance to prove–"

"No." Robert made a cutting motion. "This conversation is over. Tomorrow you're going to go back to London and buckle down to your job, and that's all there is to it."

"And what if I refuse?"

"Don't push me, Julian. I'm warning you."

For a full thirty-seconds, father and son faced each other in silence. Julian ended the staring contest by turning to go into the bathroom.

After showering and shaving, he made toast and ate it at the kitchen table, sharing titbits with Henry. Then he headed for his mum's bedroom again. He paused outside the living-room. His dad was in the reclining armchair, cradling a tumbler of whisky and staring vacantly out of the window. He looked older than his years in the unforgiving sunlight. Work and worry had carved a chessboard of creases into his forehead.

"Bit early for that, isn't it?" commented Julian. His dad had always enjoyed a drink, but he rarely reached for the bottle until the sun was over the yardarm.

"Did I ever tell you that I met Kenneth Whitcher?" Robert said without looking at Julian.

"No." There was a rise of interest in Julian's voice at the seemingly random comment.

"He came to me for a job. This was a few years before he killed those girls."

"What was he like?"

"He struck me as a bit of a simpleton."

"Did you give him a job?"

Robert nodded. "I put him to work in the packing room. Well you know what it's like in there. They're a tight knit bunch. At the end of Whitcher's first day, a couple of the old dears who've been here since year dot came to tell me they didn't think he was up to the job. I had a look at his work and, to be honest, it wasn't bad. Right then I knew something was up. So it was no surprise when the next day, half the women from the packing room came marching into my office. That's when it came out. They didn't like Whitcher. He was too quiet, he had shifty eyes, he gave them the creeps. Basically, they wanted him gone."

"So what did you do?"

"What I should have done is told them to leave the poor bugger alone. What I did is cave in to them. The business was really taking off at the time. I couldn't afford to lose any of my best workers. So I called Whitcher into the office, told him his work wasn't up to scratch."

"You lied to him." Julian's voice was low with disapproval.

"What else was I supposed to do? I could hardly tell him the truth. Besides, I'm pretty sure he had a fair idea what was really going on. He didn't get angry, or even say anything, but there was something about the way he looked at me. I got the feeling there was more going on in his head than he let on." Robert took a thoughtful sip of whisky. "I gave him a week's pay and sent him on his way. I don't know why I paid him for a week. I suppose I felt sorry for him. He was forty-years-old. Lived with his mum. No wife or kids." He turned to Julian. "Is that how you want to end up?"

A tingle climbed Julian's spine at the suggestion that he might end up like Kenneth Whitcher. "Of course not."

"Then go back to London." Robert's voice verged on pleading.

"I can't."

"Why not? Don't tell me you're still afraid of those ridiculous dreams. Because believe me, Julian, if you'd met Whitcher you'd know you have nothing to be afraid of. A sad-sack like him wouldn't have dared raise a hand against someone who might hit back."

"I'm not afraid." Hearing the telltale hollowness in his reply, Julian wished he'd remained silent.

Robert arched an eyebrow. "Is there something you're not telling me? Has this got something to do with a girl?"

Phoebe. The name rang out in Julian's mind. A cleft appeared between his eyebrows. Had his dad chanced on the truth? Could Phoebe be part of, or even the main reason he wanted to stay? Was he simply using his mum as an excuse? From the first moment he'd seen Phoebe she'd captivated him like no other girl ever had. Not because he desired her more than other girls, but because... Because of what? *We're damaged goods.* Her words came back to him. Was that it? Were they kindred spirits? There'd never been anyone else, not even Eleanor, that he'd felt able to open up to about the dreams without fear of judgement.

A longing to see Phoebe swept over him. He wanted to apologise for looking in her diary and explain why he couldn't take part in a séance. He wanted to kiss her again and find out how it felt. But most of all he just wanted to make sure she was OK.

"It is a girl, isn't it?" Robert exclaimed with relief that here was something he could finally understand. "Who is she? Obviously it's not Eleanor? I heard how you stood her up."

"There's no–" Julian broke off. His dad was far too shrewd to tell even a half-truth to. Besides, he had nothing to hide. "Actually there is someone, but I don't know if... I mean, nothing's happened..." He paused awkwardly, before adding, "Anyway, whatever happens with this girl, I want to live near Mum." He echoed his dad's earlier conversation stopper. "And that's all there is to it."

Julian put a final full stop on his words by turning to continue on his way. He brought up Phoebe's Facebook page on his phone. There had been no updates. He messaged her 'I feel like shit about last night. Can we meet up?' He stared at the phone for a moment. There was no response. Sighing, he entered his mum's bedroom. She was snoring softly through her oxygen tube. He pulled up a chair to her bedside and sat fidgeting with his phone, thinking about Phoebe and trying not to think about her, torn between wanting to see her and wishing he'd never set eyes on her.

CHAPTER 14

Julian glanced out the window. Clouds were moving in to obscure the late-afternoon sun. For the hundredth time that day, his gaze returned to his phone. It had been hours since he'd messaged Phoebe, and still no response. Was she ignoring him because of last night? He hoped that's all it was. His stomach knotted as he thought about the things Ash had said. He should never have left her alone with that scumbag.

His eyes lifted to his mum. She was staring blearily back at him. She'd woken up several times throughout the day, but only for ten or fifteen minutes at a time. "What's the matter, Julian?" she asked in a croaky voice.

"Nothing," he replied.

Christine shuffled into a sitting position, cocking her head as if to say, *Really?* "Every time I open my eyes you're staring at your phone as if waiting for a call. Is it Eleanor?"

He didn't answer her question. He couldn't lie to her, and neither could he burden her with the truth. All he could do was hide behind uncomfortable silence.

"Why don't you go see her?" suggested Christine.

Julian shook his head. "I want to stay here with you."

"I know, darling, but I'm feeling a lot better. Really I am. And anyway, I need some prescriptions picking up. Lily usually does it, but seeing as she isn't here..." She trailed off meaningfully.

Julian took the hint. "I can do that." He gave his mum a look of lingering concern. "As long as you're OK."

Christine's lips crooked up into a smile. "I'm fine, like I always am." There was a tongue-in-cheek note to her reply that brought a wry smile to Julian's face too. She told him where to pick up the prescriptions, adding, "Now go on. Go and beg for forgiveness."

"I won't be long."

Julian hurried to the door. On his way out of the house, he paused by the living-room. His dad was snoring in the armchair. There was a two-thirds empty bottle of whisky and an empty tumbler on the coffee-table. Julian considered waking him, but he couldn't face the thought of being dragged back into their earlier conversation.

He headed for his car, wondering how best to go about tracking down Phoebe. He knew she lived on Hope Road. He could just knock on doors until he got the right house. Another idea came to him. After Kenneth Whitcher's arrest, his mum's house had been all over the newspapers. He Googled 'Kenneth Whitcher. Mr Moonlight House'. An image of a small, pebble-dashed semi came up under the link 'Houses of Horror: The homes of Britain's most notorious murderers'. The garden had a low privet hedge with a wooden slatted gate at its centre. The house's front door was red. Floral curtains were drawn in its two front windows. Other than that it was utterly nondescript.

Julian followed the link and scrolled down past '10 Rillington Place' and '25 Cromwell Street' to '64 Hope Road'. Underneath a photo of the house was a brief paragraph – 'The two-bedroomed Godthorne council property where Kenneth Whitcher lived with his mother Doreen. Whitcher, dubbed Mr Moonlight, murdered five women over an eight-month period in 2004-2005 and buried their bodies in The New Forest. Doreen Whitcher died in 2014 and the council have since re-let the house.'

Julian accelerated out of the driveway. A steady trickle of cars and people were heading away from the town centre. It was half-past six. Godthorne's rush-hour, such as it was, was almost over. He was soon turning past the blocks of maisonettes at the east end of Hope Road. A group of boys in school uniforms were kicking a ball about on a patch of grass.

Beyond the maisonettes was a long row of pebble-dashed semis with small gardens. He braked outside number 64 and sat staring at the house where Kenneth Whitcher had grown up. A white uPVC door had replaced the red door. The privet hedge had been removed to make way for a tarmac driveway.

How can anyone stand to live in that house? he wondered.

He knew what Phoebe's reply would be – *Not everyone gets to choose where they live, rich boy.*

He counted four doors down. His gaze passed over a blonde-haired girl hurrying along the pavement and came to land on a scruffy house. The front lawn simultaneously managed to be overgrown and threadbare. The downstairs curtains were closed. There were no curtains in the upstairs window. Someone had graffitied 'NO MORE DRUGS' on the front door, but some joker had crossed out the 'NO'.

After lingering on the house for a second, Julian's eyes darted towards the blonde. There had been something familiar about her. She had her head down as if she didn't want to see or be seen by anyone. He reversed past her and braked. His eyes widened.

The girl was Phoebe... And yet it wasn't her. Gone were the torn fishnets, leather jacket, heavy makeup and facial piercings. A long-sleeved – perhaps to conceal the cuts on her arms – knee-length pastel pink summer dress clung to her pencil waist. Pink lipstick glistened on her lips. Her hair was dyed sandy blonde and tied back in a ponytail.

That cold, slimy feeling coiled itself around Julian's internal organs. It was as if Phoebe had found an old newspaper photo of Susan Simmons and got herself up to look like it.

Julian lowered his window. "Phoebe."

She hurried onwards, seeming not to hear. He got out of the car, calling her name again. She looked up with a start. A frown gathered between her eyes. "What are you doing here?"

"Did you get my message?"

"Yeah."

Stung by the obvious implication of Phoebe's reply, Julian asked, "Why do you look like... that?"

Phoebe laughed down her nose. "You just can't help sticking your nose into other peoples' business, can you?"

How much is enough? The question scribbled in the diary rose into Julian's mind, along with Mr Ugly's repulsive face. "Has this got something to do with him?"

"Who?"

"You know who – Mr Ugly. He's real, isn't–"

Phoebe's sharp hiss silenced Julian. She turned away and continued walking. When he began to follow her, she flashed an angry glance at him. "Look, rich boy, just fuck off, will you?"

"If you're in some kind of trouble–"

"Why are you doing this?" cut in Phoebe. "We're not friends. You don't even want to fuck me."

"I..." Julian stumbled over his words. "I don't want anything bad to happen to you."

Phoebe stopped and turned to him. Her eyes were softer, but there was a sort of contempt in them too. "You're too late. The bad thing already happened."

He shook his head. "It's not too late. You're still here. Still alive."

"Am I? Just cos something looks alive on the outside doesn't mean it's alive in here." She stabbed a finger at her chest.

"So open up. Show me what's inside you. It can't be any worse than what's inside me."

Phoebe snorted, the contempt at the front of her eyes now. "There are no dreams inside me, rich boy. I can't afford them. I'm rotten, just like this shitty town. Can't you smell me? I stink."

She resumed walking. Julian followed once again, saying, "You don't have to do this, Phoebe." She ignored him, but he persisted, "Whatever it is, I can help you. Just tell me how."

Without warning, she whirled and slapped him, her nails drawing blood.

They stared at each other for a breathless moment, Julian with his mouth hanging open, Phoebe po-faced. Then she walked away. This time he remained where he was.

"You know who you look like, don't you?" he called after her. "Susan Simmons was wearing a dress just like that when she went missing. Someone's using you for their sick game. The same as they did Chloe."

Phoebe ignored him. Cheek smarting, he watched her dwindle from sight. He thought about Susan, missing all these years, her parents still not knowing for sure what happened to her. He thought about Chloe, her maggoty eye sockets, her livid, bloated flesh.

"No." The word whistled between his teeth. "No fucking way."

He ran back to the car and drove after Phoebe, spotting her a short distance beyond the police station. He braked at a set of red lights, drumming his fingers on the steering-wheel, muttering, "C'mon, c'mon," as she crossed the road and turned a corner.

The lights changed. He accelerated around the corner. Phoebe was nowhere to be seen. Jerking his gaze all around, he caught sight of her again on a lonely side street. She was approaching a black Mercedes with tinted windows. Who the hell would she know with a car like that? As she opened the back door to duck inside, he saw two figures – one in the driver's seat, the other in the backseat. The driver had a dark beard and shades. He was bull-necked and broad-shouldered, not a guy to tangle with. The figure beside Phoebe was a busty woman in a low-cut black dress, red hair piled in coils, good looking, but with a hard-bitten edge.

Then the door was closing and the Mercedes was turning to accelerate past Julian. Phoebe lowered her window. She was looking in his direction, but she didn't appear to see him. She was wearing a somewhere-else expression that he recognised only too well from staring at his own reflection day after mind-numbing day in his office window.

The Mercedes headed for the southern suburbs. Julian tailed it at what he judged to be an inconspicuous distance, his mind whirring with the possibilities of what Phoebe might be getting herself into. He pictured Mr Ugly sniffing at her like a hungry pig. A fat slug of a tongue emerged from those leering lips to lick her face. Thick fingers clamped onto her throat. Saliva-dripping teeth sank into her flesh. The scene swept before him in nauseatingly vivid detail.

The Mercedes put on a sudden burst of speed, jumping a red light. Julian's VW lurched as he shoved at the accelerator. There was a screech of brakes, then the world seemed to explode. His car span crazily, jolting him sideways. A white light flashed in front of his eyes as his head slammed into the driver's door window.

His vision wobbled back into focus. The front left-hand side of the bonnet was a crumpled mess. The car that had crashed into him had come to a stop twenty or so metres away. Fragments of glass and plastic were scattered across the road. An electric shock of pain crackled down his spine as he twisted to look over his shoulder. The Mercedes was speeding into the distance. As it passed out of sight, a thought slid through him like a knife – *That's it, Phoebe's gone and you'll never see her again.*

CHAPTER 15

Julian lay pretending to be asleep as the doctor reassured Robert that, except for bruising and whiplash, his son was unhurt. "He's been very lucky," said the doctor.

Julian didn't feel lucky. He felt about as low as he ever had in his life.

"We'll keep him in overnight for observation," continued the doctor. "If his condition remains unchanged, he can go home in the morning."

One set of footsteps headed out of the room.

"Are you awake, Julian?" asked Robert. There was no discernible sympathy in his voice.

Julian didn't open his eyes. He knew he was in for an earful – before the doctor arrived, his dad and a constable had been talking in the hallway. Through a haze of painkillers, Julian had overheard snippets like – 'miracle no one was seriously hurt' and 'dangerous driving'.

For what seemed like a long moment, he sensed his dad looking at him. Heaving a sigh, Robert left the room too.

Julian still didn't open his eyes. The painkillers were taking him to a place where he was willing to let go. As usual, the dream was lurking in the shadows of sleep. Only this time it was Phoebe in her Susan Simmons getup that writhed beneath him. Lowering his head, he bit her windpipe, ravenously chewing deeper and deeper, blood spurting around his jaw. He saw his face reflected in her dying eyes, mutated by violent ecstasy into something even uglier than the face in her diary.

He snapped awake with a choking sob in his throat and Phoebe's words echoing in his mind. *You're too late. The bad thing already happened. Too late. Too late…*

He didn't go back to sleep.

In the morning, after giving Julian the once over, the doctor declared him fit to go home. As Julian was getting dressed, his dad turned up.

"How are you feeling?" asked Robert.

"Like I was in a car crash," Julian replied tetchily, manoeuvring his t-shirt over the neck brace he'd been instructed to wear until the whiplash cleared up. The pain was something else. Even with the brace and painkillers, every movement made him wince.

They slowly made their way to the carpark. At the very least, Julian expected a lecture about running red lights, but all Robert said during the drive home was, "The garage called. Looks like your car's a write-off." He wore the tight-lipped expression of someone who'd been warned to keep his thoughts to himself.

I couldn't give a shit about the car, Julian felt like replying. Right that moment, all he cared about was finding out if Phoebe was OK. If it hadn't been for his neck, he would have already been searching for her.

His mum, Lily and Henry were waiting at the front door. Christine was pale and drawn, but it lifted Julian's heart to see her up and about. Her lips formed a lopsided O at the sight of him. "That looks like it hurts."

"It looks worse than it is," he said, dredging up a smile.

"What did the doctor say?"

"That my neck should be OK after a few days of total rest."

"Then we'd better get you to bed," put in Lily. "I'll bring you some breakfast. I bet you're hungry after that hospital food, aren't you?"

Julian nodded and wished he hadn't.

Robert looked on with ill-disguised disapproval as the women fussed over Julian, almost as if he suspected his son had somehow contrived to injure himself for the attention. Once Julian was propped up in bed with everything he needed close to hand and everyone but his mum and Henry had left the room, he said, "I'm sorry, Mum."

"What for?"

"For causing all this trouble."

Christine rested her cold, soft hand on his. "It was an accident."

Julian looked at her guiltily from under his eyebrows. "I'm not just talking about the crash."

Christine smiled and nodded as if to say, *I know.* "Try not to worry about any of that." She gave his hand a squeeze. "Hey, everything's going to be OK. I remember what it was like to be your age. Not knowing where you want to be or what you want to do. It's perfectly normal."

Looking into his mum's concerned eyes, Julian wanted to break down and tell her everything, talk until he was as empty as a drained cesspool. He couldn't bring himself to open up, though. Partly because she already had enough to contend with, but mainly because the prospect of describing the dreams made him shrivel with shame.

Can't you smell me?

Phoebe's parting words came into his mind. Perhaps, in some strange way, he had smelled her. Not simply her external smell, but what was inside of her, and through that, had felt safe opening up to her.

"You know I love you, right?" said Christine.

Julian smiled back. "Of course I do."

"Just shout if you need anything." She looked at Henry, who was stretched out on the end of the bed. "Keep an eye on him for me, Henry. Make sure he stays put."

Henry yawned and flapped his tail.

When his mum left the room, Julian navigated to Facebook on his phone. He clicked on '*Send Dolor a message*' and wrote 'Are you OK? That's all I want to know'.

Throughout the rest of the day, despite not hearing a message alert, he checked his inbox every few minutes. It remained empty. He sent more messages with the same result. He considered phoning Kyle and asking him to look for Phoebe, but decided against it. After the other night, Kyle would probably tell him to go fuck himself. Besides, there was only one person he could really rely on – Eleanor. What's more, she had access to her dad's files. It was an open secret that Mike kept a file on everyone he deemed of interest in Godthorne. The Bradshaws were bound to be in there. But Julian was reluctant to contact her. It wasn't just the thought of coming clean about why he'd stood her up and fielding the awkward questions that would inevitably follow. It was the thought of getting her involved at all, of exposing her to something she wasn't equipped to handle, something which, although he had no idea what it was, he sensed in his heart and in his brain to be not merely ugly, but sordid and degenerate.

His mum and Lily looked in on him several times during the day. His dad didn't show his face, perhaps fearing he wouldn't be able to hold his tongue. That evening, after Lily had gone home, Julian heard raised voices. The voices were muffled, but he caught enough snatches of speech to know his parents were arguing about him.

He grimaced, but not from the pain in his neck, as his dad barked, "He's making you ill, Christine." Robert's voice dropped, before rising loud enough for Julian to hear, "…back to London."

Julian's eyebrows bunched. Maybe his dad was right. Maybe it would be best for everyone if he went back.

Night came on and seemed to go on and on. Julian staved off sleep for as long as possible, but the painkillers made him drowsy. Eventually, with dawn only a few hours away, he nodded off. He jolted awake some time later with the bitter taste of blood in his mouth and found that he'd taken a bite out of his lower lip.

Dabbing away the blood with a tissue, he reached for his phone. His heart slumped at the empty inbox. He put down the phone, picked it up again, started to dial, then hung up. With every passing minute, the sense that something was wrong, that something terrible had happened to Phoebe grew in him. At last, it got so strong he couldn't resist it. He phoned Eleanor.

CHAPTER 16

Eleanor picked up and asked sleepily, "What is it now, Julian?"

"I want to explain why I stood you up." There was a moment of expectant silence. Julian took a long breath, like someone about to dive into deep water. "I was with Phoebe Bradshaw."

"Who?"

"She was best mates with Chloe Crawley." He added quickly, "There's nothing going on between us."

"So if there's nothing going on, what exactly is Phoebe Bradshaw to you?"

"She's..." Julian's voice faltered as he struggled to find the words to define what she was to him. "She's someone I feel responsible for."

"Why?"

"I guess because I'm the one who found Chloe." That was only part of the reason, but Julian wasn't about to try to explain something to Eleanor that he couldn't explain to himself.

After a pause heavy with doubt, she said, "I suppose I sort of get that."

Julian drew in another deep breath. "The thing is, Eleanor, I need a favour."

She clicked her tongue in exasperation. "Now we're getting down to the real reason you called."

"This isn't about me. It's about Phoebe. I need you to find out if she's OK."

"Why wouldn't she be?"

"I think she might be in trouble."

"What do you mean? What kind of trouble?"

"I'm not sure. I've just got a bad feeling. I think Chloe's death has made her do something stupid."

"'Stupid' as in what? Are we talking suicide levels of stupid?"

Julian's stomach screwed into a tight ball as he thought about the cuts on Phoebe's forearms. "No. No way."

"You sound as if you're trying to convince yourself."

"Maybe I am," Julian admitted. "I don't know. I just think there's more to this."

"Why do you need me? Why can't you find out for yourself if she's OK?"

Julian told Eleanor about the crash, leaving out the reason behind it. He didn't want to get her more involved than was absolutely necessary.

"Oh my god," she exclaimed. "Are you OK?"

"I will be in a day or two."

Silence filled the phone line. Julian could sense Eleanor's mind ticking over. He knew her well enough to guess what was coming. "Perhaps you should call the police," she said. "I mean, if Phoebe's hurt herself, it might be the difference between her living or dying."

Eleanor was right, of course, but Julian was reluctant to follow her suggestion until he had no other option. If he got the police involved, Phoebe would never forgive him. "Look, all I'm asking is that you go to her house and see if she's there."

Eleanor sighed. "OK, Julian, I'll do it. But if she's not there–"

"Then I'll phone the police."

"What does Phoebe look like?"

Julian started describing her as she'd looked when he first saw her. Realising his mistake, he broke off and described her as she'd looked the previous evening. "That's a pretty radical image change," said Eleanor. "They sound like two different people. Hey, didn't Chloe Crawley also dye her hair blonde before she went missing?"

"Yes."

"Hmm." The reluctance was back in Eleanor's voice. "That's weird. Why would they both do that?"

"Phoebe lives on Hope Road," said Julian, skipping past the troubling question. He told Eleanor the address, "You needn't knock on the door. Just park up nearby and–"

"Stake the place out like Magnum P.I.," Eleanor cut in wryly.

A small smile found its way onto Julian's face. "Something like that."

"Well If I'm going to do this, I'd better get over there. I'll be in touch as soon as there's anything to tell."

"Be careful."

"Relax. You know me. Little Miss Sensible."

Julian's smile broadened. Little Miss Sensible had been his nickname for Eleanor at school. She'd hated it. Which, of course, had made him call her it all the more.

The hours seemed to stretch as Julian waited to hear from Eleanor. Lily brought him breakfast, but he couldn't stomach more than a few bites of toast. He asked where his dad was and was relieved to hear that he'd gone into work. His mum came to see him, but his attention kept drifting to his phone, and she soon gave up trying to have a conversation. "Turn that thing off and get some rest," she remonstrated gently but firmly.

Julian put his phone down, but the moment his mum was gone he reached for it again. He tried phoning Eleanor twice, but to his frustration she didn't answer. By late afternoon he was wound so tight that he flinched at a knock on his bedroom door.

Lily poked her head around the door, sporting a broad smile. "You've got a visitor."

Eleanor stepped into the room. Her chestnut brown hair was pinned up, exposing her swan neck. Her cheeks were flushed as if she'd been out in the sun too long. A folder was tucked under her arm.

The instant Julian saw her face he knew something was up, and the ball in his stomach contracted.

"I'll leave you two to it," said Lily, flashing a meaningful glance at Julian as she closed the door.

"You didn't find her, did you?" Julian said to Eleanor.

"I've been melting in my car outside her house all day. No one's in. How's your neck?"

Julian waved away her concern. He pointed at the folder. "What's that?"

Eleanor sat on the edge of the bed and flipped open the folder. Julian found himself staring at a photo of a thirty-something woman with shoulder-length mousey blonde hair and freckled cheeks. He'd seen the woman before, only she'd been bright-eyed and clear-skinned. Now she had a dead-eyed expression and broken veins marred her complexion. "Phoebe carries a photo of this woman around with her," he said.

"That's Tasmin Bradshaw. Phoebe's mum. She was only seventeen when she had Phoebe and Dylan. She was an alcoholic. She died of cirrhosis in February this year."

A pained breath escaped Julian as his mind turned to his own mum. The mere thought of losing her was enough to break him up inside. "What about their dad?"

"Unknown. Rumour has it Tasmin was a prostitute. So in the space of six months Phoebe's lost her mum and her best friend. And to top it all off, Dylan's wanted by the police for burglaries and drug offences. I'd say all that puts her in the at-risk-of-doing-something-stupid category. Wouldn't you?"

Heaving a sigh, Julian nodded.

Eleanor spread her hands as if to say, *So what now?*

Julian knew what she wanted him to do. He slowly reached for his phone. In some ways, Eleanor's words had made him more, not less reluctant to contact the police. Phoebe had been through so much in her short life. Did she really need the police prying into her business? "What if we're wrong? Her life's tough enough. I don't want to make it any worse."

"The only way it could be any worse is if she dies because we do nothing."

There was a scrabbling at the door. Eleanor rose to open it. Henry bounded into the room, delighted to see her. "Hi Henry," she said, ruffling his fur. He rolled onto his back for her to scratch his tummy. She obliged, saying, "Who's turning into a fatty fudge-cake?"

Springing to his feet, the dog darted forwards to thrust his head under the bed. "Get out from under there, Henry," said Julian, wincing as the bed shook.

Henry retreated with what looked to be a twig dangling from his jaws. "Have you got a present for me?" said Eleanor as the over-excited Labrador turned to her. She held out her hand, and he dropped the object into it. Wrinkles crowded her forehead as she looked at her 'present'. "What is–" She broke off with a sharp intake of breath, casting the thing away from her. It landed on the bed. Henry made to retrieve it, but Julian shooed him away.

Oblivious to the pain in his neck, Julian bent forwards for a closer look. The thing was five or six centimetres long, tapering to a point. It was as brown and shrivelled as sun-baked leather. "It's a finger," he said in a hushed voice as if he was poring over some sacred relic.

"No shit it's a finger," said Eleanor. "Where did it come from?"

Julian's mind flashed back to Henry tearing something from Chloe's corpse and running off with it. "Chloe Crawley."

"Uh-uh, no way. That finger looks like it's been mummified."

"I didn't say it was her finger. I said it *came* from her." Julian picked up the finger. It had the hard, dry texture of beef jerky. He ran his fingertips over what appeared to be an arthritically-swollen knuckle. The bump was too uniformly smooth and circular to be bone. He scratched its surface, exposing a glint of silver.

"Is that a ring?" Eleanor asked as Julian scratched away more of the discolouration.

"Looks like it."

The ring had fused with the finger. Strips of paper-thin skin peeled away as Julian worked the ring free. He dunked it into a glass of water and cleaned it with a tissue, revealing a simple silver band with no decoration on its exterior. He held it up to the light. A tremor took hold of his voice as he read aloud the inscription on its inner surface, "You are the joy in our hearts." He looked at Eleanor in slack-jawed astonishment. "This ring belonged to Susan Simmons."

"As in the Susan Simmons who was murdered by–"

"Yes," interrupted Julian, not wanting to hear that hated name.

"How is that possible?"

"I've no idea."

Their gazes returned to the finger. Glimpses of yellowed bone showed through the torn skin. The end of the finger was bent as if beckoning to them.

"*Now* will you phone the police?" said Eleanor.

CHAPTER 17

Tom Henson, Eleanor, Christine and Lily gathered around the coffee-table as Julian unfolded the tissue. Lily gave out a shriek at the sight of the wrinkly brown thing the tissue contained. "What in god's name is *that*?"

Christine pressed a hand to her mouth, swallowing as if she felt queasy.

"I'd say sat that's a finger," said Tom, stooping closer. "Mm-hmm, definitely a finger."

"I didn't think you were squeamish, Mrs Harris," Eleanor said with a half-hearted attempt at a smile.

"Yes well..." Christine swallowed hard again. "This is the first time I've seen a severed finger."

"'Severed' is the right word," said Tom, pointing to the knuckle end of the finger. "The bone's been cleanly cut through." His dark, steady eyes slid towards Julian. "You say Henry took this from Chloe Crawley?"

"Yes."

"Chloe wasn't missing any fingers."

"It's Susan Simmons's finger."

Tom's eyebrows lifted. "And just how would you know that?"

Julian pointed to the silver ring beside the finger. "Look at the inscription."

Tom crooked his neck to read the words etched into the ring's underside. His eyes returned to Julian, narrowing slightly. "You seem to have an *unusually* deep knowledge of the Kenneth Whitcher case."

The way he stressed the word 'unusually' made Julian shift on his feet.

"I don't see what that has to do with anything," Christine put in spikily. "Surely what you should be asking yourself is – where did Chloe find that finger? And does it have anything to do with her death?"

"I haven't got the first clue where she found it," admitted Tom. "I was a detective constable back when Susan went missing. Dozens of us spent days searching the forest. We didn't find so much as a hair."

"It must have been somewhere extremely cold, wet or dry," offered Eleanor. "Those are the three environments that would preserve a body." As all eyes turned to her, she added somewhat self-consciously, "I looked it up online. Bodies have been preserved for hundreds, even thousands of years in glaciers, deserts and bogs."

"Well there aren't any glaciers or deserts around here," said Lily.

Tom glanced at her sardonically as if to say, *Thanks for that nugget of invaluable information.*

"But we do have plenty of bogs," pointed out Christine. "I suggest you and your men get out there and start searching them ASAP, Tom."

The chief inspector replied with a respectful nod, clearly knowing better than to step on her toes again. He pulled on a latex glove and transferred the ring and finger to evidence bags. "A Forensic team will be along shortly to have a look around. Just in case Henry brought in anything else."

"Well they'd better not make a mess," warned Lily, crossing her arms.

"Can I have a word in private?" Tom asked Julian.

"As long as you make it quick," said Christine. "Julian's supposed to be resting."

Moving as stiffly as a robot, Julian led Tom to the kitchen. "A penknife with a small saw was found on Chloe," said the chief inspector, subjecting him to one of his assessing looks.

"That explains how she cut off Susan's finger."

Tom made a, "Hmm," as if he was undecided on that point. He tapped the bag containing the finger. "Are you sure it wasn't you and not Henry who took this from Chloe?"

Julian frowned. "Why would I do that?"

"Perhaps this sort of thing floats your boat. I've met all types during my time on The Force. We once picked up a bloke who kept pestering Doreen Whitcher to sell him things from her house – ornaments, pictures, books. Turned out he ran a website selling murder memorabilia. There's a big market for that stuff." Tom shook his head. "The mind boggles."

"Yeah well I'm not into that." Julian pointed to the finger. "If I was, I would hardly have left that thing lying around under my bed."

Tom nodded as if that made sense to him. "Sorry, but I had to ask."

There was a disingenuous edge to the apology that raised Julian's hackles. He didn't let his irritation distract him from what really mattered. "There's something else I need to talk to you about. I'm worried about Phoebe."

"Why? What's she done now?"

Restraining another jolt of annoyance at Tom's eye-rolling tone, Julian gave him the full story of the previous night's encounter with Phoebe. "It just seemed so odd," he said. "Her hair. Her clothes. It was like she was dressed up to play a part."

"Doesn't sound odd to me. I have a teenage daughter myself who changes her hair almost as often as she does her clothes. By all accounts, Chloe was the same. Her mum says she dyed her hair four different colours in the space of a month before she went missing."

"What about the Mercedes?"

"Did you take down the registration number?"

Julian clicked his tongue in self-recrimination. "No."

"That's a shame, but it's probably not important. After all, it's not illegal to get dressed up and go out with whoever you please." Tom leaned in close, his voice dropping as if to make extra sure there was no chance of being overheard. "But it is illegal to drive under the influence of drugs. Your blood-screen showed a positive reading of cannabis."

Julian felt his face reddening. "I'd had two joints the night before the crash. That's all."

"It makes no difference whether or not you were stoned at the time of the crash. All that matters is the level of cannabis in your system. Do you know what the penalty for drug driving is, Julian? A one year driving ban. A fine. And up to six months in prison."

"Prison?" Julian exclaimed. "Seriously?"

"Do I look like I'm joking? I warned you, didn't I, that hanging around with that Bradshaw girl would bring you nothing but trouble? Your family has a good reputation in this town."

"What does this have to do with my family's reputation?"

"Don't be naïve, Julian. Reputation is everything in a place like Godthorne. Your father built his business on his reputation for honesty. I know he wants you to take over the business one day, which means its continued success..."

"Depends on my reputation." Julian finished Tom's sentence in a voice weighed down by responsibility. He heaved a sigh, imagining everything his dad had worked so hard to build falling apart and what that would do to his parents.

Tom smiled. "Don't look so worried. I can put in a good word with the magistrate. See to it that you're let off with a slap on the wrist."

"Why would you do that?"

"Because you're a good lad. And this town needs you. The factory employs a lot of people. I'd hate to see them suffer because you made one stupid little mistake. But you have to do something for me in return – stay away from Phoebe Bradshaw."

"That won't be difficult since she's missing."

"'Missing. That's an emotive word. Believe me, Julian, if I thought for one second that she was missing, we wouldn't be chatting like this. I'd have already hauled you down the station, neck-brace n'all. And I'd have every available man out searching for her. But she's not missing. She's holed up in some dive, drugged up to her eyeballs. I guarantee you, she'll come crawling home in a day or two. That girl's got a history as long as my arm of pulling these sorts of stunts. So what do you say? Are you going to stay away from her?"

Julian sucked his upper lip. The mere thought of saying *OK* felt like a betrayal of Phoebe. He glanced around at the whirr of his mum's wheelchair. The sight of her approaching drew the word from him, "OK."

Tom nodded approvingly. "Good. And let's hope we don't need to have any more of these chats." He smiled at Christine. "I'd better get these to the lab boys," he said, pointing to the evidence bags. "Thanks for your patience, Christine. Say hello to Robert for me."

His heart heavy with unease, Julian watched Tom leave. It wasn't only the chief inspector's unwillingness to take his concerns seriously that disturbed him. He felt that he'd been backed into a corner, forced to choose between safeguarding his own future and abandoning Phoebe to whatever fate she might have brought upon herself, and he was disgusted at the ease with which he'd capitulated. Phoebe was right, he *was* just a rich boy.

* * *

Julian lay on a sun-lounger in the garden, staring at the forest. Over his shoulder, latex-gloved figures could be seen methodically combing the house's interior. Eleanor emerged from the back door and approached him, saying, "They haven't found anything."

He made a disinterested, "Mm."

Eleanor frowned. "What's wrong?"

"My neck's killing me."

She eyed him as if she suspected there was more to it than that. Her gaze moved to the ranks of trees. She shivered as if a shadow had passed over the sun. "Sometimes I feel like the forest is watching. Watching and waiting for a chance to reclaim the land we've taken from it." She was silent for a moment, then added, "God, I hope Phoebe's OK."

Do you? Do you honestly give a shit? Julian was tempted to ask, but he knew it would be undeserved. Eleanor was one of the few people he'd come across in Godthorne, or anywhere, who genuinely cared for everyone whose life she touched.

"First Chloe, now Phoebe." Eleanor shook her head. "What is going on in this town?"

"How the fuck should I know?" Julian instantly felt a bite of remorse for snapping at her. "Sorry, Eleanor. It's just..." He trailed off into a sigh. "Actually, you know what, I don't want to talk about this anymore."

She laid her hand on his wrist. Her touch was even softer than he remembered. It stirred the desire he'd always felt for her.

"I have to go." She flexed her fingers lightly. "Will you call me?"

Summoning up a small smile, Julian nodded. "Thanks, Eleanor."

He watched her head back into the house, then his gaze returned to the forest.

CHAPTER 18

One day passed. Julian didn't call Eleanor. He didn't want to speak to her or, for that matter, anyone else. Not that there *was* anyone to talk to besides Lily. A migraine had consigned his mum to her darkened bedroom. His dad was pulling twelve-hour-days at the factory. Julian didn't look at his phone, didn't read, didn't watch television. He did sleep, though, long and restlessly. Even the dreams were preferable to the guilt that coursed through him whenever he thought about Phoebe.

Two days dragged by. There was no word from Tom Henson. The pain in Julian's neck eased off to a nagging ache. Pale as a ghost, he showered, shaved and headed to the kitchen for breakfast. His mum had surfaced too, a little glassy-eyed but with a soft strength in her voice as, giving him a worried look, she asked, "Are you sure you should be up and about?"

"My neck's much better."

His dad entered the kitchen, adjusting the knot of his tie. Without looking at Julian, he poured himself a coffee and sat down. His expression was impassive, but Julian could sense his annoyance. There was an uneasy silence. Julian guessed what was coming.

"Your father and I have been talking," said Christine. "And we've come to a decision, haven't we Robert?"

"Yes." It was obvious from Robert's tight-lipped response that the 'we've' was inaccurate.

"We've decided to give you a job at the factory."

"On one condition," put in Robert. "I've spoken to Angus. He's agreed to keep your job open for you for three months."

Julian wasn't surprised. His boss owned a second home in Godthorne. Robert and Angus met up several times a year to play golf. Despite his dad's *you have to work for everything in this life* mantra, Julian wasn't so naïve as to believe he'd got the job on merit alone.

"That way you leave your options open in case you change your mind," said Christine.

"I won't change my mind," Julian said flatly. Normally it would have given him some satisfaction to get his own way against his dad's wishes, even with an issue that called forth so many mixed emotions. But at that moment he had no room for anything other than the dreadful hollow guilt festering deep down inside him. He made to leave the kitchen.

"Where are you going?" asked Robert.

"To get dressed for work."

"You don't have to start today," said Christine. "Rest up a few more days."

"I told you, I'm fine." *Besides*, Julian might have added, *anything's better than lying around thinking about Phoebe.*

"You'll have to be quick about it, if you want a lift," said Robert. "I'm leaving in five minutes."

Julian removed the neck brace and put on a shirt and trousers. When he returned to the kitchen, his dad was gone. "He's waiting in the car," Christine told him. Julian kissed her goodbye and headed for the Audi.

Julian and Robert didn't exchange a word, didn't even look at each other during the drive. The factory was on a small industrial estate, screened from view by pine trees on the north-eastern outskirts of town. 'Harris Shoes. Finest quality handmade shoes for gents, ladies and children' said the no-nonsense sign over the entrance to the hanger-like building.

Julian had once asked his dad, *Why shoes?* To which his dad had replied, *People always need shoes.*

The workers were taking their places at the cutting presses, stitching machines and hundred-metre-long assembly line, but the equipment hadn't yet cranked into motion. When it did, Julian knew, the noise would be loud enough to vibrate his diaphragm. The workers nodded hello, casting curious glances at Julian as he followed his dad to the soundproofed offices at the rear of the factory. Seating himself in a leather swivel chair behind his desk, Robert began flipping through the day's mail. Julian sat opposite him. Several minutes passed. The dull rumbling of the machines starting up penetrated the walls.

"Have you considered investing in new technology?" asked Julian.

"Mm?" Robert looked up at him as if he'd forgotten he was there.

"Some of those machines out there haven't been upgraded since the factory opened. It would cost in the short-term, but I bet we'd be able to cut down on employees."

"No, I haven't considered it, Julian. For one thing, every Harris shoe is hand finished. That's why people choose us over our competitors. For another, we're not in the business of putting people on the dole. Besides, those decisions are for management to make. You said you wanted to start at the bottom. So you can start by making me a coffee. My secretary's off sick."

With a low sigh, Julian made his way to a small kitchen. He returned with the coffee. "What shall I do now?"

"Sit down and be quiet while I think of something."

Julian watched his dad drink coffee, make phone calls and have a chat with one of the factory foremen. Half-an-hour passed. An hour. "Have you thought of anything or shall I just sit here all day?" he asked.

Robert looked at him with a thoughtful frown. "Come with me." He led Julian through the din of the factory floor to a door marked 'Cripples'. Beyond it was a gloomy storeroom cluttered with thousands of mismatched shoes, some in boxes on shelves, most in piles on the floor. "You can sort these seconds into pairs."

"Why?"

"It doesn't matter why. It's simply a job that needs doing. So do it." Robert was closing the door even as he spoke.

The room smelled of leather and glue. Its thin stud walls barely muffled the noise of the machines. A sigh broke from Julian as he rolled up his shirt sleeves. He worked as fast as possible, gladly retreating into an oblivion of monotonous movement. When the lunchtime whistle blew, he became suddenly conscious that several hours had passed.

Sitting on a wall outside the back of the factory, he ate the sandwiches Lily had made for him. Some factory floor workers were smoking and chatting there. They cast him curious glances, but didn't approach him. Perhaps they were wary of the boss's son. Perhaps they just had nothing to say to him. Whatever, it suited Julian fine if they kept their distance.

The afternoon swept by in the same way as the morning. Julian found himself almost reluctant to stop when five o'clock came around. Robert poked his head into the room, looking over his work without comment. "So how do you think your first day went?" he asked with a disingenuous smile.

Julian made himself smile back. *I know what you're trying to do*, he felt like saying, *but giving me shitty jobs won't send me running back to London*. He didn't want to give his dad the satisfaction of that answer, though. "Better than I expected."

"Good. Great. Glad to hear it." Robert's tone was offhand, disinterested. "Do you want a lift home?"

"No thanks. I feel like walking."

As much as Julian wanted to see his mum, he couldn't bear the thought of another silent car journey.

As he made his way home, he noted that the missing person posters with Chloe's face on them had been removed from the lampposts. They hadn't been replaced with posters bearing Phoebe's face. Was that a good thing? Or did it simply mean that Phoebe had no one to look out for her? A leaden feeling of guilt spread through him, slowing his feet to a stop. Phoebe's house was only a short walk away. It wouldn't take long to find out if she was home.

Reputation is everything in a place like Godthorne.

Lines gathered between Julian's eyes as Tom Henson's words of warning echoed back to him. His head bent, he continued on his way.

When he got home, Lily was setting the kitchen table. Christine was on the patio, reading a book in the early evening sun. "How did it go?" she asked, smiling at him.

He gave her the same reply as he had his dad. "Better than I expected."

Lily poked her head outside. "Tea's ready."

"Do you mind if I skip tea?" Julian massaged the back of his neck. "My neck's aching. I need to lie down."

"Of course, darling," said Christine.

"I'll bring a plate to your room," Lily said in a disapproving tone. "A working man needs to eat properly."

Henry followed Julian to his bedroom and snuggled up beside him. Now that Julian had stopped moving, a heavy blanket of weariness settled over him. He quickly slid into sleep...

He jerked awake with Phoebe's screams ringing in his ears and the smell of her blood stinging his nostrils. The room was bathed in moonlight. Henry was growling at the end of the bed, his curved canines glimmering in the sickly light. "It's OK boy," said Julian, reaching to stroke him.

The Labrador's growls grew louder. Julian warily drew his hand back. Henry jumped off the bed, pawed the door open and slunk from the room.

Julian lay for a long while shivering in the moonlight before sleep took him again.

He wore jeans and a t-shirt to work the next day. He didn't bother asking his dad what to do, he just went straight to the 'Cripples' room. The fact that he was the only one working in there made him wonder whether his dad was hiding him away out of embarrassment. Not that he cared if that were the case. He was actually relieved to get in there and close the door, close out everything. After work, he walked home again.

Two more days passed in this monotonous cycle – wake, slide from beneath sweat-dampened duvet, shower, eat, work, walk home, eat, sleep, dream. He spent any spare energy on chatting or simply being with his mum. But always Phoebe lingered in the back of his mind like a shameful secret, stealing the joy from those moments. He stopped going outside at lunch, instead staying in the 'Cripples' room all day. Alone in that dim, rumbling place, he felt detached from the world. If anyone else came into the room – which they rarely did – he'd turn to them blinking like someone roused from sleep.

On Friday, on his way home he bumped into Kyle. It flashed through his mind to dodge out of sight, but it was too late. "Hey, Julian," called Kyle, hurrying over to him, eyes wide with surprise. "What are you still doing here? I assumed you'd gone back to London."

"I'm not going back."

"Seriously? How come?"

Julian shrugged. "I hated the job. Didn't much like the place either."

Kyle's surprise gave way to incredulity. "But you couldn't wait to get away from this town."

"Things have changed."

"What things?"

Julian shrugged again. The last thing he wanted was to get into all that with Kyle. "Just things."

"So what are you doing with yourself?"

"Working for my dad."

"No way! I thought you hated the factory."

"Yeah, well, like I said, things have changed." Julian sighed, his head aching from the effort of conversation.

"You can say that again," laughed Kyle. "I'm off to The White Rabbit later. Why don't you come along? You look like you could do with a beer."

"Thanks but I'm knackered."

"If you change your mind, you know where to find me."

Julian was about to continue on his way when Kyle added, "Hey, did you hear about that crazy bitch Phoebe Bradshaw?"

A tightness clutched at Julian's chest as all the images of Phoebe lying mutilated and dead that he'd been blocking out tore through him. Sounding short of breath, he asked, "What about her?"

"No one knows where she is. I heard she's taken off with some guy."

"Heard from who?"

"A friend of a friend who hangs around with Phoebe. You OK? You've gone really pale."

"What guy? Ash?"

"Who?"

"The guy with red flames on his car."

"Oh, that dickhead. Nah, I saw him in The White Rabbit the night before last. It's probably a load of bollocks anyway. Maybe Phoebe's OD'd like her best buddy. Either way, if you ask me, it's no big loss."

Julian clenched his jaw, suppressing an urge to smash his fist into Kyle's smug face. Stepping around him, he resumed walking. Kyle called something after him, but he wasn't listening. His head was swirling with all the things he wanted to say to Tom Henson. His gaze swept along the street at shop windows, bus-stops and lampposts. Suddenly, the absence of posters with Phoebe's face on them didn't seem hopeful, it seemed bewildering, sinister even.

He searched his phone for the chief inspector's number. As the dial tone rang in his ear, he strove to reign in his anger, but the instant Tom picked up, he blurted out in an accusatory voice, "You were wrong. You said Phoebe would come crawling home in a day or two, but she's still missing. And what are you doing about it? Sod all."

"That's simply not true, Julian," countered Tom. "We're doing everything we can."

"Then why haven't I seen any appeals for information? You were all over the news when Chloe disappeared."

"Chloe was fifteen. Phoebe's an adult. If she wants to up and leave without telling anyone, that's her decision."

"In other words, you couldn't care less what's happened to her."

With exaggerated slowness, as if explaining something to a child, Tom said, "No. As I told you, we're doing everything we can." An unmistakable note of warning came into his voice. "Do you remember what we spoke about last time I saw you?"

Julian replied through his teeth. "Yes."

"Good, because I'm going out on a limb for you, Julian. Don't make me regret it."

Am I supposed to be grateful? Julian stopped himself from retorting. Tom seemed to have his best interests at heart, but something about the business made him feel manipulated. "What about the finger? Is it Susan Simmons's?"

"I'm still waiting to hear from the lab. But whatever result comes back, it's really none of your concern. Do you understand what I'm saying, Julian?"

After a brief silence, another, "Yes," whistled through Julian's teeth. He cut off the call. "You should never have listened to that fucking policeman," he muttered with bitter self-reproach as he broke into a run.

CHAPTER 19

As on the previous occasion Julian had been there, the downstairs curtains of Phoebe's house were closed. Junk mail was sticking out of the letterbox. He listened at the graffiti-scarred front door. Silence. The place had an air of abandonment. He knocked. Nothing. He knocked again, calling out, "Phoebe, it's Julian." Just more nothing.

At the side of the house was a mouldy gate. Its rusty hinges squealed in protest as he opened it. Picking his way through a tangle of brambles, he headed around back. Shaggy privet hedges enclosed a little wilderness of weeds. On the back door step was a chipped mug overflowing with cigarette butts. The rear curtains were closed too. He tried the door handle. Locked.

Julian frowned in thought for a moment, before returning to the street. He made his way to the main road into town, turned left and jogged past the 'Welcome to Godthorne' sign. Soft shadows enfolded him as he passed into the eaves of the forest.

He left the road at the 'Foxwood' sign. Twenty or so minutes later, he reached the sun-dappled glade with the ash-filled circle of stones at its centre. The ashes were cold. No one appeared to have been there in some time.

Sometimes I think Chloe's lucky. At least she's out of this shit.

Recalling what Phoebe had said when he was last there, he turned full circle, staring into the shadows, half-expecting to see her slumped amidst the undergrowth, wrists slashed open. All he saw was trees, trees and more trees. What had he expected to find?

A suffocating sense of shame settled over him as he returned to the road. *You tried to help Phoebe,* he kept telling himself. But the shame wouldn't go away. The two of them had shared some nameless connection. She'd felt it and reached out to him, but he'd failed her – and, in doing so, he'd failed himself too.

His head snapped backwards as something hit him hard between the shoulder blades, knocking him over like a skittle. He flung out his hands to break his fall. Someone grabbed him and flipped him over. A hollowed-out face, wolfish teeth and shaved head loomed into view. "What the fuck have you done to my sister?" demanded their owner.

"Nothing." Pain lanced through Julian's neck as he attempted to get up. A galaxy of stars burst into life in front of his eyes as Dylan Bradshaw knocked him down again with a punch in the mouth.

"Liar!"

"It's the truth."

Dylan drew back his fist for another punch. His head swivelled at the sound of a car pulling over. A man lowered the driver's side window, shouting, "Hey, leave him alone!"

Like a startled wild animal, Dylan jerked upright. His khaki army surplus jacket flapping behind him, he sprinted away into the forest.

"Wait, Dylan, I want to talk to you," Julian gasped, fighting off waves of wooziness.

The man hurried from the car to help him up. "Are you OK?"

"Yes." Julian licked his lips, shuddering involuntarily at the taste of blood.

The man took out a phone. "I'll call the police."

"There's no need. We were just messing around."

"It didn't look like you were messing around."

Julian thanked the man and staggered towards town, wondering who'd put Dylan onto him. Most likely it was Ash or Gemma. He knew one thing for certain – if Dylan didn't know where Phoebe was, there was no way she'd simply left town.

The wooziness had receded to a fuzzy headache by the time he arrived at the Davis' house. As he knocked on the front door, he self-consciously sucked in his bottom lip, which had swollen to what felt like twice its normal size. Mike opened the door, an ever-present cigarette in the corner of his mouth. Spectacles were perched on his bald head. He lowered them to take a better look at Julian. "Bloody hell, what happened to you?"

"Dylan Bradshaw."

Mike's bushy eyebrows lifted. "Dylan attacked you. Where did this happen?"

"It doesn't matter. What matters is why. He thinks I've got something to do with his sister going missing."

"Ah." From the lack of surprise in Mike's tone, Julian guessed that Eleanor had filled him in on recent goings-on. "You'd better come in." As Julian stepped into the hallway, Mike added, "Eleanor's in her bedroom."

"Actually, I wanted to speak to you."

Mike nodded as if he'd suspected as much. Motioning for Julian to go into the study, he disappeared through a door across the hallway. He returned with a damp flannel for Julian.

"Thanks," said Julian, sitting down and dabbing at his split lip.

Mike settled into the reclining chair behind his desk, lighting a fresh cigarette with the end of his old one. He exhaled a stream of smoke, eyeing Julian expectantly.

"I..." Julian began hesitantly, unsure how to put his jumbled thoughts into something resembling a coherent order.

"You think Phoebe Bradshaw's disappearance and Chloe Crawley's death are connected," prompted Mike.

"I'm sure of it. Just like I'm sure this is all somehow connected to Susan Simmons. Think about it, first Chloe's murdered after finding Susan's finger. Then Phoebe vanishes–"

Mike held up a cautioning hand. "We don't know that Chloe was murdered."

"Yes we do. Someone gave her an overdose to silence her because she found Susan."

"Again, we don't know that the finger is Susan's. Tom tells me the lab—"

"I couldn't care less what that bloke says," cut in Julian. "He doesn't give a toss about Phoebe. I get the impression he'd be happy if she stayed gone for good."

"You may be right. The Bradshaw's have caused him a lot of trouble over the years. Phoebe and Dylan's mum, Tasmin, was a drunk and a chronic shoplifter, amongst other things. Dylan's a thief and a suspected drug dealer. And Phoebe, well, she's not a criminal, but she has a long history of substance abuse and mental health issues. Did you know she's been hospitalised on two occasions for attempting suicide?"

"No, but it doesn't surprise me. Did Tom tell you Phoebe was done up to look like Susan Simmons the last time I saw her?"

Mike cocked an eyebrow in interest. "No."

"I thought she was involved in prostitution or pornography or something like that. But now I'm thinking maybe she was trying to retrace Chloe's steps to Susan's body."

"And how would she go about doing that?"

Julian shrugged. "If we could find Susan, maybe we could make some sense out of all this."

"What if there is no sense to be made of it? Bad things happen, Julian, especially to vulnerable girls like Phoebe and Chloe. They OD. Sometimes they drop off the face of the earth. It's hard to accept, but that's the way it is."

Julian shook his head. "This isn't just some random series of events. Susan Simmons – she's the key to whatever's going on here."

"Even if you're right, what can you do about it?" asked a voice from the doorway.

Julian turned to Eleanor. She had on an old vest and tracksuit bottoms. Without make-up, she looked as if she'd barely aged a day since high school. Her eyebrows angled into a V at the sight of his busted lip.

"I don't know," he said, "But I have to do *something*."

"You'll get yourself into serious trouble, Julian."

"It doesn't matter."

"It matters to me," Eleanor shot back.

Julian lowered his eyes apologetically. "I'd better go."

"Hang on," said Mike as Julian rose to his feet. He opened a filing cabinet, flipped through the files, withdrew one and proffered it to Julian. "My advice would be to leave this matter to the police. I can see you're not going to do that, though. So maybe this will be of some help."

The folder was labelled 'Susan Simmons'. Julian accepted it with a thanks.

Avoiding Eleanor's gaze, he headed for the front door. Mike followed him outside and said in a hushed voice, "Do me a favour, Julian. As long as you're going to be involved in… in whatever this is, keep your distance from Eleanor, will you?"

"You needn't worry about that," Julian assured him.

A look of concern played on Mike's tobacco-weathered face. "And for Christ's sake, watch your step. You may not care about yourself, but a lot of people around here care very much about you."

CHAPTER 20

Julian went into the first pub he came to, ordered a pint and took it to a quiet corner. He didn't feel like explaining his split lip to his parents. If he gave it an hour or two, his mum would be in bed and his dad would most likely have had one too many whiskies to pay him any notice. He sipped his pint whilst reading the file.

Susan was Godthorne born and bred. She was the only child of Greg and Margaret Simmons. They were a respectable middle class family. Back in 2005, Greg was a chartered accountant, working for Taylor & Co Accountancy, a long-established local firm. Margaret was a housewife.

At the time of her disappearance, Susan was a twenty-three-year-old trainee solicitor at JBR Solicitors, another local firm. She'd recently moved into a flat on Clay Street, just off the High Street. She was a quiet girl who spent much of her spare time hiking and horse riding in the forest.

On Wednesday 23rd June 2005, the night of her disappearance, Susan met up for an early drink with two female friends at The Horse & Jockey pub on the High Street. At approximately a quarter-to-eight, complaining of an upset stomach, she left the pub. Her friends wanted to walk her home, but she insisted on walking alone.

Faint lines touched Julian's brow. He'd often wondered why Susan walked home alone. Perhaps she thought she was safe because Whitcher had already claimed a victim that month. But Whitcher's kills were becoming more frequent. After Sophia Philips went missing in November 2004, he didn't strike again until Charlotte King disappeared in March 2005. Two months then passed before Daisy Russell was taken. One month later it was Zoe Aslett's turn. It seemed whatever rage or perversion was driving Whitcher was becoming increasingly irresistible. How else to explain the fact that only two days after Zoe's disappearance, even though the area was crawling with police and journalists, he'd taken to the streets before dark in search of another victim?

Susan had fitted the bill perfectly. She was last seen heading towards Clay Street, but seemingly never made it to her flat. When she didn't turn up to work the next day or respond to repeated phone calls, her parents were contacted. Her landlord let them into her flat. There were no signs of anything untoward. Susan's parents hadn't seen much of her in recent weeks, but still it was out of character for her to leave town without letting them know. There was a message on her answerphone from a local garage to say her car had passed its MOT and was ready to pick up. Greg phoned the garage. Susan hadn't been to collect her car. He then phoned the police.

That July a huge Thunder Moon had spanned the sky. The night of the true full moon was, in fact, sandwiched between Zoe and Susan's disappearance. To the naked eye, though, the moon had appeared to be full for all three days, sparking speculation that Susan had fallen victim to Mr Moonlight. A full-scale search was launched.

A sweep of Susan's flat revealed one item of interest – a pregnancy testing stick showing a positive result. DNA tests confirmed that traces of urine on the stick belonged to Susan. Her parents, friends and colleagues were unaware that she was in a relationship, let alone pregnant. A financial record search showed that she'd purchased a pregnancy test kit five months previously.

The lines on Julian's forehead deepened. As far as he was aware, it hadn't been made public that Susan was pregnant. Why the secrecy? Had she been in some sort of illicit relationship? Perhaps she'd been having an affair with a married man. In which case, maybe there'd been speculation over whether she'd run off with said man or even if he'd played a more sinister role in her disappearance. Possibly the police hadn't wanted to alert the man that they were pursuing such a line of inquiry. There was no mention as to the identity of Susan's lover, boyfriend, or whatever he was to her.

A month after Susan's disappearance, Kenneth Whitcher was caught. Despite Susan still being missing and the unanswered questions over her pregnancy, Whitcher was charged with her murder. That was pretty much it, except for a nasty little epilogue. The strain of losing his daughter proved too much for Greg Simmons. Two years later, he suffered a fatal heart attack. Six months after his death, Margaret suffered a psychotic episode and was sectioned to Florence House psychiatric hospital in Bournemouth. She claimed the ghost of Kenneth Whitcher had come to her and promised that if she cut off one of her fingers, he would tell her where to find Susan. She underwent emergency surgery after severing her left index finger. She was diagnosed with trauma-induced schizophrenia and spent the next decade in and out of psychiatric units before succumbing to cancer in 2017.

Julian hunched his shoulders as if a cold hand had touched his neck. He was well aware, of course, that Margaret had believed in ghosts. Why else would she have visited his grandma? But even so, cutting off her finger…

His thoughts turned to the withered finger Henry had brought into the house. "A finger for a finger," he murmured. *You're seeing connections where none exist, just like with your dreams and Chloe,* he told himself. *Whitcher didn't keep his promise because there's no such thing as ghosts or spirits or any of that crap.* But his mind kept looping back to the strange symmetry between Margaret cutting off her finger and Chloe retrieving Susan's finger.

A shudder passed through him as Grandma Alice's contorted, drooling mouth and bulging, hate-filled eyes rose into his mind. What if there was a way to find Susan? What if Whitcher's spirit was ready to reveal where she was? Maybe Phoebe was right. Maybe something *had* called him back here. He shook his head hard enough to make his neck twinge. It was bullshit mumbo jumbo. That's all… But what if… what if… what if…

With a sudden movement, he shut the file and rose to hurry from the pub. He headed into the town centre.

"This is so stupid," he kept telling himself, but he didn't slow down until he came to the street of redbrick terraced houses. He lifted a hand to wipe away the sweat dribbling down his face as he approached his grandma's house. He stopped at the garden gate and stood staring, dry-mouthed. Dusk was falling. A light glowed behind the net curtains in the living-room window.

"Fuck it," he muttered, opening the garden gate and slowly – very slowly – ascending the steps. He knocked on the door, almost flinching at how loud it sounded.

His grandma's muffled voice came through the door. "Who is it?"

"It's Julian."

There was the sound of a key turning and the door swung open. Alice was wearing a dressing gown as shapeless and grey with age as her face. Her silver-white hair was wound around rollers. She stared up at Julian, her eyes as bright and round as marbles. "Why are you still here?" she demanded sternly. "I warned you. *He's* looking for you."

Julian opened his mouth. For a few seconds his voice wouldn't come, then he managed to push the words out. "I need to speak to him."

Alice cupped a hand to her ear as if she doubted her hearing. "Eh?"

Julian raised his voice. "I need to speak to Mr Moonlight."

Alice's eyes widened. "Why in god's name would you want to do that?"

"A girl's life might be in danger. I thought maybe..." He trailed off with a shake of his head. "So stupid," he said to himself, starting to turn away.

"Wait, Julian." Alice's voice took on a softer tone. "You look tired. Why don't you come in and sit down?"

Julian's gaze returned to her hesitantly. A smile quivering on her thin lips, she beckoned to him with a bony, liver-spotted hand. He stepped past her, tensing as she put a hand on his back and ushered him into the living-room. He dropped heavily onto the sofa, feeling a deep ache of weariness in his legs. Alice took two glasses from a dark wood cabinet, filled them with bubbling lemonade and handed one to Julian. He took a sip. The taste transported him back to all the times he'd lain on the sofa watching cartoons while she spoiled him with cakes, sweets and fizzy drinks.

"That was your favourite lemonade," said Alice, arthritically lowering herself into an armchair. "I think of you whenever I drink it." Sadness glimmered in her eyes. "I wish things could have been different."

The same sadness filled Julian's eyes. "So do I."

There was a brief silence. Alice wafted her hand as if shooing away the regret of what might have been. "Tell me about this girl."

"Her name's Phoebe. She's missing. I think she went looking for Susan Simmons. If I find Susan, I might find Phoebe."

Alice sipped her lemonade, eyeing Julian over the rim of her glass. "Do you believe?"

"In what?"

"In the other side."

"No."

"Then a séance won't work. To summon the spirits, you have at least to be open to the possibility of their existence."

Julian thought about Margaret Simmons's severed finger. "I guess I wouldn't be here if there wasn't some part of me that... y'know..." He faltered, struggling to put his feelings into words.

Nodding understanding, Alice rose to open a polished wooden box. She took a bundle of dried green leaves bound with red string from it.

"You'll do the séance?" asked Julian.

Alice looked at him intently. "I'll try to contact Kenneth Whitcher. But what you must realise is that spirits – especially evil spirits – only commune with the living when it suits them. If this spirit answers your question, it's not because he wants to help, it's because he's using you to serve his purpose. You still dream about him, don't you?"

"Yes."

"I don't know why, Julian, but this spirit is fixated on you. He's been attacking you all these years, but the door between you and him is not open wide enough for him to get through. By summoning him, we're flinging that door open. The attacks may become much, much worse. Are you willing to accept that risk?"

"Yes."

"You must care deeply for this girl."

"I do." Julian blinked away from his grandma's keen eyes as if it was an admittance of guilt.

She smiled. "That's good. Those feelings will give you more protection than any prayer."

Julian followed Alice to the dining-room. She pulled out a chair for him, then left the room. She returned after a moment with a bowl of steaming soup and a salt cellar. "This was supposed to be my supper," she said. "Oh well, I'll just have to make do with a bit of toast."

Alice placed the bowl in the centre of the table and arranged the candles at equal distances around it. She poured two small mounds of salt out on the table – one in front of Julian and one in front of the opposite chair. Rifling through a sideboard drawer, she said, "Aha, here it is." She took out a photograph. "I used this when Margaret and Greg came to me." She winced as if at a sharp pain. "Poor Margaret. She came here again after Greg died, wanting to talk to him. I tried to help her, but her grief was too intense. It clouded everything."

Some might say you exploited her grief, Julian was almost tempted to say.

Alice shot him a squinty look as if sensing his judgement. The photo was a mugshot of a man with a cue-ball head and mismatched features – pudgy, almost cherubic cheeks; thin lips; small, angular nose. His muddy-brown eyes slanted inwards beneath bushy eyebrows, giving him the look of a worried dog.

Julian's Adam's apple bobbed at the sight of Kenneth Whitcher.

"Don't bring your fear to the table, Julian," cautioned Alice. "There's no use for it here."

She struck a match and held it to the bundle of dried leaves. She waited for the flames to take hold, then blew them out and walked clockwise around the table, wafting smoke and chanting, "Dominus illuminato mea. Divine light surround us. Divine light cleanse and purify us. Divine light guide and protect us. Divine light free our hearts from fear."

The smoke's minty, earthy scent eased the tightness in Julian's throat and made him a little lightheaded.

Alice dimmed the lights, lit the candles and sat down facing Julian. "Before we begin, there are some rules you must abide by," she began stridently, like an actor reciting well-worn lines. "No matter what happens, you must not break the circle. Doing so will allow the spirit to attack you at will. Do not enter into conversation with the spirit. Ask it only what you wish to know. At the end of the séance, I will blow out the candles and say the words of closure, then we will both throw a pinch of salt over our shoulder. Is this understood?"

"Yes."

"Then let us begin. Place your hands palm down on the table." Alice and Julian both did so. "Clear your mind, focus on your surroundings. What can you smell? What can you hear? What can you feel?"

Julian inhaled through his nose. The room smelled of smoky incense and soup. There were no sounds except the faint sizzle of the candles. The air was neither hot nor cold.

After a minute or two, Alice continued, "Now focus on the photo. Take in every detail."

Reluctantly, Julian looked at Kenneth Whitcher. Kenneth's mouth turned down at the corners. There were small pits on his cheeks that might have been acne or chickenpox scars. His left eye was slightly larger than his right. But what he noticed most of all was how utterly unremarkable Kenneth was.

He was the sort of bloke you could walk past in the street a hundred times without ever noticing him.

Alice drew in a slow, deep breath, closing her eyes. "Are there any spirits here with us? If so, give us a sign."

Julian held himself motionless, hardly breathing. Several seconds passed. A minute. Nothing.

"I'm calling on any spirits in this house," went on Alice, her voice rising. "Can you hear me?"

Another minute passed.

"Nothing's happening," said Julian.

"Patience," Alice softly rebuked. "These things take—" She broke off, cocking her head. "Did you feel that?"

"What?"

"A vibration in the air." She pointed at the soup. "Look."

Julian looked at the soup. A ripple passed over its surface, so slight as to be almost indiscernible. Or was it just a trick of the candlelight?

"Is there someone there who's willing to talk to us?" asked Alice. She lowered her head, rolling it from side to side as if stretching her neck. She lifted her gaze back to Julian. "There was someone here for a moment, but they've gone." She gave a sudden shudder. "Something else is here. A dark energy. That's why the other spirit left."

"Is it him?" There was a tremor in Julian's voice.

"I don't know. Remember what I said, Julian. Fear is of no use." She closed her eyes again. "Kenneth Whitcher is that you?"

There was a loud, echoing knock at the front door. Julian reflexively made to stand.

"Don't move," snapped Alice, her eyes springing open. As Julian sat back down, she added, "Someone is playing games with us."

Her bright, quick eyes scrutinised the room as if trying to see beyond the visible. She bent her head, her wrinkles deepening in concentration.

"Kenneth Whitcher, we wish to commune with you. If you are there, I ask you to respond."

Ten seconds passed. Twenty seconds. Thirty...

Alice gave out a low, rattling moan that seemed to originate from deep in her scrawny chest. Very slowly, she rolled her head, the moan growing louder. As if jerking to attention, her head snapped up. Her lips peeled away from her gums, revealing notched and yellowed teeth. Her nostrils flared as she snorted out a breath. But it was her eyes that grabbed Julian and squeezed the air from his lungs. They were black holes of hate that made him want to spring to his feet and flee.

He trembled with the effort of resisting the urge, silently telling himself, *Only you have the power to take control of your life. There's nothing to be afraid of. You have to hurt to heal. Hurt to heal. Hurt to heal...*

As he repeated the mantra, he brought his breathing back to normal. He tried to speak and a whisper came out, "Where is Susan Simmons?"

Alice's lips pulled up into a leering grin. She gnashed her teeth as if taking a bite out of something. Sweat glistened on her face. Her pallor was so ashen that the thought flashed through Julian's mind, *What if she dies?*

Breathlessness threatened to engulf him again. He fought it with the affirmation – *There's nothing to be afraid of. You have to hurt to heal. Hurt to heal...*

"Where is Susan Simmons?" Voice strengthening, he repeated, "Where is Susan Simmons? Where is Susan–"

He broke off as Alice's mouth dropped wide open and the same growl of a voice that had drawn him to the dining-room all those years ago spat at him, "Well, well, well."

Instantly, he was back in the firelit clearing with Phoebe. *We made a crappy Ouija board,* he heard her saying. *The coin spelled out one word three times – well, well, well.*

He clutched the edge of the table as if he was dangling from a clifftop. His voice scraped out. "What does that mean?"

"Well, well, fucking well!" the voice boomed, propelling strings of saliva into his face. Alice leaned forward, her eyes so blacked out with anger that he half-expected her to lurch across the table and attack him. She huffed out a breath that had just barely enough strength to extinguish a candle. The neighbouring candle's flame wobbled but remained lit as she blew on it. Julian leaned in to blow out the other candles.

"Thank you spirit." Alice's voice was hoarse and faint, but it was her own again. The blue had returned to her eyes. "Now leave. This circle is closed." She threw salt over her shoulder. Julian did likewise.

Alice slumped back into her chair, her face drawn with exertion. "I'm sorry, Julian," she murmured. "I couldn't continue. He was too much for me."

He hurried around the table to her side. "Can I do anything?" There was none of the usual mistrust in his voice. There was only concern.

She smiled faintly at his tone. "Give me a moment and I'll be right as rain."

"I'm sorry, Grandma. I thought you were crazy or a fraud, but..." Julian shook his head as if he couldn't believe what he was saying. "Well, well, well. There's no way you could've known that... *something* said those same words to Phoebe and Chloe through a Ouija board."

"Ouija boards." Alice scrunched her nose disapprovingly. "That's a dangerous game." She reached for Julian's hand. Her skin had the soft, thin texture of tissue paper. "Help me up."

Hooking his other hand under her armpit, Julian helped Alice to her feet. He'd used the same technique many times to manoeuvre his mum into and out of her wheelchair. They shuffled to the living-room and Alice dropped into an armchair. She took a swallow of lemonade and heaved a sigh. "That's better."

Julian's eyes travelled uneasily around the room. "Is he still here?"

"No. But that doesn't mean he's gone." Alice eyed Julian with worry and curiosity. "He has such hate for you, Julian. I've never felt anything like it before."

"But why would he hate me?"

"Perhaps because you remind him of everything he wasn't in life. There's nothing evil hates more than the sight of goodness."

Julian shook his head again, thinking not only about the dreams, but about all the years he'd wasted on resentment and anger. "I'm not a good person, Grandma. I blamed you for all my problems. Even worse, I was too much of a coward to be there for Mum when she needed me most."

"You're not a coward, Julian. You're too brave for your own good. If it was up to me, you'd be back in London now." A flicker of sadness came into her eyes again. "Besides, you're right to blame me. I blame myself. I should never have let you and your mum come over here that night, but you see I'm a lonely old woman. But I've paid for what I did. It's been fourteen years since I spoke to my daughter. My only child."

"Perhaps we can change that."

"I doubt it. Christine hates me."

This time, Julian reached for his grandma's hand. "I'll speak to her. It's got to be worth a try."

Alice smiled in a way that suggested she didn't hold out much hope. "At least I have my darling grandson back. That's more than I ever hoped for." Anxiety seeped into her voice. "Promise me you'll be careful, Julian. There's something evil at work in this town."

"I promise I'll be careful." His brow creased. "Well, well, well," he murmured. "What does it mean?"

"Whatever it means, remember this – Kenneth Whitcher is not trying to help you. He's manipulating you."

Well, well, well. Julian turned the words over in his mind. They'd seemingly led Chloe to Susan. Had they led Phoebe to the same place? A sense of urgency gripped him. "I have to go." A little awkwardly, he leaned in to kiss his grandma's cheek. In response, she clasped her hands to either side of his face and planted a kiss on his forehead.

"Will you come to see me again soon?" she asked.

He nodded. "Bye grandma."

Alice waved as he turned to head for the front door. Darkness was softening the outlines of the street, but every detail seemed sharply defined to him. As the humid night wrapped itself around him, he was struck by the feeling that he was stepping out into a strange new world.

CHAPTER 21

When Julian got home, instead of going into the house he headed for the back garden gate. Rumour had it Dylan was hiding out somewhere in the sprawling tangle of trees. If true, it could take days or even weeks to find him. Still, even if it was futile, searching the forest was preferable to the agony of waiting for something to happen.

He thought about where he'd found Chloe. It was only a short walk from there to the derelict sawmill where hypodermic needles had been found. What if she'd been on her way to see Dylan?

He hiked along the sandy trail, alert to the slightest sound, glancing over his shoulder every few minutes as if he expected to see the spirit of Kenneth Whitcher stalking him. Scraps of blue and white plastic tape bearing the words 'POLICE LINE DO NOT CROSS' dangled like banners of shame from the trees where Chloe had lain decomposing. He quickened his pace.

The sawmill was a brick building with a partially collapsed corrugated iron roof. A rusty wire fence dotted with 'Private Property. No Trespassing' signs enclosed it. The fence had been pulled up and pushed down in numerous places. Julian shone his phone's torch through a door hanging off its hinges. The mill had long since been stripped of its machinery and anything else of value, but the sweet, resinous fragrance of cut lumber was still detectable beneath the sour reek of old urine and the bacon-like scent of wood-smoke. The walls were decorated with graffiti and the concrete floor was littered with cigarette butts, broken glass, beer and aerosol cans and other rubbish. A torn, stained mattress was pulled up close to a mound of ash.

"Anyone in here?" Julian called into the dank gloom.

The only reply was the echo of his voice. Cautiously, he approached the ashes and poked at them with his foot. They gave off a faint heat. He glanced behind a corrugated panel propped against a wall. A rolled up sleeping-bag was stowed there.

"Dylan, this is Julian Harris." His voice bounced eerily off the walls. "I need to talk to you about Phoebe."

Again, silence. He sat on the mattress, figuring that whoever the sleeping-bag belonged to would show up sooner or later. The gibbous moon came out, slithering through holes in the roof and windows. He stared at the pockmarked three-quarter sphere. The full moon was only a couple of days away.

He jerked around at a crunch of dry leaves. Dylan's scowling skull-like face loomed at him through the murk. "What the fuck do you know about my sister?" he demanded, one hand darting out to encircle Julian's throat, the other raised and clenched.

Blinking rapidly in anticipation of being punched, Julian said, "I know she needs my help."

"Why would she need your help?"

"I think she's in danger." *If she's not already dead,* a voice in his mind added grimly.

Dylan's eyes glared at him from deep hollows. "Ash told me about you. He said you've got a thing for Phoebe. Did you fuck her?"

"No."

Dylan hawked and spat out the side of his mouth. "Bollocks you didn't."

"Believe what you like, but it's true."

"So why do you give a shit what's happened to her?"

There was that question again. With every asking, it seemed to assume more significance. Why did this girl that he'd only known for a few days haunt him like a spectre? "She... she..." Julian reached for but failed to grasp the words he wanted.

Dylan's grip tightened. "Spit it out."

"I don't know, alright? I don't know why I give a shit. I just do."

Dylan stared at Julian as if unsure what to make of him. After what felt like a long moment, Dylan let go of him and, with the wariness of a cat, circled towards the other side of the ashes. Julian heaved a breath of relief, rubbing at the indents Dylan's fingers had left in his neck. The skin-headed boy dropped to his haunches, knees poking through tears in his grubby blue jeans. He dug at the ash with a stick, exposing glowing embers. He fed them handfuls of leaves and twigs. Flames crackled into life, shooting shadows up the walls. Julian studied Dylan's androgynous teenage face, struck by how much he looked like Phoebe. If Dylan grew his hair and put on a few pounds, the two of them would be difficult to tell apart.

Darting glances at Julian, Dylan added bigger sticks to the fire. There was a coiled tension about his wiry frame, as if at any second he might spring to strike or flee. "So let's hear it then. Why is Phoebe in danger?"

Julian told him why, minus the supernatural component. Some small part of him still couldn't quite accept that his changing dreams, the severed fingers, the Ouija board and the séance were strung together by anything more than monumental coincidence. After all, *well, well, well* was a common enough phrase. What if Dylan laughed in his face and discounted everything else that came out of his mouth?

As the story unfolded, Dylan betrayed no clue as to his emotions. "Let me get this straight in my head," he said, when Julian was finished. "You reckon this Mr Ugly killed Chloe cos she found Susan Simmons, and now he's done the same thing to Phoebe?"

"I hope he hasn't done the same to Phoebe, but yeah, that's about it. Don't suppose you have any idea who Mr Ugly is?"

"Whoever the fuck he is, he'd better pray I never find out cos I'll cut his dick off and feed it to him." There was a quiet menace in Dylan's voice that suggested the threat wasn't empty bravado.

"What about the man and the woman in the Mercedes? Any idea who they are?"

Dylan took out a cigarette, lit it with a stick from the fire, and ran his tongue over his sharp canines. "You say the woman was a redhead? Big tits?" When Julian nodded, Dylan's face wrinkled thoughtfully. "Could be Ginger."

"Who's Ginger?"

"She was a mate of my mum's." His tone matter-of-fact, Dylan added, "They used to turn tricks together."

A sympathetic gleam found its way into Julian's eyes as he wondered what Dylan's life must have been like to harden him so much. "Do you know where she lives?"

"Yeah." Dylan rose to his feet.

"Where are you going?"

"I'm gonna have a friendly chat with Ginger." The way Dylan said 'friendly' made it clear the chat would be anything but.

Julian stood up to follow him. "I'll come with you."

Dylan eyed him narrowly again. "You sure you didn't fuck my sister? Cos if I find out you're lying…" He made a cutting motion at his groin.

Julian cringed at the gruesome image the threat conjured up. "I'm a thousand percent sure."

Dylan nodded as if satisfied he was telling the truth. "It's miles to Ginger's place. You got a car?"

"No, but I might be able to get hold of my dad's car."

"In that case…" Dylan motioned for Julian to lead the way.

"You're not going to hurt Ginger, are you?"

"Depends on what that bitch has gotten my sister into. I know for a fact she was giving Chloe free junk."

"Junk?"

"Heroin. A few days before she went missing, Chloe and me got blasted together. It wasn't the usual weak shit you get round here. One hit knocked me on my arse, and I only smoked it. Chloe was shooting the stuff up. I didn't even blink when I heard she'd OD'd."

"Did she mention... I don't know, anything about what she'd been up to or any plans she had?"

"*Plans.*" Dylan chuckled as if amused by the word. "The only plans she had were to get as fucked up as possible as fast as possible." He pointed to the mattress. "She spent most of the night passed out on that. She left when it got light. Said she'd see me soon."

"So she *was* she looking for you when she died?"

"Can't see why else she would've been out here."

"Were you at the mill?"

"Not that night. I move around. Keeps the coppers off my track."

"Why would Ginger give Chloe free junk?"

"I say free, but nothing's ever really free, is it? You let that shit get on top of you and you'll do anything for another hit. And Chloe was using way too much." Dylan drew a long breath as if suppressing a sudden pain. "Phoebe reckons that if I hurt myself she feels it. She says the souls of twins are linked by ES... ES something."

"ESP," offered Julian.

"Yeah, that's it." Dylan looked at Julian with an almost child-like appeal in his eyes. "Do you reckon that's true?"

A few hours ago Julian would have replied with a flat no, but now... He shrugged. "Maybe."

"If it is true, it means Phoebe can't be dead. Cos I'd have felt something, wouldn't I?"

Dylan puffed on his cigarette, nodding to himself as if reinforcing his belief in the possibility. They walked on in silence to the back garden gate. As they entered the garden, Dylan gave out a low whistle. "Ash said you were loaded, but fuck... I didn't realise you were *this* loaded." There was a sullen resentment in his voice that reminded Julian of Phoebe, as he added,

"Someday I'm gonna have a big fuck-off house like this, Ultra HD TV and a shit-hot sound system in every room, and all the rest of it."

"It's not everything you think it is."

Dylan hawked and spat near Julian's feet. "You should try being skint. It's just as shit as you'd think."

Julian opened his mouth to say sorry, but realised an apology would be as patronising as his previous comment. His gaze scanned over the dark windows. "Looks like my parents have gone to bed. I'll get the car keys."

"What if your parents clock you?"

"Then I'll pretend to go to bed and sneak out when I can." Julian pointed to the left of the house. "Go around the front and wait by the gate. Stay close to the hedge or you'll trip the motion-sensor lights."

Dylan flicked away his cigarette. Dropping into a semi-crouch, he moved off into the darkness as swiftly and silently as someone for whom sneaking around was second-nature.

Julian approached the back door. A spotlight attached to the eaves clicked on, bathing him in white halogen light. Hoping his dad was either asleep or too drunk to look and see what had tripped the sensor, he eased his key into the lock, opened the door and padded into the kitchen. Henry pattered over to greet him, whining for a stroke.

"Hello boy," whispered Julian, ruffling the Labrador's fur.

He straightened to lift a set of keys from a rack. 'I've borrowed the car. Julian' he scribbled on a stick-it note, then crept from the kitchen. He tensed at a snort from the living-room. It was followed by what sounded like someone crying. It wasn't his mum. The sobs were too deep. Was Dad crying? His chest contracted. Had something happened to Mum?

He tiptoed to the living-room. The door was ajar. His dad was crashed-out in the reclining chair. Robert's right arm dangled towards the floor. His fingertips rested on an upturned tumbler. His arm twitched as another sob shook him, followed by several snorts.

He's crying in his sleep, realised Julian. Guilt nibbled at him. His dad had so much to contend with – a chronically ill wife, a business that sucked up most of his time, a son who'd just thrown away a career most people would give an arm for – no wonder he was crying in his sleep.

For a second, Julian considered putting the keys back and telling Dylan he wasn't going with him. But then, like an extension of his nightmare in a waking state, an image rose into his mind of Mr Ugly pressing himself against Phoebe, sniffing and licking her like a randy dog. With a shudder, he turned to head for the front door.

His dad's Audi was parked in front of the garage. Julian put it into neutral, released the handbrake and pushed it to the front gate.

Dylan appeared from behind a bush, saying admiringly, "Nice."

Julian couldn't tell whether he was referring to the car or praising his sneak-thievery. He punched in the gate code and they rolled the car into the street. As the gate slid shut, he started the engine. "Where to?"

"Just drive, rich boy. I'll tell you as we go."

Julian threw Dylan a frowning glance. Had Phoebe used that nickname when talking to Dylan about him? He could just hear her saying, *I got pissed with this rich boy...* Or perhaps the twins really were somehow psychically connected. "Don't call me that."

"Why not? That's what you are, isn't it? That's what I'll be too one day. A big, fat rich fuck."

Julian sighed, not for himself, but for Dylan. He couldn't imagine him ever being any of those things. Dylan directed him to the north side of town to a street of grey pebble-dashed houses not far from Hope Road. Julian pulled over and Dylan pointed to a mid-terraced house on the opposite side of the street. "That's Ginger's place." A light glowed behind the upstairs curtains. A black-and-chrome low-rider motorbike was parked on a little driveway.

"Looks like she's got someone with her," observed Julian.

"Probably a punter."

"So what now?"

"Now we wait."

They sat in silence for a while. Dylan fidgeted with an unlit cigarette, his eyes drifting off into the same thousand-yard-stare Julian had seen in Phoebe's.

"Maybe Phoebe's really done it," Dylan murmured.

"Done what?"

"Killed herself. She always said she would one day."

Doubts crowded in on Julian. Perhaps Dylan was right. He thrust the possibility away. He had to keep telling himself there was more to Phoebe's disappearance, because at least that way there was a chance, however slim, that she was alive. "I don't believe she's killed herself."

Dylan's eyes blinked back to Julian. "When Phoebe and me were like ten or eleven and mum was hitting the bottle big time, we were sent to live with a foster family. Nice people. They really tried to make us feel part of the family. We had our own bedrooms, new clothes. They even took us on holiday. It was only a week in a crappy caravan in Cornwall, but it was nice. We went to the beach, built sandcastles, ate ice creams, played in the sea." His eyes drifted again. "When I think about it now, it's like I dreamed it or something."

"So what happened?"

"Phoebe fucked it all up, that's what." Dylan ground his teeth at the memory. "One day Mum turned up at the house pissed out of her skull as usual. Our foster parents called the coppers, and they came and carted her away. Phoebe started acting all weird, doing that staring off into space thing she does. Then she just went nuts. Started smashing everything up. She smashed the TV and loads of other stuff. Then she locked herself in the bathroom, smashed the mirror, slashed herself up with broken glass. She was out cold from blood loss by the time our foster dad kicked in the door.

She was in hospital for ages and when she got better she refused to go back to our foster parents. So we ended up in a children's home cos they wouldn't split us up. A couple of months later, mum got on the wagon for like the hundredth time and we went home. And just look how well that worked out for us." Dylan let out a bitter little laugh.

There was another silence, then Julian said, "My dad was brought up on this estate. He says it was a good place until Thatcher started dumping problem families here."

Dylan gave him a sidelong look. "You mean families like mine?"

"Seems to me that all families are problem families," remarked Julian. "When I was born, Dad was working like crazy to get the factory up and running. I have hardly any memories of him from childhood. I don't think he took a day off until I was about seven." A sudden vehemence took hold of his voice. "No way am I going to waste my life working fifteen hours a day. If I ever have kids, I'll spend as much time as I can with them."

Dylan eyed Julian as if reassessing him. He proffered the cigarette. "Smoke?"

"We can't smoke in my dad's–" Julian started to say, but broke off. "You know what? Fuck it." He accepted the cigarette. "Thanks."

Dylan lit it and one for himself. He took out a short black-handled knife and thumbed its blade.

"What's that for?" Julian asked uneasily.

"Protection. You ever stabbed anyone?" Dylan answered his own question. "Of course you haven't. Me neither. I stabbed a forest pony once. I dunno why I did it. For a laugh I suppose." There was a musing, almost sad tone to his voice. "It's weird. The skin was kind of tough to get through. But then it was like the knife was falling into the pony. Do you reckon it would feel the same to stab a person?"

"I don't know." *And I don't want to find out,* Julian added silently. He took a nervous drag on his cigarette. "What if Ginger *is* the woman from the Mercedes, what then?"

"We ask her where she took Phoebe."

"What if she won't tell us?"

Dylan twisted the blade's point into his palm. "She will."

The sight gave Julian a sliding feeling in his stomach. "Maybe it would be better to call the police."

"No fucking coppers," scowled Dylan, that animal light flaring in his eyes again. "We do this ourselves, right?"

Before Julian could reply, Dylan pointed out of the window with the knife. A bald, bearded man, wearing torn blue jeans and a black leather jacket lumbered out of Ginger's front door. The man had the bloated body of a steroidal weightlifter gone to seed. He looked like he could have picked up Julian and Dylan, one in each hand, and cracked their heads together. Behind him was a slim, busty woman in a silky kimono that left little to the imagination.

"Is it her?" asked Dylan.

Julian squinted. The woman in the Mercedes had worn her hair up, but Ginger's auburn hair was spread over her shoulders. It was difficult to make out her face. "I–" Julian broke off with an intake of breath as Ginger stepped forwards into a lamppost's pool of light. "Yes, it's her." His tone was tinged with disbelief. He hadn't really expected it to be her. "And I think the biker's the guy that was driving the Merc."

Ginger sparked up a cigarette as the biker strapped on a WW2 style German helmet and climbed astride his low-rider. She gave a perfunctory wave as he fired up the engine and roared away.

Dylan reached for the door handle. "Showtime."

CHAPTER 22

Julian hurried after Dylan to Ginger's front door. With each step, he had the unnerving sense that he was drawing closer to some unseen edge. They got to the door as it clicked shut.

"Stay out of sight while I talk to her," said Dylan.

Julian ducked behind a wheelie bin as Dylan knocked on the door. Peeping around the bin, he saw that Dylan had one hand – doubtless the hand holding the knife – inside his jacket. Julian ran his tongue dryly over lips.

"That you, Bear?" A husky female voice asked through the door. "Did you forget something?"

"It's Dylan."

"Dylan Bradshaw? What do you want?" There was a rise of surprise in the question and, perhaps, a trace of unease.

"It's about Phoebe."

A brief pause followed, then the click of a lock and the squeak of the door opening. "What about her?"

"Have you seen her recently?"

"No." The reply was spoken without hesitation, almost as if Ginger had been ready with it before Dylan asked the question.

"You sure?"

"I just said so, didn't I? Now, is that all? It's late."

"Yeah, unless you wanna suck my cock."

Ginger frowned, her plump pink lips turning down with distaste. "What? Is that your idea of a joke?"

"Do I look like I'm joking? I've got twenty quid here. That's the going rate, isn't it?"

"Piss off, you filthy little shit," retorted Ginger, starting to close the door.

Dylan shoved his foot between it and the doorframe. "Oh yeah," he grinned as Ginger tried to kick his foot out of the way. "That's it, baby, I like it when you get rough."

"I'm warning you," she yelled.

Dylan whipped his hand out of his jacket. He wasn't holding the knife. Instead, he was gripping a crowbar. "Don't, Dylan," exclaimed Julian, springing up. Ignoring him, Dylan brought the crowbar down with bone-breaking force on Ginger's hand. With a cry, she snatched her hand away from the door handle and reeled backwards onto the floor.

Dylan caught hold of Julian and yanked him into the house. He slammed the door, then stood over Ginger, brandishing the crowbar. "Where's my fucking sister?"

"Jesus Christ, Dylan, there was no need for that," gasped Julian, his heart pounding in his voice.

"This bitch lied to me. Now she's gonna tell me the truth or I'm gonna crack her head open."

Ginger's eyes flicked between Dylan and Julian, wide with pain and anger. "You're crazy," she groaned. "Bear's going to kill you when he finds out about this."

Dylan's lips curled into a sneer. "Ooh, I'm shaking." He jabbed Ginger with the crowbar. "If you don't tell me what you were doing in a Merc with Phoebe and Bear the other night, you won't be in any state to tell anyone anything, you get me?"

Ginger blinked at the mention of the Mercedes, the anger in her eyes shading to a sort of hesitating fear. She looked at Julian. "You'd better tell your pal to back off before he goes too far."

Noting that she didn't deny Bear had been in the car, Julian spread his hands as if to say, *Sorry, but there's nothing I can do.* There was a mute appeal in his eyes for Ginger to tell Dylan what he wanted to know.

"You've got to the count of five," said Dylan. "Then I start breaking bones. One... two–"

"Don't make me laugh. Run away, little boy, while you still can," said Ginger, grinning contemptuously up at him. But it was bravado, and they all knew it.

"Three... four..."

Ginger threw up her uninjured hand in surrender. "OK, OK." She heaved a shaky breath. "Yeah, I was with Phoebe, but how could you know that unless you've spoken to her?"

"Don't you worry your empty little head about that. You just tell me why."

"We were on a job."

"Do you mean like prostitutes?" asked Julian.

"No, I mean like Jehovah's Witnesses," Ginger retorted sarcastically.

Julian was hardly surprised by the revelation, but even so, part of him had clung to the hope that he was wrong. He held in a sigh. "Where did you take Phoebe?"

"To the client's house."

"Whose is the Mercedes?"

"It belongs to the client. He's got this whole thing about treating us properly. Y'know, chauffeur-driven car, champagne and all that."

"Sounds like a real prince charming," sneered Dylan.

Ginger threw him a look that said, *And what would you know about that?* "Like I was saying, we went to the client's house and serviced him–"

"Serviced?" echoed Julian.

"Yeah, *serviced*," Ginger emphasised with a sleazy smirk. "Do you need me to paint you a picture?"

"Don't get mouthy," warned Dylan. "So this prince charming's into threesomes, is he?"

"No."

"Then why were you there?" asked Julian.

"The client pays a lot of money for a very particular service. I was there to make sure Phoebe gave him exactly what he wanted."

"Ooh, 'a very particular service'," said Dylan, putting on a bad cut-glass accent. "How come these posh fucks are always the biggest pervs of all?"

"Nothing perverted about it," countered Ginger. "Unless you think wanting girls to dress nicely and speak nicely is perverted."

"What happened after the client had been *serviced*?" asked Julian, his mouth twisting around the word as if it tasted bad.

"Bear drove us back to town. Phoebe went her way and we went ours, and that's all there is to tell."

"So Phoebe was fine when you left her?"

"Yeah." There was something not entirely convincing about Ginger's tone. Julian heard it. Dylan did too. He made a threatening movement with the crowbar, prompting Ginger to add swiftly, "She was a bit quiet. Y'know, kind of faraway. But then again, she's always like that after we do a job."

"You mean this wasn't her first time?" asked Julian.

"It was the first time she'd been with this guy, but I've done other jobs with her. I hadn't spoken to Phoebe in months. Then about a week ago, she called and said she needed money. So I set the job up."

"Did she say what she needed money for?"

"No. Probably for junk."

Dylan's face contracted into a scowl. "My sister isn't a junkie."

"OK fine, she isn't a junkie, but she needed money for something."

"Yeah, to get the fuck out of this town."

"Who's the client?" asked Julian.

Ginger compressed her lips.

"Who's the fucking client?" growled Dylan.

"Just some guy," said Ginger. "What does it matter?"

"What does it matter?" Julian repeated incredulously, his anger flaring like oil spilled into flames. He snatched the crowbar off Dylan and shoved it into Ginger's stomach hard enough to force her breath out in an *oof!* She tried to push him away, but he caught hold of her hand. "Phoebe's missing. Maybe hurt or in danger. So you're going to tell us who this fucker is, understand?"

"He calls himself Rupert," gasped Ginger. "But no way is that his real name."

"What does he look like? Is he ugly?"

"No. He's average looking."

Julian's face scrunched in contempt. "So just some average guy with average fucked up fantasies, eh?"

"Look, this guy says he wants me to keep an eye out for girls like Chloe and Phoebe. So I took Chloe to his house, but she wasn't what he was looking for. Too young."

"Was that the day Chloe went missing?"

Ginger shook her head. "It was one… No, two days before that."

Julian's brow creased. Did that mean this Rupert hadn't killed Chloe? "Could Chloe have gone back to the client's house on her own?"

"I suppose so, but I don't see why she would have. Like I told you, she wasn't his type."

"But Phoebe was?"

"Oh yeah. You should have seen Rupert's face when he saw her. I thought he was going to cry."

"Why? Because she looked so much like Susan?"

Ginger gave Julian a look in which surprise blended with unease. "How do you know that's what he always calls the girls?"

A cold thrill coursed through Julian at the confirmation that his suspicion was correct. He responded with a question of his own. "Why does he call them Susan?"

"I've never asked. It's none of my business." Ginger's matter-of-fact tone had the ring of truth.

"How many 'Susans' have there been?"

"I don't keep count. A fair few over the years."

"Have any of the other ones gone missing?"

Ginger looked at Julian as if the question was beyond absurd. "Are you deaf or something? How many times do I have to say it? Rupert's a proper gentleman." She flashed a glare at Dylan. "Unlike some others around here. I've no idea what the deal is with Phoebe, but he didn't do anything bad to her."

Julian stared darkly into Ginger's faded blue eyes. "Yes, he did. Now tell us where he lives."

"Uh-uh. No way." Ginger's gaze returned to Dylan. "Your mum was a good mate of mine, so I'll give you one more chance. Leave now and I promise I won't tell Bear about this."

A grin splitting his undernourished face, Dylan reached to yank free her dressing-gown cord. The kimono fell open, exposing fake-looking watermelon breasts and skimpy underwear. He bared his teeth in admiration. "Not bad for an old whore."

"Fuck you," spat Ginger.

Chuckling, Dylan set about tying her hands with the cord. He took no care to be gentle with her injured hand, which was already swelling black and blue. "Fetch the car," he said to Julian.

Julian hesitated, his gaze fixated by Ginger's bound hands. That shrivelling sensation of running towards a clifftop in blackness was back. One more step might be all it took to fall over the edge...

"Go on," Dylan snarled so fiercely that Julian flinched.

Julian ran to the car. His shaking hands fumbled the key twice before managing to insert it into the ignition. He pulled onto the driveway, keeping the motor running. Dylan poked his head outside, glancing from side to side to check no one was around. He emerged from the house, holding Ginger by an arm. He'd put away the crowbar. The knife glinted in his hand, the point of its blade touching Ginger's side. He shoved her onto the backseat and got in beside her.

"Which way?" asked Julian.

Ginger said nothing.

Dylan twisted the blade into her ribs, drawing a dribble of blood. Flinching, she jerked her bound hands up to point.

As they set off, Dylan closed the dressing-gown over her breasts. "Don't want anyone getting a free eyeful, do we now?" he chuckled.

CHAPTER 23

Julian followed Ginger's finger across town towards the southern suburbs. He wondered uneasily if Rupert was someone his parents knew. Perhaps he was a family man. Perhaps his wife and kids were tucked up in bed, blissfully ignorant that the man they loved was about to be exposed as a sexual deviant and very possibly worse.

Leaning forwards, Ginger spoke in his ear. "You're a good-looking boy. What do you think you'll look like when Bear's finished with you?"

Dylan chuckled. "Fuck Bear."

Ginger treated him to a mocking grin. "I know you, Dylan Bradshaw. You're a nothing. A little boy trying to cover up how shit-scared he is with a lot of big talk."

"I'm a nothing?" Dylan laughed louder. "Says the cheap whore."

"I'm not that cheap. Not compared to your mum. She practically had to give it away."

With violence lurking in his eyes, Dylan yanked Ginger backwards. "Do you want me to put this knife in you, or what?"

"Go on then, do it." There was a sneering challenge in Ginger's voice. "Do it."

Dylan's lips drew back into a snarl. "Fuck you! Fucking bitch! Skank!"

As Dylan hurled obscenities at Ginger, an image swirled into Julian's mind of Grandma Alice's possessed face – the hate-swollen eyes, the flaring nostrils, the leering grin. Feeling as if a vice were tightening against his lungs, he squeezed out a hoarse, "Stop! Enough!"

Ginger's eyed him intently. "You come from money, don't you? I can tell. I should be able to. I've fucked enough of your kind in my time. What I can't work out is what you're doing here."

"I'm a friend of Phoebe's."

"So how come I've never seen you with her?"

"I haven't known her long."

"Then you're not her friend. Kids like her don't make friends easy. Especially not with people like you." Ginger narrowed her eyes. "No, you're something else. You look like a nice boy, but there's something about you. You've got shifty eyes. Like you've got something to hide."

Julian couldn't help but blink rapidly. *Shifty eyes.* That was how the packing room women had described Kenneth Whitcher.

"There it is." Ginger turned to Dylan. "Can't you see it?"

"Huh? What you on about?" said Dylan. He frowned at Julian. "Do you know what this bitch is on about?"

Julian shook his head. He couldn't speak. The vice in his chest was airlessly tight.

"Course he knows," said Ginger. "It's in his eyes."

Her voice went through him like fingernails on a blackboard. All he could think about was shutting her up. He shot her a sidelong glare.

"I bet you'd like to get your hands on my throat, wouldn't you?" taunted Ginger. "Bet you'd like to fuck me while you squeeze. That what you did to Phoebe, is it, hmm?"

That was more than Julian could take. He found enough breath to shout, "You're sick!"

Dylan pointed the knife at Julian, suspicion rife in his eyes. "Are you sure it's her who's the sicko?"

Seeing Dylan's violent blue eyes in the rearview mirror, it was all Julian could do not to be overcome by another fit of blinking. "She's trying to turn you against me."

After a moment of silence, Dylan returned the knife to Ginger's ribs.

Julian's attention was drawn away from the backseat. They were nearing his street. A kernel of relief opened in him as they passed the turning and left behind the outskirts of the town. The dark walls of the forest reared up on either side of the road.

His gaze shifted to Ginger. "Fifteen. Chloe was only fifteen. How do you live with yourself?"

She pushed her face towards him, nostrils flaring indignantly. "I was the same age when I started turning tricks."

"That doesn't make it right."

"Fuck you. Don't you sit there with your silver spoon up your arse judging me."

Dylan grabbed Ginger's shoulders and slammed her against the back seat. "One more word, bitch, and I'll gag you. Just keep your gob shut and point the way."

Her mouth twisting into a contemptuous smile, Ginger raised her hands and pointed to the only way – straight ahead.

"What about your other clients?" Julian asked her. "Anyone we might know?"

Ginger remained silent.

"Tom Henson? Does that name ring a bell?"

Still no reply.

"Answer him," said Dylan.

"You told me to keep my gob shut," shot back Ginger.

Dylan gave a low chuckle. "Oh yeah, so I did. Well now I'm telling you to talk."

"I've got nothing more to say to you two little pricks."

"I'd say that's a yes," laughed Dylan. "Henson's a proper arsehole. Wouldn't surprise me one bit if that fucker's bent. Probably fucked Chloe himself."

Deeper and deeper into the forest they drove. At first, they passed an occasional house tucked back into the trees. Then there were only trees, clustering as thick as the night.

"You sure this is the right way?" Julian asked after several more miles. He knew the forest well enough to know there were no houses in this part of it – or at least he thought he did.

"Yeah, I'm sure," said Ginger.

"You better not be shitting us," warned Dylan.

Ginger suddenly pointed into the trees on their left. At first Julian couldn't see anywhere to turn off, but then he spotted a narrow track so overgrown as to be almost invisible. 'Private Road' read a sign on a padlocked wooden farm-style gate. Julian pulled over in front of it.

"Keep an eye on her," said Dylan, getting out of the car to attack the padlock with his crowbar.

Julian watched Ginger. His nose wrinkled as he found himself picturing Phoebe 'servicing' Mr Ugly.

"You've no right to look at me like that," she said. "You think I chose this life? My parents kicked me out at fourteen. I did what I had to do to survive." She expelled a sharp breath. "Why am I telling you this? Unless you've been there, you can't understand how it is."

"But I want to understand," said Julian, thinking maybe it would help him understand Phoebe.

"No you don't. You're just a white knight, playing at being a nice guy because you want to stick your cock in Phoebe. I can read your dirty little mind like a book."

Julian couldn't keep a quiver of anger out of his voice. "I thought I'd already done that while I was strangling her?"

Ginger smiled thinly. "Maybe you have, maybe you haven't. To be honest, I couldn't give a shit either way. Don't get me wrong, I like Phoebe, but..." She gave an indifferent shrug. "At the end of the day, it's just business."

"Just business," murmured Julian, shaking his head. He was half-tempted to add, *You should meet my dad. You two would get on like a house on fire.*

Ginger watched Dylan wrenching at the padlock. "That boy will end up in the hospital or a box because of you."

"Why because of me?"

"Someone must have seen me in the Merc with Phoebe, and I'm guessing that someone was you."

The chain wrapped around the gatepost clattered loose. Dylan kicked open the gate and ducked back into the car, beaming with self-satisfaction. Julian squeezed the Audi along the narrow stony track, wincing as branches scraped the paintwork.

"Have you been to this part of the forest before?" he asked Dylan.

"No. You?"

"I'm not sure. You know what the forest's like. It all looks the same."

After about half-a-mile, the track forked. At Ginger's direction, they took the right-hand fork, which descended into a heavily wooded valley. As the trees crowded ever more densely, Julian had a familiar sense that he was entering a hidden world – a world he'd felt more comfortable in than anywhere else as a child, but which at that moment made him acutely aware of how isolated they were.

He checked his phone.

"You won't get a signal out here," said Ginger. She was right.

"Ah, this is bollo–" Dylan started to say, but broke off as, after climbing a steep incline, they rounded a curve and came to a wrought-iron gate topped with spikes. A brick wall overgrown with ivy stretched away to either side. Beyond the rusty bars, a gravel driveway curved to the right, disappearing behind trees that shivered in the night breeze.

"Back up." Dylan pointed to a gap in the trees.

Julian reversed into it.

Dylan got out of the car, dragging Ginger after him. "Open the boot."

Julian pulled the boot-release lever and got out too.

"Wait," said Ginger as Dylan shoved her into the boot. "Don't do this. I'm telling you, Phoebe's not here."

Dylan hawked and spat at her, before closing the boot and turning to Julian. "You coming?"

"What if she's telling the truth?"

Dylan spat out another ball of phlegm, narrowly missing Julian. "Fuck her and fuck you."

Hunkering into a low run, Dylan melted into the darkness. Julian stared after him a few heartbeats, his face twitching with uncertainty. Then he too broke into a run. He caught up with Dylan a stone's throw to the left of the gate. Dylan was using handfuls of ivy to haul himself up the wall. Julian attempted to do likewise, but his neck spasmed and he lost his grip. Dylan reached down to grab his hand and pull him up. Julian hooked his leg over the the wall and slithered down its far side. Breathing heavily, he squinted at his surrounds. A half-circle of moon peeping from behind a cloud dimly illuminated an expansive, overgrown lawn split by the driveway. At the end of the weed-riddled driveway a sloping roof was outlined against the star-speckled sky.

Dylan darted forwards, using the thickets of bushes that dotted the lawn for cover. Gradually, a house almost as overgrown with ivy as the garden wall took shape. On the ground floor, two sash windows flanked a panelled front door. The place had an air of disuse. There was no Mercedes, or indeed any vehicle, in the driveway.

"Doesn't look like anyone's in," whispered Dylan. He took out his crowbar and dug at a rotten window frame. The wood splintered as he jimmied the crowbar up and down. Julian cringed. Every noise seemed magnified a hundred times in the deep silence. The window popped open. Dylan shoved it upwards and slunk through the gap. Heart hammering in his ears, Julian followed. A faint damp smell tickled his nostrils.

Dylan took out a torch. The light swept over a pale green three-piece-suite, floor-to-ceiling floral curtains, antique-looking coffee-table and deep-pile rug. A pair of candles in elegant silver holders bookended a cast-iron mantelpiece. The hearth was empty, except for a few strands of cobwebs. There were no pictures, ornaments, potted plants or personal objects, giving the room an unlived-in feel, like a shop window display.

They padded across creaking floorboards into a high-ceilinged hallway. Dylan shone the torch over vacant coat hooks and an empty shoe rack by the pillar-box red front door. Straight ahead was a varnished door. To their right, a stairway whose carpet matched the front door rose into darkness. At the far end of the hallway was a third door.

Dylan nudged open the nearest door. It led to a dining room. A rectangular dark-wood table was set as if for an elaborate meal for two – china plates and bowls, wine glasses, silver cutlery and candelabra. Again, the scene had a staged quality. Julian wouldn't have been particularly surprised to see mannequins occupying the chairs in poses of eating, drinking and talking.

They slunk to the final door. Beyond it was a kitchen with dark wood cupboards, speckled marble work surfaces, a deep farmhouse-style sink, a big old Rayburn and a fridge-freezer. Julian looked in the cupboards. One contained a few plates, bowls, glasses and bundles of candles. The rest were empty. He opened the fridge. No light came on. It was empty too.

"I don't think there's any electricity," he whispered.

Dylan directed his torch at the ceiling. The bulb socket was empty. He approached the sink and turned the taps. No water came out. He made a low growl in his throat like a dog sensing something it didn't like.

No longer bothering to tiptoe, he left the kitchen. Julian followed him upstairs. There were four doors on a square landing. Dylan threw them all open. One led to an empty room, its floorboards coated in grey dust. Another led to a bedroom furnished with a shabby-chic antique double bed, bedside tables, dressing-table, chest of drawers and a wardrobe. The bed was made up with silky crimson sheets and pillows. The dressing-table was bare, the drawers and wardrobe were empty. Beyond the third door was a ceramic and marble bathroom. No towels, toilet paper or soap. Dylan depressed the toilet handle. The cistern was empty. The fourth door opened onto a nursery, its walls painted pastel pink. A rocking-chair was pulled up to an empty cot. The air hung stale and dead. A thick layer of dust indicated that no one had been in the room in a long time.

"That bitch is full of shit," scowled Dylan. "No one lives here."

"Perhaps they just use this place for somewhere to bring girls," suggested Julian.

"Phoebe!" shouted Dylan. His voice echoed into silence. "Ah fuck this. That lying whore's gonna wish she hadn't fucked with me."

He darted back downstairs. Julian ran after him. Dylan ducked through the open window and sprang to the lawn. Sweat broke out on Julian's forehead as he struggled to keep up. The moon had fully emerged from the clouds, palely lighting their way. They were halfway across the lawn when Julian stopped as abruptly as if someone had grabbed him, his eyes wide with something between incomprehension and disbelief.

"Dylan!" he shouted.

Dylan looked back at him. "What?"

"Well."

Dylan frowned in bemusement. "Well what?"

Julian stabbed a finger at a circular structure partly concealed by bushes. "Well, well, fucking well!"

Dylan aimed his torch at the well. It was constructed of grey stone bricks. A pair of Y-shaped wooden uprights supported a peaked roof. A bucket dangled from a rope attached to a horizontal thick wooden bar.

"Yeah it's a well," said Dylan. "So what?"

Julian started towards the well, slowly at first, but breaking into a run after a few steps. Almost as if he doubted it was real, he tentatively touched the low stone wall. It was cool and smooth. He peered over its rim into impenetrable blackness. The well breathed a cold, dank breath into his face. Dylan appeared at his side, demanding to know, "What the fuck are you doing?"

Julian snatched the torch from him and shone it into the well. Crumbling, mossy bricks lined its interior. The torchlight glimmered on a mirror of black water ten or fifteen metres down. He leaned out over the aperture to yank at the braided hessian rope. It seemed strong enough to hold his weight. He stepped up onto the wall and pointed to the iron winding handle. "I need you to lower me down."

Dylan looked at him as if questioning his sanity. "What for?"

"Just do it!"

As an afterthought, Julian pulled out his phone and dropped it to the ground. Gripping the torch between his teeth, he reached for the rope with both hands. He waited for Dylan to take hold of the iron handle, then balanced his feet on opposite sides of the bucket's rim. The rope creaked ominously under the strain. Dylan began to wind the handle, lowering Julian centimetre by centimetre. The bucket wobbled, tilting Julian into the wall.

Dylan's voice echoed down the well. "Stay still or you'll make me drop you."

Julian regained his balance and held himself as steady as possible. Tremors ran through him at the expectation that the rope would break any second, but it held fast. He was three metres down. Goose pimples prickled his flesh. The temperature was dropping. Five metres. Slimy green-brown lichen filmed the walls. Ten metres. He had the impression that he was being lowered into the throat of some giant worm. Without warning, the bucket dropped fast enough to make Julian's stomach rise into his gullet. The torch fell out of his mouth and the air whooshed from his lungs as he plunged into water so cold it stole his breath. For a few rapid heartbeats, his head was submerged. Then his feet found purchase on the bottom of the well and he pushed to the surface.

Gasping, he clutched at the walls. A brick came away in his hand and splashed into the water. His panic subsided as he realised that the water only came up to his chest.

"You alright?" Dylan called down to him.

"Yeah." Julian groped for the rope. He exhaled with relief upon discovering that it was intact. Dylan must have lost control of the winding mechanism. Swiping his wet hair out of his eyes, Julian peered downwards. The torch was still shining at the bottom of the water, hazily illuminating bricks piled against a collapsed section of wall.

Julian sucked in a sharp breath. A pale green, skeletally delicate hand poked out of the rubble as if stretching for the surface. There was a bony stump where the index finger should have been.

"Susan." Julian's voice was hushed with a kind of fearful awe. He reached as if to take her hand, but stiffened at a sound as faint as a distant whisper of wind. For a moment, he couldn't breathe. All he could do was listen. There it was again! Something was down here with him. Something alive. Or perhaps something not alive, yet not entirely… gone.

With a jerky movement, as if breaking an invisible grip, he ducked underwater to retrieve the torch. Teeth chattering uncontrollably, he resurfaced and whirled in a circle. The light stopped on a shallow alcove above the pile of rubble. The collapse had created a small shelf just above the waterline. A figure was curled into a foetal ball on the shelf.

Saucer-eyed, Julian took in the dirty pink dress, the scratched and scabbed limbs, the blonde hair matted with blood. "Phoebe!"

She didn't respond. Her eyes were closed. Her skin had a bluish tint.

"What's going on?" shouted Dylan.

"It's Phoebe," Julian called back.

"What the fuck?" Dylan's voice was shrill with disbelief and fear. "Is she…" He faltered, unable to bring himself to ask the obvious question.

Julian reached for Phoebe's wrist. She felt almost as cold as the water. After several seconds of anxious searching, he found a pulse, just barely. "She's unconscious, but alive!" He focused the torch on her head. There was a deep-looking gash above her left temple. "Phoebe, it's Julian," he said softly. "Dylan's here too. We're going to get you out of here."

"I'm coming down," said Dylan.

"No. Give me as much slack as possible. I'll tie the rope around Phoebe and you take her up."

The rope coiled on the water as Dylan resumed turning the handle. Julian quickly checked Phoebe over. Her nails were jaggedly broken as if she'd tried to climb the walls, but there didn't appear to be any other injuries. He looped the rope under her armpits, tied it across her chest, then he wound it around her thighs so that they were supported by the bucket.

"OK. Take her up."

As the rope tautened, Phoebe's dress rode up, exposing the red rose tattoo with its bloody thorns. She hung as limp as a rag doll, but the bucket held her in place. The seconds stretched like elastic as Julian watched her rise up the well. Relief flooded through him when she reached the top and Dylan leaned into view to pull her over the wall. The winding mechanism squeaked as Dylan swiftly lowered the bucket again.

Julian's gaze returned to the three-fingered hand. There was no time to dig Susan free. She would have to wait a while longer. "Sorry," he murmured through rattling teeth.

This time, he wrapped his legs around the rope and sat on the bucket. Dylan hoisted him out of the water. Going up seemed to take much longer than going down. At last, the rim of the wall came within reach. Julian hauled himself over it and dropped soggily to his knees beside Phoebe. Her face was sheet-white in the moonlight.

"She looks dead," Dylan said breathlessly, blinking sweat from his eyes.

"She's not fucking dead," Julian retorted with a ferocity that took him by surprise. He snatched up his phone, then hooked his hands under Phoebe's armpits. Dylan took hold of her legs. With simultaneous grunts, they lifted her and carried her towards the gate. "Just hold on a little longer, Phoebe," pleaded Julian. "We're taking you to hospital."

"How did you know she was in there?" asked Dylan, the suspicion back in his eyes.

Julian didn't have the energy to explain.

Upon reaching the gate, they carefully put down Phoebe. Dylan whipped out his crowbar. Metal grated against metal as he prised at the gate's lock. After a minute or two of frantic but futile effort, he hammered the gate with the crowbar. "Shit! Shit!"

Julian darted to the wall. "Give me a boost."

"We'll never get her over that."

"We won't need to. Just stand well back from the gate."

His eyes flashing with understanding, Dylan hastened to cup his hands under Julian's foot and heave him upwards. Julian caught the top of the wall and dragged himself over, heedless of the pain in his neck. He dropped to the ground on the other side and sprinted for the car. When it came into sight, he slowed down, his brow creasing. The boot was open and empty. His eyes darted around. Ginger was nowhere to be seen.

He yanked open the driver's side door, got behind the steering-wheel and clicked his seatbelt into place. The engine flared into life and he reversed onto the track, facing the gate. The wheels spat sand as, shoving the gearstick into first, he floored the accelerator. He pushed himself back against the seat, arms braced as straight as ramrods.

There was a screech of rending metal as the car slammed into the gate. The airbag blew out, smacking him in the face. He sat momentarily dazed, before clearing his head with a shake and clambering out of the car. The front wheels were resting on the gate, which had been torn from its hinges, collapsing a small section of the wall.

Dylan appeared in the headlights, carrying Phoebe. Julian helped him manoeuvre her onto the backseat. Seeing him glance at the open boot, Julian said, "Ginger's gone."

"Good fucking riddance. She'd better never show her skank face around here again."

Dylan got in alongside Phoebe, cradling her head. Julian pushed on the airbag to deflate it and threw the gearstick into reverse. The front wheels squealed in protest, struggling to dislodge themselves from the gate.

"Come on!" shouted Julian, pounding the steering-wheel with his palm.

As if in response, the wheels jerked free. Hissing triumphantly, Julian turned the car around and raced towards the main road. Stones kicked up, cracking the windscreen. Phoebe gave out a low moan as she was bounced around by potholes. Her eyelids fluttered but didn't open.

"It's OK, sis." Dylan held her steady, stroking her hair. "I'm here."

Her lips moved a fraction.

"She's trying to say something." Dylan bent to put his ear close to her lips. After a moment, he straightened with a look on his face like he was ready to murder someone.

"What did she say?" asked Julian.

"She said, 'Someone pushed me'."

CHAPTER 24

Someone pushed me, those words kept turning over in Julian's head as he waited in the A&E reception area. Who was that 'someone'? He watched Dylan prowling back and forth like a caged tiger. It had been almost an hour since Phoebe was rushed away on a trolley-bed.

"What's taking so long?" muttered Dylan. "Ah fuck this." He tried to open the double doors Phoebe had been wheeled through, but they were locked.

"You can't go in there," a receptionist informed him.

Dylan glared at her. "I want to see my sister."

"Someone will come and speak to you as soon as–"

"I want to see her *now,*" broke in Dylan, slamming his palm against the doors. "Open this fucking door."

"We have a zero tolerance on verbal abuse," warned the receptionist.

Julian moved to intervene. "Sorry," he said, ushering Dylan to a seat. Still eyeballing the receptionist, Dylan reluctantly sat down.

The automatic door at A&E's entrance slid open. Tom Henson strode in accompanied by two constables. In the blink of an eye, Dylan was back on his feet. His eyes darted around as if seeking an escape route. The constables took up a position at the entrance. Tom approached Julian and Dylan. He eyed Julian for a moment as if trying to make his mind up about something. His gaze shifted to Dylan. "We've been looking for you for quite some time, Dylan."

Dylan stared defiantly back at him, his lips compressed in silence.

"Have you searched the well?" asked Julian.

"Officers are at the property," said Tom. "It's going to take some time to find out what's at the bottom of that well."

"What about the house? Who owns it?"

The chief inspector sighed as if wearied by Julian's questions. "A Mr Martin Jones."

"Who is he?"

"That's a good question. Mr Jones is ninety-two-year's old, no wife or children. That's about all we know right now."

"Ninety-two," Dylan said incredulously. "I'm surprised the guy can stand up to take a piss on his own, never mind throw my sister down a well."

Tom treated him to the sort of look that might be reserved for a particularly intelligent breed of rodent. "Maybe so, but we can't know that until we track him down."

"Someone around here must know him," said Julian. "You can't live around here for long without your face being known."

Dylan humphed as if to say, *Tell me about it.*

"Regardless of that, you two have a lot of questions to answer," said Tom. "You can start by telling me what led you to Mr Jones's house."

Dylan's lips curled into a sneer. "Why don't *you* start by thanking us for doing your job for you?"

A palpable tension crackling between them, Dylan and Tom eyeballed each other. Tom flexed his fingers as if he was itching to get them on the wild-eyed boy. A slow smile spread over Dylan's face as if daring him to try it.

"Ginger," said Julian.

Tom turned frowning eyes on him.

"Yeah, you recognise that junkie whore's name, don't you?" Dylan said in an insinuating tone.

Tom threw him such a glare that it appeared as if he might actually take a swing at him.

That boy will end up in the hospital or a box because of you. Determined not to let Ginger's prediction come true, Julian tensed in readiness to get between the policeman and Dylan.

The double doors swung open. A bespectacled man with a stethoscope slung around the collar of his shirt stepped between them. A different kind of tension took over as Tom said, "Dr Enfield, how is she?"

Julian's stomach clenched in anticipation.

"She has a fractured skull, hypothermia, malnutrition," Dr Enfield replied in a dry matter-of-fact tone.

"But she's going to live, isn't she?" asked Dylan. His tremulous voice drew a glance from Julian. Dylan's hard-bitten mask had dropped away. He looked like what Ginger had accused him of being – a little boy trying to cover up how shit-scared he was.

"We're administering intravenous fluids and humidified oxygen to raise her body temperature."

"What the fuck does that mean in English?"

"It means we're doing everything we can. And at the moment, your sister is responding positively to treatment."

"Did you hear that?" Dylan turned to Julian, his voice clogged, his eyes close to tears. "I fucking knew it would take more than this to finish off Phoebe."

Julian smiled. "She's tougher than any of us."

As if embarrassed by his show of emotion, Dylan lowered his gaze to the floor.

"Can we see her?" asked Julian.

"Yes, but family and police only at this time," said Dr Enfield. He glanced at Tom. "And don't expect much from her."

A flicker of disappointment passed over Julian's face. He sat back down as Dylan and Tom accompanied the doctor through the doors. He wondered whether to call his parents, but decided against it. There was too much to explain over the phone. Besides, it would be a minor miracle if either of them was fit to make it to the phone.

The minutes crawled by. At last, Dylan came slamming back into the waiting area. "Fucking Ginger!" he spat. "I told you she's a lying bitch. Her and Bear never took Phoebe back to town. They just dumped her at that house and fucked off to another job. Phoebe didn't even see this Rupert wanker. She was looking down the well when some sneaky fucker pushed her in."

The knowledge that Phoebe was awake and talking alleviated Julian's disappointment that she couldn't identify her would-be killer. "Did she say anything else?"

"Nah, she only opened her eyes for a minute." Dylan leaned in close, his voice dropping. "Listen, don't breathe a word about what we did to Ginger or you'll drop us in the shit. You get me?"

Julian nodded, his gaze moving beyond Dylan as Tom opened the doors. "You two are coming with me to the station," said the chief inspector. His tone left them under no illusion that they had any choice in the matter.

CHAPTER 25

The soft pink glow of dawn was seeping through the windows when Julian stepped out of the interview room. Rubbing his stinging eyes, he headed for the exit. His feet dragged as if he was wearing lead boots. He felt as if he could sleep for a year.

"Julian."

He turned to the speaker. Tom looked like Julian felt. Dark bags hung under his bloodshot eyes. "I thought you might be interested to know," said the chief inspector. "We've recovered the body of a female from the well. It looks like she's been down there a long time."

"Fourteen years."

Tom eyed him curiously. "I still don't understand what made you look down the well."

"I told you, it was what Eleanor said about bodies being preserved in wet environments."

Tom arched a sceptical eyebrow. "OK, but what about Chloe and Phoebe? Why did they look in the well?"

Julian shrugged. He was tempted to tell Tom about the Ouija board just to see his reaction, but he knew it would only further muddy the waters. "Have you contacted my parents?"

"No. Why would I? You're a grown man, Julian. You don't need them to hold your hand."

There was something new in chief inspector's tone – a respectful yet vaguely threatening note. Julian blinked away from Tom, then forced himself to meet his gaze again. "Where's Dylan?"

"He's being interviewed. I wouldn't waste your time waiting around. He won't be leaving here anytime soon."

"Is he going to prison?"

"Possibly." A humourless smile crossed Tom's face. "I would tell you to let us deal with this from here on in, but I know I'd be wasting my breath."

Julian held his gaze, wishing he had the courage to say exactly what he thought of him. But even if he spoke his mind, it would amount to nothing more than an empty accusation. He had no evidence that Tom was crooked, just speculation. His lips compressed into a tight line, he turned to leave

"Good luck with telling your dad you've written off his Audi," Tom called after him.

Fuck the Audi and fuck you, Julian bit on the urge to reply.

A constable was waiting to give him a lift home. Julian settled wearily into the passenger seat. His thoughts turned to Phoebe. He desperately wanted to see her, but there was no chance until visiting hours. Maybe not even then, depending on how she was doing.

His eyelids drifted down. Catching himself on the brink of sleep, he lowered the window and hauled in a lungful of cool air. The last thing he needed was to fall into a dream about murdering Susan or Phoebe or whoever. *But will you have the dream?* he wondered. Kenneth Whitcher had seemingly wanted Susan to be found. Perhaps now he'd gotten what he wanted, the dreams would stop. With a tingle of anxious excitement, Julian found himself anticipating collapsing into bed and giving in to sleep.

He asked the constable to drop him at the gate. He put the code into the keypad and trudged towards the house. Before Julian could open the front door, his dad stormed out with rage in his eyes.

"Where's my car?" Robert demanded to know.

"I needed it. I'm sorry."

"You're not bloody sorry," spat Robert. "You're a selfish little shit, you always have been. You never think of anyone but yourself. What if your mum had needed rushing to the hospital? What then?"

Julian was too tired to argue. Releasing a heavy sigh, he stepped around his dad into the hallway.

Robert yelled after him, "Don't you dare walk away from me!"

Christine and Lily were watching from the kitchen doorway. Christine looked as though she didn't know what worried her more – Julian's haggard face or her husband's furious puce face.

Robert grabbed Julian's arm and yanked him around to face him. "I said don't walk away from me."

"Let go," said Julian, his cheeks reddening.

Robert jabbed a finger into his son's breastbone. "Not until I get answers. I'm sick and tired of your games, Julian. We're going to get to the bottom of this right now. Where have you been all night? Why do you look as if you've been punched in the face? And where's my car?"

Julian had been anticipating telling his parents about Phoebe with mixed emotions. He knew there would be awkward questions, but surely even his dad would be proud of him for saving a girl's life. At that moment, though, the stubborn side of him didn't want to give the bastard the satisfaction of any answers.

His eyes were set hard, mirroring his dad's. For a full thirty seconds, they eyeballed each other. Then Julian brought his fist down on his dad's hand, knocking it away. Robert's eyes widened, more in shock than pain. Turning, Julian made for his bedroom. Robert lunged after him, catching hold of his t-shirt. Julian twisted, struggling to shove his dad, who was several stones heavier than him, away.

"Stop it," said Christine, her voice shrill and quivering.

"Answers," shouted Robert.

"Fuck you," retorted Julian. "I don't care what you think of me. I did what I had to do to find Phoebe and Susan."

Robert's face wrinkled in bemusement. "Who the hell are Phoebe and Susan?"

"You found Susan Simmons?" Christine asked slowly as if each word was a sentence.

"Yes," said Julian, keeping his glare fixed on his dad. "Now let go of me!"

There was a sound of tearing material as Julian jerked away from his dad. The two of them staggered a few steps and toppled over in front of Christine. The breath whistled between Julian's teeth as he hit the floorboards. Winded, he scrambled to his knees.

"Stop it," Christine cried out again. "Stop–" She broke off with a sudden choke, her head jolting back, clench-toothed, body taut and shaking. Henry ran to her side, barking in alarm.

"Christine," gasped Robert, scrambling to hold her arms and legs steady whilst Lily cradled her head.

"Phone an ambulance," Lily calmly told Julian.

Panic flushing through him, his hand darted to his phone. He'd seen his mum have seizures before. Most only lasted a few seconds or minutes and passed without causing lasting harm. There was always the chance, though, that one could lead to further paralysis, even death. By the time he got off the phone, the spasms had subsided and Lily was checking to make sure Christine hadn't swallowed her tongue.

"Can you hear me, darling?" asked Robert. A low grunt from Christine brought a loud exhalation of relief from him.

Julian looked on with his arms hugged across his chest. "Is she going to be OK?"

"She'll be fine," Lily said reassuringly. "Won't you, Christine?"

Another grunt. Christine's breathing was ragged. Her eyes were unfocused.

"You see?" Robert hissed at Julian. "You see what happens when you–"

Lily silenced him with a sharp, "Shh. Go open the gate."

As Robert hurried to do so, Lily wheeled Christine to her bedroom. She applied the oxygen nose prongs and spread a blanket over Christine's lap.

Tears glazing his eyes, Julian took his mum's hand. "I'm sorry, Mum."

"Leave her be, Julian," Lily gently remonstrated.

When Robert came into the room, Julian avoided his gaze. The ambulance seemed to take an eternity to arrive. Christine's condition showed no further signs of improving, but neither did it deteriorate. At the sound of sirens, Lily trundled her to the front door.

The paramedics checked Christine's vitals, transferred her to a trolley stretcher and slid her into the back of the ambulance.

"If it's OK with you, Robert, I'll go in the ambulance," said Lily. "You take my car."

She handed him the keys to her little Nissan, and he jogged over to it. Julian got into the passenger seat. Robert barely gave him chance to close the door before accelerating after the ambulance. Neither of them looked at the other. The wail of the ambulance's siren offset their frosty silence.

At A&E, Julian and Robert continued to avoid speaking or eye contact, whilst Lily nattered on nervously about petty concerns. An inevitable sense of déjà vu washed over Julian as he stared at the double doors. He couldn't stop thinking, *If she dies, it'll be my fault.* From the occasional glowering looks his dad cast at him, it was clear he would have agreed.

The three of them rose to their feet when Dr Enfield appeared through the doors. The doctor informed them that Christine's blood pressure and heart rate had returned to normal. Her brain waves were also within the normal range. However, she'd been given a strong sedative to help her sleep off the after-effects of the seizure.

A breath swelled from Julian's stomach, puffing his cheeks. Dr Enfield led them to Christine's bedside. They stood looking down at her, Robert holding her good hand in both of his. A familiar feeling of helplessness swept through Julian at the sight of her chalky, lopsided face.

For a while, Phoebe had been driven from his thoughts, but now her face rose into his mind again. He stooped to kiss his mum's forehead. "I love you," he whispered, then he straightened and turned to leave.

"Where are you going?" Robert asked brusquely.

"That other girl I mentioned. Phoebe. She's in this hospital. I need to..." Julian trailed off. Why should he bother trying to explain himself like a naughty child? "I'll be back soon."

Robert gave a flick of his wrist as if to say, *Do as you please.*

Julian summoned up a small smile for Lily. "See you later."

She smiled back and nodded.

Julian glanced at his dad. Robert refused to meet his gaze. *So much for him being proud of me,* Julian thought bitterly as he left the room.

CHAPTER 26

Julian pressed the intercom button and told the nurse on duty he was there to see Phoebe. She replied that she would have to check if it was OK with the police. After several minutes, the nurse came back on the intercom and buzzed him into the ward.

She pointed Julian to Phoebe's room, saying, "She managed some breakfast this morning, but she's still very weak."

Butterflies fluttering in his stomach like he was heading into a job interview, he opened the door and peered inside. Phoebe was lying on her back, eyes closed. A gauze pad covered the cut on her head. An IV snaked from her arm. The room was stuffily warm. The blue tinge was gone from her lips, and there was a faint flush in her cheeks. He padded to her bedside, afraid to wake her, yet hoping she would open her eyes.

He smiled when her eyelids fluttered apart, his heart quickening as her bottomless blue eyes focussed on him.

"Hi." Phoebe's voice was hoarse and whispery.

"How are you feeling?"

"How the fuck do you think I'm feeling?"

Julian's smile broadened at the tetchy response. "I think you're going to be just fine."

They looked at each other for a moment. "I'm sorry," said Phoebe, her chapped lips shaping the words slowly as if they were foreign to her.

"What for?"

"For being such a bitch."

Julian shook his head. "I'm the one who should be sorry. I thought I knew it all, but I knew nothing." He glanced around as if to make sure they were alone, before murmuring, *"Well, well, well."*

Phoebe shuddered as if a draught had touched her. "She spoke to me."

"Who did?"

"Susan."

Now it was Julian's turn to give a little shudder. "What did she say?"

"She said, *I'm so happy you're here. I've been so lonely for so long.*" Phoebe's voice hitched as if she was fighting tears. "I thought I'd be down there with her forever."

As if reaching to stroke a temperamental cat, Julian tentatively laid his hand on hers. His heart quickened again as she turned her hand over and curled her fingers into his.

"She told me other stuff," went on Phoebe. "About her family, her job, her Rupert."

Julian frowned. "Rupert? The man you were supposed to meet?"

"*We're in love. We're starting a family of our own.* She kept saying that over and over, like a song stuck on fucking repeat." Phoebe squeezed her eyes shut. "I can still hear her voice in my head."

Seeing her distress, Julian changed the subject. "Have they said how long you'll be in here?"

"No. Where's Dylan?"

"The police have got him. I don't think they're going to let him go."

Phoebe's face contracted into a faint scowl. "Fucking coppers." Her gaze drifted away from Julian. "My best mate's dead. My brother's locked up. Perhaps it would have been better if you hadn't found me. At least then neither me nor Susan would be alone."

You're not alone. I'm here. Julian wanted to say, but experience had taught him that it would only annoy Phoebe.

They sat in silence. After a while, Phoebe's eyelids slid back shut. Her fingers uncurled from his. Tearing his gaze away from her sleeping face, Julian left the room.

I've been so lonely for so long. Those words kept going round in his head as he made his way back to his mum. He found his dad and Lily sat at either side of the bed. His mum was still deep in sedated sleep. She looked as fragile as one of her dying roses.

"How's your friend?" asked Lily.

"She's OK."

Lily smiled as if to say, *That's good.*

Robert remained pointedly silent as Julian pulled up a chair next to Lily. As the minutes of their bedside vigil dragged by, Robert kept glancing at his wristwatch. It was obvious he was itching to be somewhere else. And it didn't take a genius to work out where. He stood up suddenly, saying, "I have to go to the factory for a while. Can I take your car, Lily?"

"Go ahead. I won't be needing it."

"I'll try to be quick."

"Yeah right," Julian muttered before he could stop himself.

Robert's eyebrows bunched together. "What's that supposed to mean?"

"You're just using work as an excuse to escape. Same as you always do."

"You mean like you use your stupid bloody dreams–"

"Not here," Lily interjected firmly. "If you're going to argue, take it outside."

Julian and Robert stared at each other, their jaw muscles tense from biting down on the urge to hurl recrimination back and forth. With a sharp shake of his head, Robert turned on his heel and left.

Julian's gaze returned to his mum. *I've been so lonely for so long.* That was how he'd felt in London. He never wanted to feel that way again. *You can't die,* he silently told his mum. *I need you.*

The morning edged towards midday. The sun moved round to shine into the white-walled room. Julian stifled a yawn. His head was so heavy he could hardly hold it up.

"Why don't you go home and get some sleep?" suggested Lily. "Your mum will be out cold for hours yet."

As reluctant as he was to leave his mum's side, Julian's body was screaming for rest. He kissed his mum on the cheek, then turned to do the same to Lily. "Thanks, Lily. I really don't know what we'd do without you."

"Neither do I," she said matter-of-factly, but with an appreciative smile.

Striving not to get lost in a fog of exhaustion, Julian made his way to the taxi rank near the hospital's main entrance. Somehow he kept his eyes open during the minicab ride.

The house felt jarringly empty when he stepped through the front door. *House.* That's exactly what it was without his mum. Just a soulless box. It was her who made it a home.

His footsteps seemed to echo more loudly than usual on the hardwood floor as he headed to the kitchen. Henry pattered over to him, tail between his legs, whining. Julian stroked him, saying with a conviction he didn't feel, "It's OK boy. "Mum's going to be fine."

He fed Henry and let him onto the garden, before staggering, drunk with fatigue, to his bedroom. Not bothering to undress, he flopped face-first onto the bed, equal parts anxious and eager to discover what sleep would bring.

CHAPTER 27

Julian jerked awake, trembling with impotent disgust and rage. The room was cloaked in purple twilight. Phoebe's blood-spattered disembodied face flickered in front of his eyes. He blinked and the spectral image vanished, leaving him faced by his own reflection. He snatched up a mug and hurled it at the wardrobe-door mirror. There was a pop of breaking glass. The distorted, fragmented face that now stared back at him seemed like a revelation of his inner being.

"I found Susan," he shouted at the empty room. "What more do you want from me?"

The muffled sound of music drew his gaze to the door. He rose to leave the room. The mellow tones of some Sinatra-like crooner were floating from the living-room. A slurring voice sang along to the lyrics. "I'm the luckiest man alive. I'm the luckiest..."

Julian peered into living-room. His dad was stretched out on the sofa with a tumbler of whisky. The glaze over his pupils indicated that he already had more than a few glasses under his belt.

"Julian," Robert exclaimed, seemingly delighted to see him. He waved for him to come into the room.

As if he suspected a trick, Julian warily approached an armchair and sat down. Robert wobbled to his feet to pour another tumbler of whisky and proffered it to Julian.

"No thanks," said Julian.

"Take it," Robert insisted. "You've earned it."

Julian narrowed his eyes. Was his dad being sarcastic? He couldn't tell. Seeing that his dad wasn't going to take no for an answer, he accepted the glass. "How's Mum?"

"Same." Slumping back onto the sofa, Robert sang along tunelessly to the song's chorus again. "I'm the luckiest man alive. The luckiest–" He broke off, looking at Julian. "Did I ever tell you this song was playing when I met your mother?"

"No."

"Well it was. She was in The Swan with her mates. I couldn't take my eyes off her. She was the most beautiful girl I'd ever seen." Robert closed his eyes as if savouring the memory. "Took every bit of courage I had to ask her out. When she said yes, I really did feel like the luckiest man alive." Sadness clouded his face. He dispelled it with a gulp of whisky and poured himself another generous measure. He clicked his fingers as if he'd remembered something else. "Oh, I spoke to Tom. He's been singing your praises."

Julian's eyebrows lifted. "Really?"

"A hero. That's what he called you." An unmistakable gleam of pride shone in Robert's eyes.

A flush of surprise and pleasure stole over Julian's cheeks. His dad had never looked at him like that before. "Hardly."

Robert shook his head as if he wouldn't hear otherwise. "You saved that girl's life and... and..." He trailed off momentarily as if forgetting what he wanted to say. "And I owe you an apology. I'm sorry for the way I spoke to you this morning."

Julian sipped his drink, unsure how to respond. First praise, now an unheard-of apology. What next?

"I know we don't always get along," continued Robert. "And I know I haven't always been there when you needed me. But that doesn't mean I don't care about you. You're my son, my little boy. Although you're not so little anymore." He faded into silence, his eyes growing even mistier.

Jesus, he's going to cry, thought Julian. When his mum had first suffered her stroke and it was touch and go whether she'd survive, his dad never once broke down in tears – at least not in public. The day she went into hospital, Julian had woken in the dead of night and thought he heard sobbing through the walls. But he hadn't been sure.

He wanted to reach out, put an arm around his dad, but he didn't know how. Sometime during his teenage years – he wasn't exactly sure when – his dad had stopped hugging him. It was like an intangible barrier had sprung up between them. It would take more than an apology to break it down.

With a sharp sniff, Robert sucked back his tears before they could fully form. "I've put so much into the factory. Too bloody much. But I was trying to build us a–" He broke off with a shake of his head. "No. No more bullshit. Truth is, Julian, sometimes I just can't bear to look at your mum's face."

Julian thought about how his stomach always tied itself into a painful knot at the sight of mum's lopsided face. "I know how you feel."

Robert threw him a look as if to say, *Do you really?* "It broke her heart, you know, you staying away all those years."

Julian winced at the words. "It broke mine too, but I'm here now and I want to do whatever I can to help, both with Mum and the factory. I've spent three years working in finance. If the business is struggling, maybe we can put our heads together and come up with a solution."

"A solution?" Robert gave a sour laugh. He took a big mouthful of his drink, grimacing as if it burned his mouth. "Have you got a spare five hundred grand?"

"The business is in debt?"

"Five hundred grand. Five hundred grand," sang Robert, sloshing whisky over himself as he raised his glass to toast the figure.

"Do we owe suppliers? The bank? Back taxes? What?"

"Back taxes," echoed Robert, chuckling as if Julian had told a joke. "Yes, back taxes."

"How bad is it? Are we talking bankruptcy?"

Robert didn't reply. Julian saw that his eyes had fallen shut. The tumbler was balancing precariously on Robert's chest. A sudden loud snore shook him and the glass toppled to the floor with a clunk. Julian picked it up and put it on the coffee-table. He stared at his dad's sleeping face with a mixture of curiosity and sympathy. *Half a million in back taxes. No wonder he's been hitting the bottle.* Julian wondered how things had got so out of hand. His dad was usually scrupulous about taxes. Had everything simply got too much for him? It would hardly be surprising if it had.

Julian frowned in thought. There had to be a way to raise the money – sell non-essential assets, reduce overheads, cut production costs. If the worst came to the worst, Dad would just have to accept the need for redundancies. Anything was preferable to the business going into administration.

The first thing was to put together a plan. Something to prove to HMRC and any other debtors that the business could be brought back onto a profitable footing.

Julian fetched a blanket and laid it over his dad. He went to the kitchen, plucked two sets of keys from the rack, then hurried to Lily's car.

CHAPTER 28

Night closed in as Julian drove to the factory. The alarm beeped as he opened the door beneath the 'Harris Shoes' sign. He punched a code – his date of birth – into a keypad and made his way to the office. A deep hush hung over the building, as if the machines were sleeping.

He opened a filing cabinet. Inside was twenty-five years' worth of business accounts. He plucked out folders containing the balance sheets for the previous five years. As he dropped into the leather swivel chair behind the desk, his gaze came to rest on a framed photo of his mum in her bridal dress, her smile as big and bright as the summer sun. A hand seemed to tighten around his heart. He'd almost forgotten what she looked like before she became ill. With a little wrench, his eyes shifted to the folders.

He flipped open the top one, scanning down the balance sheet, gladly losing himself in the figures. As he worked backwards through the years, a puzzled expression gathered on his face. Year on year, spending on stationary, telephone bills, insurance, equipment repairs, rent, interest on business loans and other overheads had risen. There were definitely savings to be made, but even so the bottom line appeared to be healthy enough.

He took out more files and worked through them too. It was the same story. The business and associated costs had grown steadily. Nothing suggested it was on a path to bankruptcy.

Julian's brow furrowed as he opened a file labelled 'Unaudited Income and Expenditure Account for the year ended 5ᵗʰ April 2005'. The accountants were listed as 'Taylor & Co'. The firm Susan's dad Greg had worked for. In subsequent years a different firm had been used. Julian turned to the back page. The lines on his forehead deepened. The account was signed off by Greg Simmons and dated '23:05:05' – a month before Susan went missing.

He grabbed the rest of the accounts from the filing cabinet. A cold dampness formed on his palms as he flipped through them. 2004 – Greg Simmons, 2003 – Greg Simmons, 2002 – Greg Simmons. Every year the same. Greg fucking Simmons. What did it mean? Why had his dad never mentioned that he knew Greg? Why had he switched accounting firms the year after Susan disappeared? And why did he owe so much money when the business was turning a decent profit?

The questions burned their way through his mind like a fuse to an explosive. "Rupert," he murmured. He took out his phone and Googled 'Rupert, Robert'. A Wikipedia quote came up – 'Rupert derives from the Old High German *Hruodoperht/Hruodoberht*, which is also the source of the name Robert. Thus, Rupert and Robert are different modern forms of the same name.'

Julian squeezed his eyes shut as if blocking out something he didn't want to see, but images flowed over him like blood from a gaping wound – his dad throwing Susan down the well, his dad injecting heroin into Chloe, his dad sneaking up behind Phoebe as she looked into the well. He clenched his fists as if to smash the stomach-turning scenes.

Another question seared itself into him – did Mum know?

"No." He expelled the word in a savage hiss. If she knew, she wouldn't be married to the bastard. More than that, she would have gone to the police. She'd have destroyed him.

Julian's eyes flicked open. He sat trembling and dazed like someone recovering from a blow to the head. A surge of rage jolted him into action. Snatching up a fistful of papers, he strode to the car. He raced home through the empty night-time streets, his knuckles pale on the steering-wheel. His anger propelled him through the front door.

Robert was still snoring on the sofa. Julian stood staring down at him, his jaw muscles pulsing as if he was chewing something indigestible. He flung the papers at his dad.

Robert jerked awake, flinging up his hands to shield his face. "Julian." His voice was a dehydrated rasp. "What the hell are you doing?"

"I know." Julian's reply was ominously flat.

Robert sat up, casting a bewildered glance at the scattered papers. "Know what?"

"I fucking know!" The words exploded from Julian like bullets. "It's not me Kenneth Whitcher hates. It's you."

"You're not making any sense. Have you been smoking that crap again?"

"Oh I'm making perfect sense. My head's clear for the first time since *that* night at Grandma's. You killed Susan and let Whitcher take the blame."

Robert stared at him, dumbfounded. Recovering his voice, he asked, "What in god's name would make you think such a thing?"

Julian stabbed a finger at the papers. "Greg Simmons. You stopped using him to do your accounts the year Susan went missing."

Robert spread his hands as if to say, *So what*? "Greg went to pieces after Susan's disappearance. He wasn't fit to do anyone's accounts."

"What about the five hundred thousand pounds?" shot back Julian. "I've been through the accounts. The business is in profit. So why would you owe anyone that kind of money?"

"I told you about that, did I?" Robert pinched the bridge of his nose. "Jesus, I must have been drunker than I thought."

"You're being blackmailed by Ginger, aren't you?"

Robert gave him a puzzled look. "Who's Ginger?"

Julian's lips curved into a sardonic smile. "You're a good liar, Dad. I'll give you that. Mind you, you've had plenty of practice."

"You're right on that score," Robert conceded with a sigh. "You may have a nice shiny degree, Julian, but you don't understand how business works. Yes, the company *appears* to be in profit. It's called creative accounting. Balancing the books to keep everyone happy."

"You mean you've been cooking the books?"

"I mean that you don't live in the real world." Robert's eyes glimmered with anger and hurt. "I put you through university, set you up with a job and a flat. And what do I get in return? Sick accusations. Do you know what you are, Julian? You're an overgrown child. So I have off-balance-sheet-debts. Big bloody deal. Maybe this coming out is a good thing. It's about time you had a dose of reality." He rose to stand eye to eye with Julian. "Sometimes we have to do things to protect our family."

His heart beating so hard it threatened to steal his voice, Julian said, "You mean like murdering Susan? Why did you do it? Was she threatening to tell Mum she was pregnant with your child?"

Robert's brow scrunched. "Who's been filling your head with this rubbish?"

"No one." Julian put on a childish voice. "I worked it all out by my itty-bitty self. Not bad for an overgrown child, eh?"

Robert shook his head sadly. "First I have to put up with your nightmares for year after year. Now this. I'm done with your nonsense, Julian." He stepped around Julian, heading for the door.

"Where are you going, Rupert?"

"To get a–" Robert broke off, an expression of sudden, nauseating clarity stealing over his face. He screwed his eyes shut and opened them, blinking as if unsure where he was.

"Rupert." There was a sort of bitter triumph in Julian's tone. "That was Susan's pet name for you, wasn't it? You killed her to protect your precious reputation. I get that. What I don't get is why you pay prostitutes to dress up like her. What kind of sicko are you?"

"You don't know what you're talking about!" Robert exploded, a vein pulsing down the centre of his forehead. He whirled and took a step towards Julian, his eyes spitting rage.

Julian rapidly retreated, putting the sofa between himself and his dad. His voice quivered out, "You killed Chloe and tried to kill Phoebe because they found Susan. Is it my turn now? Are you going to kill me?"

"Kill you?" Robert's anger collapsed in on itself like a bombed building, leaving behind a pained, almost pleading expression. "I *love* you, Julian."

The words, so unfamiliar coming from his dad, sliced through Julian's scorched heart. Fighting back the feelings that threatened to escape, he retorted, "I don't think you know what love is."

"How can you say that? After your mum's stroke, she was almost completely paralysed for the first year. I had to feed her, wash her and keep her alive at the same time as bringing you up."

"I seem to remember Lily doing most of that stuff."

"Then you remember wrong." Robert jabbed his chest indignantly. "I used to be up and down all night long, emptying your mum's colostomy bag, turning her over every few hours, rubbing cream into her bedsores. What's that if it's not love?"

"Guilt?"

As if the word was a blade sliding between his ribs, Robert slumped back into an armchair.

"You don't deserve Mum." Julian's nose wrinkled with revulsion. "The thought of you touching her with your filthy hands makes me want to puke."

"You don't know what you're talking about," Robert said again, his voice a drained murmur.

"Then why don't you enlighten me?" When no reply was forthcoming, Julian added contemptuously, "Yeah, that's what I thought. You've made her life a lie. Well now it's time for the truth to come out."

Robert jerked his head up, real fear showing for the first time in his eyes. "The truth would kill her."

"I don't think so. I think it's just what she needs. And if it does kill her, at least she'll be free from your lies."

"You don't mean that. You're upset. Not thinking straight. I'm not going to ask for your forgiveness, Julian. I know what I've done is unforgivable. But I am asking you to spare your mum. She's been through so much."

"So what do you suggest I do? Just let you get away with murder?"

Robert wrung his hands, his face twitching. For a moment, he looked ready to fall apart and collapse in a blubbering heap, but then he took a steadying breath. "OK, let's talk about this rationally, see if we can come to some agreement," he said, putting on his business-face. "I can't undo what's been done, but I can try to put things right as best I can."

Julian's eyes narrowed. "And just how do you intend to do that?"

"Well for starters, that girl in the hospital... What's her name again?"

"Phoebe." Julian's voice was icily soft.

"I'll help her make a better life for herself – pay for her education, find her a job, whatever she needs."

"What about Chloe? Are you going to bring her back from the dead?"

"I never laid a finger on that girl. Why would I? She was dead well before I knew she'd found Susan."

Julian had to admit the statement had a ring of truth. After all, it was days after finding Chloe that Henry had presented Susan's finger to Eleanor. Of course, the same didn't apply to the attempted murder of Phoebe. "So you admit that you tried to kill Phoebe?"

Robert's business-face started to slip. Worms of sweat wriggled down his face. "You're twisting my words." He took another slow breath. "How about this – I'll tell your mum I want a divorce. She'll be devastated, but she'll survive."

"And you get to walk away from all of this and start a new life. No, I don't think so."

"A new life?" Robert released a ragged laugh. "Christine and you are the only life I'll ever have."

Julian raised a doubting eyebrow. He was silent a moment as if considering the offer. "It's not enough. Nowhere near."

"Then you tell me what you want?"

How about a dad who loves me, cares for me and believes in me? Julian wanted to say, but the time for that was long past. Besides, this wasn't about what he wanted. "Even if you agreed to walk away with nothing but the clothes on your back, how can I know you won't do this to someone else?"

Robert's eye fell away from Julian's. "You must think I'm as much of a monster as Whitcher."

"Well, aren't you? For all I know, you killed the old guy who owns that house in the forest as well as Susan and Chloe. That would put you only one kill behind Whitcher. Maybe you're even more of a monster than him. At least he didn't pretend to be a family man, a pillar of the fucking community." Julian gave a sharp little shake of his head. "You know what? I'm done looking at your ugly mug. I think I'll just let the police decide what to do with you."

He headed for the door, giving his dad a wide berth.

"You've no idea what you're doing," said Robert.

"So you keep saying," Julian retorted in exasperation. "But what could possibly be worse than what I already think?"

A frown like a scar on his forehead, Robert's mouth worked mutely.

"Oh fuck this," said Julian. "I don't know why I bothered coming here. I should have known you're incapable of speaking the truth."

He started towards the door again. His dad's voice rang out behind him. "I didn't kill Susan!"

There was such desperate insistence in his words that Julian stopped and turned to him.

"I could never have hurt Susan," Robert continued. "She was the sweetest, kindest girl I ever knew."

A sneer touched Julian's lips. "She was fucking a married man. Oh yeah, a real sweetheart."

Robert's anger flared back into life, swelling the vein on his forehead. "You'd better watch what you–" he broke off, catching his anger. His voice grew heavy with shame. "The only reason Susan let me anywhere near her was because I lied to her about my marriage. Told her it was over in all but name. Truth was, I loved both her and Christine. I couldn't stand the thought of being without either of them."

"So you decided to have your cake and eat it?"

Robert's eyes pleaded for understanding. "I never meant to fall for Susan. It just happened."

"Just happened?" Julian laughed scornfully. "I'd have thought a master bullshitter like you could come up with something better than that."

"Maybe one day you'll fall for someone you shouldn't and then you'll understand."

Julian thought about Phoebe, the way he'd futilely tried to resist his feelings for her. From the outset he'd been both drawn to and repulsed by her vulnerability. Had his dad felt something similar for Susan? Julian dismissed the possibility as soon as he considered it. Phoebe's vulnerability was born of poverty and neglect. Susan had come from a loving middle-class family. She might have been naïve, but she wasn't vulnerable. Not in the same way as Phoebe. Like himself, she'd had the luxury of a safety net to catch her if she fell.

His dad's voice pulled him back to the moment. "When Susan fell pregnant, she didn't threaten to tell Christine. In fact, she was willing to bring the child up on her own. But I couldn't abandon her. I decided to find us a place, somewhere where we could be together without having to worry about being seen."

"The house in the forest?"

Robert nodded. "Susan and I used to go for long walks in quiet parts of the forest. We came across the house by chance one day. I remember I was just thinking how perfect it would be for us, when Susan screamed and pointed at something in the driveway. It was a dead body. It had obviously been there a long time. It was almost a skeleton. The gate wasn't locked, so I had a nose around. The house had seen better days, but it wasn't in too bad a state. There was no running water, gas or electricity. No telephone or TV. Whoever the owner was, they appeared to have been living off-grid."

"His name was Martin Jones."

"I know. I found a driver's license on the body. Susan wanted to call the police, but I persuaded her not to. I made some discreet enquiries about Mr Jones. He had no family, no living relatives. His estate would only have been auctioned off by The Treasury, so I couldn't see why we shouldn't keep it for ourselves. I buried the body in the garden. And over the next few weeks, I started doing the house up. Susan wasn't comfortable with being there at first, but as time went by, she came around to the idea."

"And just how was she going to explain the house or her pregnancy to her parents?"

"We hadn't given it much thought. I realise how crazy that sounds, considering she was five months pregnant by then and it was getting more difficult by the day to hide her bump."

"Five months," Julian echoed. The pregnancy testing stick found in Susan's flat had been purchased five months before her disappearance. It seemed his dad was finally telling the truth.

"The thing is, her parents didn't matter to us. No one did when we were at the house. You know what the forest's like, Julian. It's... It's like..." Robert struggled to explain.

"Like another world."

"Yes. Another world. A world where we felt like nothing could touch us." Robert heaved a shuddering breath. "We couldn't have been more wrong." He fell silent for a moment, then drew in another deep breath. "I still remember the day Susan died as if it was yesterday. It was a humid evening. Air so thick you could almost cut it with a knife. It felt like a thunder storm was on the way. The sky was purple..." He closed his eyes as if visualising it. "I was washing paint off my hands at the well. I'd been decorating the nursery. I was spending a lot of time working on the house. Too much. I'd lied to Christine one too many times about working late. I didn't realise it, but she'd become suspicious. Started checking up on me. That evening she dropped you off at her mum's, then drove to the factory. She arrived just in time to see me leaving. She followed me to Clay Street."

"Where Susan lived."

Robert gave a grimacing nod. "I wouldn't normally have risked being seen with her in town, but her car was in for an MOT. I can only imagine what was going through Christine's head when she saw me pick up Susan."

"I bet she felt like she wanted to–" Julian broke off as something like an electric shock shivered through him.

"We drove out to the house. Like I said, I did some work on the nursery. Afterwards, I went to the well to wash my hands. Susan came outside. I splashed her. We..." Robert faltered briefly, before continuing in a strange hollow voice. "We were laughing and kissing, when suddenly there this scream of... of pure rage. I turned and saw Christine. Her face was..." He struggled for a description. "I barely recognised her. She was running at Susan–"

"No," broke in Julian, shaking his head as if he didn't want to hear any more.

"She pushed her."

"No."

"Susan fell into the well. It happened in the blink of an eye. She didn't even have time to cry out."

Julian clasped a hand to his chest as if he was struggling to breathe. "Liar." The word hissed through his lips. "You're trying to stop me from telling Mum."

"I wish I *was* lying."

Julian wrenched his gaze away from his dad's remorseful eyes. His mind looped back to the weeks after Susan went missing. That was when his mum started suffering from the migraines that culminated in her stroke. Had her illness been brought on by guilt over Susan's death? It made sense. He rocked forwards, hugging himself. Oh god, it made sense.

A haunted light flickered in Robert's eyes. "After it happened, Christine just stood there staring into the well as if she couldn't believe what she'd done. I shouted for Susan. She didn't reply. I was about to climb down the well, but Christine stopped me. The way she looked at me... I knew it would be the end of us if I went down there. That's when it hit me. If Susan survived, Christine would go to prison. You would have lost your mum. I had to make a choice. I chose Christine and you. We got in our cars and drove home and... and that was it. We never spoke about what had happened. Not once. It was like it was all just a bad dream."

Robert's head sagged. Julian stood motionless, rooted to the floor by horror. Long seconds passed. Outside, darkness was wearing away to the blue edge of dawn.

Just a bad dream. The words kept echoing in Julian's mind. If only all this was just a dream... If only...

At last, Robert, spoke again. "I tried to forget about Susan. But as the months went by, I found myself thinking about her more, not less. I started going to the house. I'd sit by the well for hours. I just wanted to be near her. Then your mum had her stroke and everything changed again. I didn't have time for anything but work and looking after her and you. It felt like we were being punished for Susan, but gradually things improved. Your mum regained some movement. The factory was doing well, money was rolling in. The hardest thing to deal with at that time was you. Your nightmares. Every night you'd wake up screaming about Mr Moonlight." Robert spoke through his teeth. "Christ, how I hate that stupid fucking name. Constantly having it shoved in our faces ruined any chance we had of moving on. Then *I* started dreaming about Susan. She would call to me from the well, telling me how lonely she was, begging me to visit her."

I've been so lonely for so long. Julian's skin prickled as he recalled what Susan had said to Phoebe.

"I tried to resist it, honestly I did," went on Robert. "But in the end it got too much. I went to the house and sat by the well for hours, talking to Susan. It's difficult to explain, but I really felt like she could hear me. After that, I went there every chance I got. I looked after the house and garden. I used to fantasise that I lived there with Susan and our little girl." His voice thickened with unshed tears. "I always wanted a girl."

Julian let slip a *hmph*. "Well you never wanted me."

Robert grimaced as if the words tore at his heart. "That's not true. When you were born, you were everything to me. But somewhere along the line I lost sight of what I had. I messed it all up." He faded into silence, looking too exhausted to go on.

Julian's tone didn't soften. "So that's when you asked Ginger to bring you girls who looked like Susan?"

"You have to understand, your mother and I..." Robert paused awkwardly. "Our sex life was... Well it was..." He sighed. "What I'm trying to say is, I have needs. Your mum couldn't give me what I needed. But after Susan I didn't want to get emotionally involved with anyone. I used to see Ginger at the golf clubhouse with different men. It was common knowledge she was a prostitute. She wasn't my type, but I thought maybe she knew someone who was. She asked me what I was looking for and, before I'd even thought about it, I was giving her Susan's description. Ginger found me what I wanted and…" He trailed off into shameful silence.

Julian filled in the blanks. "She and her boyfriend or pimp or whatever Bear is brought you Susan lookalikes. You indulged your fucked up little fantasy, then came home to Mum and me exhausted from all your *hard work*." His voice was dripping with venomous sarcasm. "How many times a year do you use Ginger's services?"

"That depends on whether she can find the right woman."

"Ah yes, I heard how you turned away Chloe because she didn't resemble Susan closely enough."

"No. I turned her away because she was a child. I trusted Ginger's judgement, but I was wrong to do so."

"Didn't stop you from using her services again, did it though?"

"That wasn't planned. After Chloe, I told myself, *Done. Over. No more.* Then Ginger sent me a photo of another girl and when I saw it I couldn't catch my breath. She was the spitting image of Susan. I–"

"Let me guess," broke in Julian. "You tried to resist, but it in the end it got too much."

Robert heaved a sigh. "You don't know what it's like. You've never loved a woman and lost her. I've lost two women. Your mother may still be alive, but she's not the woman I fell in love with."

Julian's eyes flashed at the self-pitying words. "Because you ruined her."

Robert shook his head. "I didn't make her push Susan. She did it because… Well, because she's got it in her." He shuddered as if something slimy had touched him. "We both have."

Have I 'got it in me' too? Julian wondered. Another thought ran through him like a fever – what if the dreams weren't a product of the séance after all? Maybe that had just been the catalyst, the key that opened the door to the darkest recesses of his mind. Perhaps the dreams had been handed down through the gene pool, a sort of twisted biological keepsake.

"When I saw Phoebe by the well, I knew what I had to do," said Robert. "I had to protect your mother at all costs."

Julian's brow creased dubiously. "But that was before Susan's finger was found. How could you know Phoebe was looking for her?"

"I watched her staring into that well for what felt like hours. What else could she have been doing but looking for Susan?"

"You couldn't have known that for sure." Julian stabbed an accusing finger at his dad. "I'll tell you why you tried to kill her – because you thought you could get away with it. She's a nobody, right? What's her life worth compared to yours?"

"You're right," Robert agreed in an unapologetic tone. "That girl *is* a nobody. I provide this town with dozens of jobs. What will she ever do for Godthorne? She'll take drugs, collect her Income Support, push out a few babies who'll grow up to do the same." He made a circular motion. "And so it goes on and on. Really, I did everyone a favour by pushing her into the well."

Gobsmacked, Julian stared at his dad for a moment. Then he murmured, "You *are* worse than Whitcher."

"Why? You wanted the truth. Well here it is. You should be grateful." Robert made a sweeping motion at their surrounds. "If I wasn't the way I am, you'd have grown up without all of this."

Julian scrunched his face as if he could smell shit. "I couldn't give a toss about *all of this.*"

Now it was Robert's turn to sound dubious. "That's easy to say when you've never known anything else. And even if you don't care about all of this, you do care about your mum." He motioned to the doorway. "Go to the police. I won't stop you. But I guarantee you, Julian, doing so will kill your mum just as surely as if you pushed her down that well. It's your choice. We all have to live with our choices."

"Thanks for the words of wisdom, Dad," Julian retorted bitingly, but his face was a map of indecision. At that instant, he hated his dad, hated him with every cell of his body for forcing him to make this choice. "At least now I understand why you kept your distance from me. You were afraid I'd see you for what you really are."

"I never thought about it, but maybe you're right."

Robert's eyes were like open windows. A shock of connection thrilled through Julian, immediately followed by the soul-destroying realisation that the thing which had at long last brought them together had also torn them apart. His shoulders sagged. As if his legs couldn't support him, he put his back to the wall and slid to the floor.

Robert's face showed no relief, but he reached to pour himself another whisky. He refilled Julian's tumbler too and slid it across the floorboards towards him. Julian picked it up and stared at the finger's width of amber liquid as if trying to work out what it was.

He wished he'd never come back to Godthorne, never set eyes on Phoebe, never found his way to Susan and the truth. A lifetime of nightmares would have been preferable to knowing his mum was a murderer. He felt hollow, as if someone had reached inside him and gouged out everything that made him who he was.

His gaze shifted to the garden – its manicured lawns, well-pruned shrubs and well-composted flower beds. He looked at the trees that pressed close to the fence. *Sometimes I feel like the forest is watching. Watching and waiting for a chance to reclaim the land we've taken from it.* Eleanor's words came into his mind. How long, he wondered, would it take for the forest to reclaim the garden if there was no one to care for it? How long would it take for a lifetime's labour of love to be obliterated? Five years? Ten? Not even the blink of an eye on an evolutionary timescale.

He downed the whisky and closed his eyes, trying to focus on its throat-burning heat.

"I know how you're feeling," Robert said with uncharacteristic tenderness.

Julian threw him a sceptical glance. "Do you?"

"You feel like the world isn't what you thought it was, and neither are you. I went through the same thing after..." Robert's voice briefly caught in his throat, "after your mother did what she did."

Julian's lips twisted bitterly. "Like you said, it's about time I had a dose of reality. Well my eyes are open now and I can see that I'm just as big a piece of shit as you."

"That's not true, Julian. You saved that girl's life."

"And now I'm putting her at risk by not going to the police."

Robert put up a hand like a scout taking an oath. "I swear on your mother's life, I'll never lay another finger on that girl."

Julian gave a grunt of contemptuous doubt.

Robert let out another heavy sigh. "Not that it matters if you believe me. It doesn't even matter if you go to the police. Regardless of what you do, by this time tomorrow I'll be under arrest unless I can come up with half-a-million quid. Which I can't."

Julian's eyes widened in realisation. "You *are* being blackmailed."

"Half-a-million," repeated Robert. "That's how much it'll cost to buy Ginger's silence."

"She could be bluffing."

"She's lived in this town her entire life. Now she can never come back here. She's not bluffing."

"How much can you come up with?"

Robert peered into his whisky as if it held the answer. "I can scrape together maybe two hundred thousand."

"What about borrowing against the house?"

"That would take time. Besides, the house is mortgaged to the hilt. This may come as a surprise to you Julian, but between paying for round-the-clock care for your mother and keeping the factory afloat, there's not a hell of a lot of cash left over. I spend half my life shifting money around. Two hundred grand is just about enough to ruin me. Half-a-million and I might as well put the factory up for sale." Robert's voice cracked at the thought of it.

Julian almost felt a twinge of sympathy. Almost. "Then Ginger will just have to make do with two hundred grand."

"You don't know what these people are like."

"Don't I? How do you think I found Phoebe? Her brother Dylan and me made Ginger tell us about the house."

"Made her how?"

"We beat it out of her."

Robert's voice rose in shock. "Jesus, Julian."

A challenge gleamed in Julian's eyes. "What? Are you going to lecture me about how violence doesn't solve anything?" he scoffed. "Give me a fucking break."

"We didn't raise you that way."

"Yeah well, you know what they say about the apple and the tree."

Robert was momentarily silent as if mulling over Julian's words. "Does Ginger know you're my son?"

"No, but she will do soon enough."

"Why's that?"

"When are you meeting her?"

"Tomorrow night."

"I'm coming with you."

Robert shook his head vehemently. "No chance. I'm not putting you at risk."

"It's not up to you," stated Julian. "You don't get to tell me what to do anymore."

They stared at each other, competing in a silent battle of wills. A glimmer of satisfaction lit up Julian's eyes as Robert blinked and said, "OK, suit yourself, but I don't see what good it'll do."

"What's to stop Ginger from endlessly blackmailing you? If I'm there, she'll think twice about coming back for more."

"Why? Because she's scared of you? That woman's not scared of anyone when Bear's with her. Have you seen her pet grizzly? He could snap you in half with one hand."

"Oh I know she's not scared of me, but she is scared of Dylan. She knows he wants to cut her into little pieces and that he's crazy enough to do it. Dylan owes me. I'll convince him to leave Ginger alone."

"*If* she accepts the two hundred grand?"

Julian nodded. Robert pushed his lips out doubtfully, but said nothing. They sat in silence for a few minutes. Slowly, as if he'd aged fifty years in a day, Julian got to his feet and turned to leave.

"Where are you going?" Robert asked with a hint of nervousness.

"Bed," Julian replied flatly. He had no more energy to feel anything. He trudged to his bedroom and crawled under the duvet. He almost welcomed the thought of the dreams. At least he wouldn't have to think about this waking nightmare for a few hours.

As he closed his eyes, a sharp dropping sensation hit him. He was falling, plummeting down, down into a fog of doubt, where he saw nothing but lies. Would there even have been any point going to the police? Maybe they were all as corrupt as Tom Henson. Maybe Mike Davis was corrupt too. And what about Eleanor and Kyle? Perhaps the whole fucking town was a snake pit of liars. And now he'd made his choice. He'd chosen to be a snake too.

CHAPTER 29

"Julian. Julian."

The voice dragged Julian out of sleep. As he surfaced from the dream, his dad's razor-burned face replaced Phoebe's blood-spattered one. Robert's hair was swept back into neat wavy lines. But a wash and shave couldn't get rid of the broken veins in his eyes or the sour stink of whisky that still infested his breath. He was wearing smart-casual trousers and a polo shirt, as if he was heading out for a round of golf.

"What are you doing in my room?" Julian demanded to know, jerking into a sitting position.

Robert held up a conciliatory hand. "It's 8am. Time to visit your mum. Here, I've brought you breakfast."

He proffered Julian a plate of toast. Julian shook his head, his Adam's apple bobbing at the smell. He still seemed to taste Phoebe's blood in the back of his mouth.

"You need to eat something," said Robert.

A sardonic smile lifted one corner of Julian's lips. "Thanks for your concern."

With a sigh, Robert put the plate on the bedside table. "Eat it, don't eat, whatever. Just make sure you're ready to go in ten minutes."

"I'm not coming with you."

Robert frowned. "Your mum will be expecting you."

Julian's gaze dropped to his lap. "I can't face her. Not yet."

"But what do I tell her?"

Julian flashed a sharp look at his dad. "Just do what you do best – lie."

His hungover eyes shot through with pain, Robert stared at Julian for a moment then turned to leave. After waiting to hear the car pull away from the house, Julian headed to the bathroom. He scoured himself under the shower as if he was washing off Phoebe's blood.

Afterwards, he dressed and went to the kitchen. As if sensing Julian's unhappiness, Henry peered up at him dolefully from his basket. Julian made a cup of tea and took it to a lounger on the patio. The sun was rising into a cloudless sky. The roses swayed in a mild breeze. He watched Henry chasing butterflies, the tea untouched in his hand. He heaved a sigh. Somehow it didn't seem right that it should be such a beautiful day.

Lying is the worst thing in the world, Julian. I can forgive almost anything, but not a lie.

His mum's words from all those years ago echoed back to torment him. How could she have said that to him when she herself was living a lie? Had she been trying to warn him? Or was she a hypocrite as well as a murderer? A strange feeling took hold of him. He had the sense that he was drifting, like a rudderless boat. Where was he going? He had no idea. The world around him looked foreign, the familiar seemed unfamiliar. He felt dislocated, displaced. A stranger in his own skin.

Shuddering in the warm sunlight, he rose to go back into the house. He switched on the television, hoping to distract himself from his thoughts. But his mum's voice kept on chanting in his head, *The worst thing in the world, the worst thing in the world, the worst thing in the world...*

"You have to hurt to heal." He repeated the prescribed mantra, but the words rang hopelessly hollow.

Not knowing what to do with himself, he wandered aimlessly around the house. The hallway wall outside his mum's bedroom was a montage of family photos – birthdays, holidays, Christmases. A fit of rage gripped him at the sight. Lies. All of it lies! They crowded in on him like trees in a forest, until it was impossible to know where they stopped and the truth began. He tore the frames off the wall and hurled them to the floor.

The clatter of smashing glass brought Henry barking into the house. Julian sat down on the floor, his shoulders shaking as tears forced their way from his eyes. Henry licked the tears away. Wrapping his arms around Henry, Julian buried his face in downy black fur. A sense of calm gradually descended over him, until he felt able to let go of Henry and rise to his feet. He returned to the kitchen, made a sandwich and mechanically ate it. The afternoon was drawing to a close. He would need all the strength he could muster for what was to come.

Faint lines formed between his eyebrows at the sound of a car pulling up. The front door opened and closed. Robert entered the kitchen, shoulders slumped, face drawn with weariness. He had the air of a defeated man. In one hand he was carrying a bottle of whisky, in the other his briefcase.

Without affording Julian a glance, Robert headed for the kettle. He made himself a coffee and topped it up with a slug of whisky. He gulped the mixture down and released a long breath.

A silent moment passed. "Well, aren't you going to ask?" said Robert.

"How is she?" Julian's tone was indifferent, but a faint tremor threatened to give away his true feelings.

"She's awake, but she's weak. She'll be in hospital a few more days." Robert looked at Julian as if gauging his reaction. Julian impassively returned his stare, determined not to show how relieved he was. Robert shook his head. "You're a cold fish, Julian."

"Takes one to know one."

Robert sighed. "You really don't know me at all, do you?"

"I know *exactly* who you are, although I wish I didn't."

Julian's reply was steady and sure. He realised with a little jolt of surprise that it wasn't bravado. For the first time in his life, he had no fear of his dad, no eagerness to please or placate him. Why should he? All his life a part of him had wanted to be like his dad, but he no longer had anything to live up to. No pressure, no expectations. He was the one in control. If he wanted, he could walk out the front door and never look back.

He remained seated. Even if he'd been willing to abandon his parents to their fate, he couldn't bear the thought of leaving Phoebe behind. She needed him. And he needed her, perhaps even more so. She was the only girl he'd ever felt able to reveal the darkest corners of his mind to. He found himself picturing her intense eyes, pale skin and pouting lips, the hard curve of her jaw…

He blinked back to the room as Robert clicked open the briefcase. It contained several bricks of cash wrapped in paper bands. "How much is here?"

"A hundred-and-eighty-two-thousand. Everything I…" Robert corrected himself. "Everything we have. It won't be enough."

"Yes it will."

Clearly not sharing Julian's confidence, Robert poured himself another whisky.

"Make that your last one," said Julian.

Robert gave him a narrow look as if unsure what to make of the new authority in his son's voice. Julian didn't flinch from his gaze. Robert tossed back his drink, then upended the whisky bottle over the sink. He continued to eyeball Julian as the bitter-sweet scented liquid glugged down the plughole. When the bottle was empty, he set it down with a clunk and walked from the room.

Julian waited for the angry shout when his dad found the wreckage of the family photos, but it didn't come. His gaze returned to the cash. A ripple crossed his forehead. *Would* it be enough? What if it wasn't? His eyes slid to a block of knives. He reached to remove a long chef's knife. He placed it on the work surface and sat staring at it uncertainly.

As time ticked on, his gaze kept flitting to the kitchen clock. Nervous anticipation built inside him like an electric charge as afternoon tipped into evening. He went to look for his dad and found him in the living-room with one of the broken picture frames on his lap. It contained a photo of Julian as a blonde-haired, chubby-cheeked baby being enveloped in a double hug by his smiling parents.

Robert glanced at Julian. His eyes were red-rimmed as if he'd been crying. Julian read the question in them as if it had been asked out loud – *How did it ever get from that to this?*

A twinge of sympathy tugged at him. He mentally stamped on it. If they were going to make it through the next few hours, he couldn't afford to let emotion cloud his judgement. "When and where are we meeting Ginger?"

"I don't know." Robert took out his mobile phone and put it on the coffee-table. "She's going to call."

Julian sat down. Both men stared at the phone as twilight descended around them. Several times, Robert opened his mouth as if to speak, but no words came out. There was nothing left to say.

It was dark when the phone's ringtone eventually sliced through the silence. Running his tongue nervously over his lips, Robert answered the phone. "Yes, I've got the money," he said. "OK. I'll be there."

He hung up, rising to his feet as slowly as someone being summoned to their execution. Julian followed him to the kitchen. Robert picked up the briefcase. He looked at it for a moment, his brow wrinkled. Then, with a sort of broken resignation in his eyes, he proffered it to Julian. Julian accepted it. The briefcase dangled at his side, feeling strangely heavy. Lowering his gaze, Robert headed for the hallway.

Julian hesitated, looking at the knife. His features twitched with uncertainty. At the sound of the front door opening, he snatched up the knife, pocketed it and hurried from the house. Robert was getting into Lily's Nissan. Rewind twenty-four-hours and he would have looked out of place in such a small, cheap car. But not anymore. Not to Julian's eyes.

CHAPTER 30

As they drove out of town, Julian's gaze swept over the suburban houses. There was a time when he would have found comfort in the bland affluence of his surroundings. But now something ugly seemed to lurk behind every neatly trimmed hedge and faux-Tudor façade.

Lies. Nothing but stinking, rotten lies.

Darkness enveloped the car as they passed from the lamplit streets into the forest. The resignation had left Robert's eyes. His dark pupils gleamed with focus. Julian had seen that look many times before when his dad was preparing for a difficult business negotiation.

Deeper and deeper into the forest they drove. After several miles, the road narrowed to a single lane. There were no houses. It had been ten minutes since they'd seen another car.

Robert braked at a broad bridleway that rose gently into towering pines to the left of the road. "I think this is it." He looked at Julian with an appeal in his eyes. "You don't have to do this."

"I know." Julian's tone was resolute.

Drawing in a nerve-steadying breath, Robert turned onto the bridleway. The headlights eerily illuminated tree trunks as sinewy as old arms. The track curved out of sight of the main road. The trees opened up into a grassy clearing dotted with clumps of bracken and gorse. At the far side of the clearing was the Mercedes that had been used to chauffer Susan lookalikes to Rupert/Robert. The hulking figure of Bear unfolded himself from behind its steering-wheel. He'd shaved off his beard and exchanged his biker jacket for a polo-shirt. His thick arms were sleeved with tattoos. Ginger got out of the front passenger seat. *That* cold, slimy thing stirred inside Julian at the sight of her. Her hair had been dyed blonde and was scraped back into a ponytail. For a breath-stopping instant, he found himself looking at Susan Simmons.

He blinked and the illusion dropped away. Ginger was too hatchet-faced to make a good Susan

Julian reached for the door handle. Robert caught hold of his wrist with a clammy hand and said in a dry-mouthed voice, "Whatever happens, Julian, I want you to know that I lov–"

"Save it for someone who gives a shit," broke in Julian.

His face creasing with hurt, Robert's head drooped towards his chest. He looked as if he didn't possess enough strength to get out of his seat. But then, that steely gleam flickering back into life, he drew himself upright and opened the door.

As Julian got out of the car too, a pine-scented breeze murmured through the trees. The moon broke through a cloud, pooling in the centre of the clearing. Julian froze like a rabbit in the headlights of an oncoming car. The moon was as silver and round as a ten pence piece. The slimy thing cinched so tight around his insides that he gasped. The briefcase slipped from his fingers, hitting the grass with a soft thud.

"Julian," hissed Robert, anxiety vying with concern in his voice.

His face ghoulishly pale, Julian stared wide-eyed at the full moon.

"Julian," Robert repeated, reaching to shake him by the shoulder.

Blinking, Julian looked at his dad as if they were strangers.

Robert shook his head. "I should have known you weren't up to this." He sounded more annoyed at himself than Julian. "Get back in the car."

His dad's familiar authoritative tone snapped Julian's mind back into focus. As vividly as he saw the moon, he understood that if he did as his dad told him, things would revert to how they'd always been. He'd never amount to anything more than a frightened boy living in his dad's shadow.

Shrugging off Robert's hand, Julian retrieved the briefcase. Drawing himself tall, he approached Ginger and Bear.

"You!" gasped Ginger, her eyes springing wide.

Bear's bicep rippled as, stabbing a sausage-like finger at Julian, he growled at Robert, "What the fuck is this? You were told to come alone."

"Do you know who this fucker is?" Ginger said to Bear. "He's the one who was with Dylan."

Lips peeling away from tombstone teeth, Bear glared at Julian. His fingers curling into sledgehammer-sized fists, he started towards him. "I'm gonna twist your head off."

Robert blocked his path, hands spread, palms outwards. "This is my son, Julian."

"Your son," Ginger exclaimed with a derisive snort. "Now it starts to make sense."

Bear drew back his fist as if to pummel Robert. "Get the fuck out of my way."

"Hurt my son and you won't get a penny," said Robert, standing his ground.

Ginger lifted a hand encased in plaster of Paris. "Your son and his dickhead mate broke my hand."

"You got off lightly," put in Julian.

"Julian," snapped Robert, shooting him a silencing glance.

"Why are you scared of these people?" Julian's tone was icily contemptuous. "They're nothing but petty criminals. You're a killer."

"Julian! Shut your mouth."

"No. You shut yours." There was a quiet forcefulness in Julian's manner that rendered Robert speechless. Julian turned his dark eyes on Ginger. "They're the ones who should be afraid of us."

Her tongue flickered between her lips, like a snake tasting the air, trying to evaluate whether he was predator or prey.

Laughter rumbled from Bear's broad chest. "You've got big balls for a little prick. I'll give you that. But I'm still going to fuck you up beyond all recognition."

With an almost casual flick of his fist, Bear sent Robert staggering to the ground. Julian's hand darted into his pocket. His fingers closed around the knife's handle.

"Wait," said Ginger.

Bear stopped a stride away from Julian, his biceps twitching with the urge to carry out his threat. Ginger's eyes descended to Julian's pocketed hand, then rose to meet his gaze. They eyed each other silently. Julian noticed for the first time how blue Ginger's eyes were. Like Susan's. A shudder threatened to shatter his thin veneer of composure. The slimy thing was spreading through him like a virus, infecting every part of his body. *No, not like Susan's eyes*, he told himself. Susan had warm, smiling eyes. Ginger's eyes were cold and calculating.

"What's in the briefcase?" she asked.

"What do you think?" Julian just about kept his voice steady.

"Show me."

Julian let go of the knife and opened the case. Ginger frowned at its contents. "That doesn't look like half-a-million quid."

"It's a hundred-and-eighty-two-thousand," said Robert, sounding winded.

"That's not what we agreed on."

"It's all I could raise."

Ginger arched an eyebrow. "What about your house? Your factory?"

"There's no equity in the house. And if I sell the factory then... Well then I'll..." Robert's voice faltered.

"You'll be just as poor as the rest of us." Ginger finished his sentence with sneering glee. "Except for me, of course."

A choking little sob escaped Robert. His shoulders sagged, making him seem to sink lower into the ground. *Poor.* Julian knew there was no word more terrifying to his dad. A wave of contradictory emotions swept over him. Part of him was thrilled to see the bastard get what he deserved.

Another part couldn't help but hate to see this man, who'd once seemed like a giant to him, shrunken to a pathetic shell of himself.

"We're not selling the factory," Julian said matter-of-factly. "This money is all you're ever getting from us."

"Please let me teach this cocky little shit a lesson," snarled Bear.

"Tell me why I shouldn't let him mess your pretty face up?" Ginger asked Julian.

"One word," he replied. "Dylan."

Ginger's eyes darted around the clearing as if expecting to see the skin-headed boy lurking nearby.

"Don't worry, he's locked up," said Julian. "But he'll be out soon enough and he'll come looking for you."

"Let him," Ginger laughed. "Like I give a fuck about that little no-mark."

A faint smile played on Julian's lips. The look in Ginger's eyes contradicted her words. He tapped the briefcase. It sounded hollow. *Like the echo of a spirit's voice.* Grandma Alice's words came back to him so clearly that for a heartbeat he was ten-years-old again and staring up into her sparkling blue pupils. He blinked himself back into the here and now. "There's enough here to start a new life. Do you really want to spend that life looking over your shoulder, wondering if..." he corrected himself, "wondering *when* Dylan will stick a knife in your back?" He gave his words a moment to sink in before continuing, "I can talk to him. Convince him not to come after you."

"How?" asked Ginger.

"I saved Phoebe's life. He'll do whatever I ask."

Ginger's narrow eyes returned to the bricks of banknotes. Her tongue flickered between her lips again. "I want the full five hundred." Her voice was thick with greed.

Robert sighed, giving Julian the sort of pitying look that might be reserved for a well-meaning but clueless child.

Red splotches mottled Julian's cheeks. *You think I'm naïve?* he wanted to shout at his dad. *You think I'm not up to this? I'll fucking show you.* He snapped the briefcase shut and told Ginger, "Then you'll get nothing."

"What are you doing?" Robert asked with a rise of anxiety as Julian turned towards the Nissan.

"Get up. We're leaving."

"Do you want me to go the police?" threatened Ginger.

Julian shrugged. "Maybe I do."

"You're bluffing. If that's what you want, why are you here?"

Julian shot his dad a look of loathing. "I'm here to make sure this dirty old perv doesn't promise you more than he can afford. That factory's my inheritance." As he said it, he realised he meant it. The factory *was* his inheritance. He wasn't about to stand by while his dad sold it to finance a life of luxury for these two scumbags.

Shame dragged down Robert's eyes.

Bear let out a boom of laughter. "That's some cold-blooded shit." There was admiration in his voice.

Julian jerked his chin at his dad, repeating in a tone of savage contempt, "I said get up."

Head hanging, Robert obediently rose to trail after him.

"Walk away from me and I'll destroy your family," Ginger spat after them.

"My family's already been destroyed," said Julian. He opened the passenger-door and ducked into the car.

Robert got behind the steering-wheel, whispering, "I don't think she's gonna go for the bluff."

"Who says I'm bluffing?" Julian's expression was unreadable.

"Wait," Ginger exclaimed, throwing up her hands as Robert started the engine.

He glanced askance at Julian. At a nod, he turned off the engine.

"Stay here," said Julian, getting back out of the car.

Giving him a thin-lipped smile, Ginger clapped softly as if to say, *Well played*. "OK, Julian, a hundred-and-eighty-two-grand it is."

"Onetime payment."

Ginger nodded. "Onetime payment."

"Come back asking for more and I swear I'll go to the police myself."

Ginger chuckled. "Yeah, I bet you would." She held out her hand for the briefcase.

Julian glanced at Bear. "Tell that muscle-head to back up."

Ginger nodded at Bear. Keeping his eyes on Julian, the big man retreated towards the Mercedes. Julian and Ginger advanced to the clearing's centre. His heart lurched as she stepped into the pool of moonlight. Its ghostly rays softened her face, making her look younger. Somewhere in the depths of his mind, a voice whispered, *Susan*.

His arm jerked up to proffer the briefcase. Suddenly all he wanted to do was get this over with and leave.

Instead of taking it, Ginger said, "You love her, don't you?"

"Who?"

A *you-know-who* smile crawled up Ginger's face. "Before I put Phoebe to work, Bear road-tested her. Made sure she knew the tricks of the trade. He fucked that girl in every hole she's got. And you should see Bear's cock." She spaced her hands like a fisherman boasting about catching a big fish. "So if she feels a bit stretched down there, you know why."

A cold tentacle seemed to be slithering up Julian's throat. Swallowing, he thrust the briefcase further forwards. Ginger still didn't take it. She tilted her head, her eyes tracing over his face. The moonlight picked out a vein on her throat. "Or maybe fucking isn't your thing. Maybe you're into something else." She nodded, continuing in a tauntingly soft voice, "Yeah, you're into something else. But what?" Her forehead creased. "I've always had a talent for knowing what men want. But I can't get a read on you."

Julian's lips trembled. The pressure in his throat was becoming painful. He could barely breathe. Ginger's vein seemed to pulse in time with his hammering heart.

"Come on, Ginger. Take the money and let's get the fuck out of here," called Bear.

She showed no sign of having heard him. "There's something about you," she said to Julian, her tone spiked with sourness. "That look I saw in your eyes the other night, it reminded me of someone, but I can't put my finger on who. It's been bugging the shit out of me..." She trailed off, her eyes narrowing to slits.

Julian's ears were pounding like drums. His mouth was filling with sticky saliva as if he was about to puke. He blinked away from Ginger's gaze.

"For fuck's sake, Ginger," said Bear.

"Shut up, Bear," she retorted. She crooked her head further, seeking Julian's eyes. "What is it about Phoebe that gets you hard?" She ran her fingers down her cleavage, her voice taking on a repulsively sensuous tone. "What's she got that I don't have, hmm?" She chuckled. "Apart from being twenty-years younger. You know she could never be happy with you, don't you? I can't read you, Julian, but I can read her. She's a whore through and through." She pointed to the briefcase. "Even if she had twice as much as what's in there, she'd still go out and sell her cunt."

Julian clenched his teeth so hard it felt as if they would crack. The tentacle was thrusting at them. He could scarcely contain it. He dropped the briefcase and started to turn away. Ginger grabbed his wrist. "A whore," she repeated in a vicious hiss. "A cock-sucking whore. That's all she'll ever be."

Julian wrenched his arm free, his eyes spitting hate at Ginger.

Smile broadening, her voice lifted in realisation. "Ah! Now I know who you remind me of. This bloke came to see me one time. Years and years ago. I must have only been eighteen or nineteen. When the guy pulled down his underpants, I started laughing." She waggled her little finger. "He had a teenie weenie little dick. The smallest one I've ever seen. And I've seen a *lot* of 'em. I didn't mean to laugh, but I couldn't help it. There were tears of laughter streaming down my face. The poor sod gave me the same look you're giving me right now. I wouldn't have blamed him if he'd punched my teeth out. But all he did was pull up his pants and run away. A few years later I saw his face on the news. His name was Kenneth Whitcher."

Kenneth Whitcher. The name was a finely honed edge scraping over Julian's nerves, peeling away his resolve. He squinted at Ginger, tearing up. The moon seemed blindingly bright.

"You know what that sad sack did, don't you?" said Ginger. "He killed women. I don't remember how many, but it was a lot. And all because of this." She waggled her little finger again. "Is that your problem, Julian? Have you got a teenie weenie little dick?" She laughed. "I've got an idea. Why don't you and drop your keks? If yours is smaller than Kenneth's, you can keep your money. And if it's bigger, I'll give you a free blowjob. What do you say? Come on. What have you got to lose?"

Ginger reached to unbuckle Julian's belt. His mouth snapping open like a puppet's, he seized her hand. As if realising she'd gone too far, she took a step backwards, trying to pull her hand free. Knuckles whitening, he yanked her towards him as if to kiss her. She gave out a winded gasp, her eyeballs straining at their sockets.

He released her hand. She looked downwards, frowning as if she couldn't comprehend what she was seeing. The wooden handle of a knife protruded from her stomach. He stared at the knife too, Dylan's words ringing in his ears – *The skin was kind of tough to get through. But then it was like the knife was falling into the pony. Do you reckon it would feel the same to stab a person?* Now he knew the answer – yes.

"Ginger," said Bear, his voice edged with concern. "What's wrong?"

She locked eyes with Julian again, her mouth an O of horror. For a breathless second no sound came out, then a scream ripped through the forest. As if compelled by the sound, Julian pounced on Ginger. His fingers clamped onto her throat, silencing her. The two of them fell to the ground with him straddling her. A scratchy sound, like sandpaper on glass, found its way between her bloodless lips. She struggled to push him off, but he hardly noticed. He felt strong. So strong, so alive. It was as if lightning was coursing through his veins. The surrounding forest seemed to fall away. Nothing mattered but that feeling of strength. He wanted more. More, more, more!

The vein in Ginger's neck was throbbing beneath his fingers. More saliva welled into his mouth. He didn't feel nauseous. He felt hungry. It wasn't a normal hunger, but an all-consuming craving for the blood that vein carried. He had to taste it. He had to drain every last drop of strength from her.

"Not laughing now, are you, bitch?" he snarled, lowering his mouth towards her throat.

His teeth were centimetres away from the vein. Millimetres. Ginger's panting hot breath tickled his face. It had an acrid, bitter scent. The same scent he smelled in his dreams. It made his head reel like no drug had ever done.

His lips touched her skin. It tasted of sweet, sweet fear. His jaw contracted. The flesh pinched between his teeth. The lightning inside him was approaching a frenzy. Just one mouthful of blood and his world would surely explode, destroying and remaking him into something untouchable, godlike.

Julian's teeth lost their grip on Ginger. Hands were on his shoulders, wrenching him away from her. He let out a howl of thwarted rage as he was hurled through the air. The breath whooshed from his lungs as he landed on his back. Winded, he struggled to sit up. Through tear-misted eyes, he saw Bear looming over him. Reality came crashing back in, extinguishing the lightning. He suddenly felt weak and tiny, an ant about to be crushed underfoot. He flung up his arms as Bear aimed a size fifteen boot at him. The impact snapped his head back, rekindling the pain in his neck with a vengeance. The canopy of stars swam in front of his eyes. Rolling groggily onto his hands and knees, he scrambled away from Bear.

"I'm gonna kill you!" roared the big man, stalking after him.

The flare of an engine starting up drowned out Bear's voice. Whirling towards the sound, he just had time to cry out before the Nissan slammed into him. The bumper hit his shins, pitching him forwards. Blood exploded from his nose as it was crushed against the windscreen.

Robert kept his foot on the accelerator. There was a crunch of glass, metal, wood and bone as the car hit a tree, pinning Bear between the trunk and the bumper. He flailed about, vainly trying to free himself. His pulverised legs gave way as Robert reversed. Bear screamed as the car lurched towards him again. He was silenced by the front wheel rolling over his head, pressing it into the grass with a wet pop like a melon bursting.

Robert reversed over Bear, tangling the big man's limbs into floppy knots. Oily-looking smears stained the grass around his grotesquely misshapen head. Half his scalp had been torn away from his skull. One eye was out of its socket, dangling by a pink string of optic nerve.

Robert killed the engine, jumped out and ran over to Julian. "Are you OK?" His voice wavered between concern and wariness.

Julian didn't reply. Blood was running down the side of his face from a cut above his left eye. Tentatively feeling at the cut, he staggered to his feet. Robert made to help him, but Julian batted his hand away. A low groan from nearby drew their eyes. Ginger was crawling towards the Mercedes, leaving a bloody snail-trail in her wake.

Julian and Robert were motionless for a moment, not looking at each other, seemingly unsure what to say or do. Then, exchanging a glance, they approached Ginger. She twisted into a sitting position, her pupils shrinking with fear. Her vest clung to her curves, drenched with blood and sweat. The knife was no longer embedded in her stomach. It was gripped in her right hand. Cold flames of moonlight flickered on its blade as she thrust it out in warning. Under her other arm, she clutched the briefcase.

Her voice rasped out. "I won't tell anyone."

Julian stared down at her. The hunger was gone. In its place there was nothing. Just numbness.

"I promise you'll–" Ginger clawed in oxygen and continued, "You'll never see me again."

"I'm sorry, Ginger," Robert said with a strange sad tenderness in his voice. "It's too late for that."

"No," she sobbed. "No, no, please no."

Leaving behind the briefcase, she twisted onto her hands and knees and resumed crawling towards the Mercedes. Robert scanned the ground. He moved to pick up a grapefruit-sized stone and turned towards Ginger. Julian stepped in front of him, holding out his hand.

"We can't let her go," said Robert.

"Give me the stone." Julian's voice was flat and emotionless.

Robert's eyes widened, but there was no surprise in them, just that same mix of concern and wariness. He placed the stone in Julian's palm. Julian turned away from him and slowly, like a cat closing in on its prey, approached Ginger. She was almost at the car. She didn't hear his footfalls. A trace of relief penetrated his numbness. If he had to look her in the eyes, he wasn't sure he'd be able to do what needed to be done.

He raised the stone overhead. It wasn't like before. There was no lightning in his veins. The stone felt so heavy he could barely keep it aloft. Ginger stretched out a trembling hand. Her fingertips brushed the Mercedes.

"Julian," Robert said urgently.

He glanced at his dad. His gaze rose to the huge dead moon. "This is what you wanted all along, isn't it?" he said to it. "You never gave a shit about who killed Susan."

The moon stared down impassively.

"Well you can go fuck yourself!" Julian dropped the stone. It thudded against the ground. He turned to open the car door Ginger was pawing at. She darted him a look of frightened confusion.

"What the hell are you doing?" exclaimed Robert.

Ignoring him, Julian stooped towards Ginger. She clutched the knife in front of her. He spread his hands. "I'm not going to hurt you." He reached for the knife. She feebly thrust it at his hand. He caught hold of her wrist and pried the knife from her fingers. She gave a hoarse cry, stiffening in anticipation of it being plunged into her again.

"I'm not going to hurt you," repeated Julian.

The wrinkles of confusion on Ginger's forehead deepened. She flinched as he stretched a hand towards her again. Hooking his fingers under her arm, he lifted her towards the open door.

"I said what the hell are you doing?" Robert demanded to know.

Fear swelled Ginger's eyes as she looked past Julian. Glancing around, he saw his dad rapidly approaching. Anger had chased the wariness from Robert's face. Julian let go of Ginger. She slumped back to the grass with a moan. He straightened to face his dad, gripping the knife.

Robert halted abruptly, his gaze flitting between Julian's eyes and the blood-dappled blade.

"Back up." Julian's voice was calm but forceful.

"I don't understand. This is… It's…" Robert's bewilderment mirrored Ginger's.

"Insane. Is that the word you're looking for?" Emphasising each word, Julian repeated, "Back up."

"Julian—"

"Back the fuck up!" exploded Julian, advancing.

Robert retreated in small, quick steps.

"Keep going." Julian ushered him further away with the knife. Eyes never leaving his dad, he bent to retrieve the briefcase and returned to Ginger.

She'd dragged herself halfway into the car. An agonised whimper escaped her as he helped her into the driver's seat.

"You're killing your mum," Robert hurled the words like stones.

Julian grimaced as they hit home, but the pain in his heart didn't stop him from pressing the briefcase into Ginger's arms. The sight was too much for Robert. "No!" he cried, charging towards the Mercedes.

"Go," Julian urged Ginger. He added in a chillingly quiet voice, "And don't ever let me see you again."

She gave a quick nod of understanding. Julian closed the door. The engine started up. The Mercedes lurched towards the clearing's entrance. Robert sprang out of its path, throwing up his arms. "What have you done, Julian? What have you done? She'll go to the police."

"I don't think so, but if she does…" He spread his hands as if to say, *That's just how it goes.*

"What if she dies?"

"Can the Mercedes or anything in it be traced back to you?"

"No."

"Then what does it matter if she dies?"

Robert wrung his hands despairingly. "But what about the money?"

A sardonic smile touched Julian's lips. "Now we get down to what really matters."

"The factory could go bankrupt."

"No it won't, because you won't be mismanaging it anymore."

Robert's forehead furrowed. "What do you mean by that?"

"It's time for you to retire and hand over the reins."

A new kind of horror filled Robert's face. "That's not going to happen."

"Yes it is," Julian stated as if it was a simple fact. "Mum's latest health scare has forced you to re-evaluate. You've realised you want to spend whatever time she has left with her. Haven't you?"

Robert replied with stony silence.

"Haven't you?" Julian's voice was soft with warning.

Robert's eyes battled with Julian's, his lips clamped together like he'd been asked to swallow a spoonful of shit. A deep hush settled over the forest as if the trees were listening. Finally, dropping his gaze, Robert said in a barely-there voice, "I have."

There was no triumph on Julian's face. Like his dad, he wore the expression of someone who had accepted their fate.

After another space of silence, Robert motioned to Bear's mangled corpse. "What do we do with him?"

"Do you know of any other wells around here?"

Robert frowned as if trying to work out whether Julian was joking. "We could bury him. I know a place. It's not far from here, but far enough."

Julian nodded and they approached Bear. Julian's lips curled in revulsion. The big man looked like a waxwork dummy that had been dropped from a great height. Quivering with strain, they hoisted his deadweight between them and staggered to the car. Robert opened the boot. He took off his jacket and spread it over the base of the boot, explaining, "Should keep off most of the blood."

Bear flopped about awkwardly as they stuffed him into the boot. They hurriedly got into the car.

CHAPTER 31

The moon-splashed forest swept by in a blur. The dashboard clock read 12:46. Dawn was only a few hours away. They were in a race they couldn't afford to lose. After several miles, Robert turned onto a potholed track just about wide enough for a car.

He nosed the car along the track, the headlights illuminating encroaching tufts of marshy grass. After maybe two hundred metres, the track became too narrow to continue.

Julian glanced at the time – 01:07. It was going to be a close-run thing. They sprang out of the car. The trees were sparser here. A faint aroma of stagnant water permeated the air. A stream trickled alongside the track in a shallow, stony channel.

With grunts of effort, they hefted the corpse out of the boot. Rigor mortis was freezing its limbs, causing them to dangle at odd angles. Robert switched on his mobile phone's torch, aiming it awkwardly with a hand that also held one of Bear's tree-trunk legs.

The path was mercifully flat. Even so, they hadn't progressed far before Julian's muscles were pumped solid and stinging sweat fogged his vision. Every pore seemed to have gone into overdrive, as if he were a wet dishcloth being wrung out. Judging by his laboured breathing, his dad wasn't faring any better. Julian estimated they were about half-a-mile from the road. The grim load sagging between them felt heavier with every footstep.

"How much further?" he gasped.

"Not much," Robert replied.

After another hundred or so metres, Robert left the track. Boggy earth sucked at their shoes as they picked their way through hummocks of spiky grass. Once, twice, three times, Julian staggered to his knees. The final time, his trembling muscles refused to cooperate when he attempted to lift the corpse. Dragging it by the arms, they struggled onwards. They'd fought their way perhaps five hundred metres from the track when Robert stopped and shone his phone's light at their surroundings. There was nothing to be seen except clumps of birch, beech and oak interspersed with reed-fringed pools.

"This'll do," said Robert.

Too out of breath to speak, Julian nodded agreement. Few people visited this part of the forest at any time of the year. In the summer biting midges infested the murky pools and in the winter the area was one big bog.

Robert fixed the light on a bowl-shaped grassy depression deep enough to hide them from immediate view. He approached a copse of trees and searched the ground until he found what he was looking for – two thick, straight sticks. "Give me the knife," he said to Julian.

Julian handed it over and Robert set about carving one end of each stick into a chisel shape. He descended to the bottom of the depression and thrust one of the sharpened sticks into the ground. He nodded in satisfaction. "It's soft enough to dig here." As Julian took up a position beside him with the other stick, Robert added, "Try to keep the turf intact. Like this." He repeatedly drove the stick into the grass, marking out and levering up a rectangle of turf.

They worked in breathless silence, piling the turves to one side. When a patch of earth roughly two-by-one-metres had been exposed, they started digging downwards. The soil was strength-sappingly water-logged. They shovelled it out of the hole with their hands. It was slow going. "This will take all night," said Julian, pausing to wipe sweat from his eyes.

"Keep digging," urged Robert. "It has to be deep enough to keep a dog from digging him up."

Julian smiled mirthlessly, reflecting that murderers must fucking hate dog walkers.

Gradually, the hole deepened. Above Julian and Robert's bent backs, the stars were disappearing into a sky that was shifting towards sunrise. The fading moon grinned at them as if amused by their frantic exertions. Julian could feel blisters forming on his palms. A scum of exhaustion caked his lips. His throat burned for a drink.

At last, their shoulders were level with the rim of the hole. Julian rested his head against it, fighting off waves of faintness. The earth beneath his feet looked strangely inviting. Part of him wanted to lie down and close his eyes. It would be so easy to drift off, drift so far from this world that he would never find his way back.

They heaved themselves out of the hole, rolled Bear's body into it and dropped the digging sticks and knife in after him. The grave wasn't quite long enough. Bear's head rested at an awkward angle, a flap of torn scalp hanging over his face. Julian stared at him, feeling as if he should say something, but not knowing what.

"No one besides Ginger will miss this bastard," said Robert, scooping up a handful of soil and upending it over Bear.

They swiftly pushed the rest of the soil back into place. When the grave was full, they stamped the earth flat and laid the turves over it. They each gathered an armful of leaves to scatter over the grave, then stood back, scrutinising their handiwork.

Julian shook his head in dissatisfaction. "It's obvious someone's been digging here."

"It's only obvious because you know. And it won't take long for the grass to grow over the joins between the turves." Robert glanced skywards. The first blush of pink was ushering in a new day. "Besides, we're out of time."

The dawn chorus broke out as they hurried to the track. By the time they reached the car, Julian's legs could barely support him. He all but collapsed into the passenger seat. Robert slumped down alongside him. There was no time to rest. Come daybreak, the forest roads could get surprisingly busy during the height of summer. The fewer people that saw their car, the better.

Robert reversed to the road and put his foot down. The journey passed in silence. Julian was hardly surprised. Nothing had been said after his mum pushed Susan into the well. Why should now be any different? Perhaps it was for the best. What good would talking about it do anyhow?

As Robert turned into the driveway, the sun peeked over the trees behind the house. He cut the engine, rested his head against the steering-wheel and released a long breath.

Aching as if he'd been in a fight with an actual bear, Julian got out of the car and inspected its front end. One headlight was smashed and the bumper was dented. There were brown smears on the wheel trims that might have been mud, blood or both.

Robert went into the garage. He returned with a bucket and sponges. They set to work on the car, cleaning it inside and out with hot soapy water and disinfectant, then rinsing the exterior with a hosepipe. When they were done, Robert parked the car in the garage.

As they trudged into the house, Henry emerged from the kitchen to greet them. Julian wearily patted him and dragged himself to the bathroom. He scrubbed himself from head to toe in the shower, reopening the cut above his eye. Looking in the mirror to put a plaster on the cut, he closed his eyes as if he couldn't stand his reflection. His shoulders quaked at the thought of how close he'd been to tearing Ginger's throat out. One more second and he would have become... Become what? Tremors raced up and down his spine. As if in response to a silent challenge, he murmured, "Only I have the power to control my life. No one else. The circle is closed. The circle is–" Flinching at a knock on the bathroom door, he asked sharply, "What is it?"

"I need your clothes and shoes," said Robert.

Fighting down the tremors, Julian opened the door and handed over the required items. Robert had cleaned himself up and put on clean clothes. Julian followed him to the living-room where the log-burner was ablaze.

Robert fed the mud-caked clothes and shoes to the fire. They watched them burn and bubble into globs of black ash.

Robert glanced at his wristwatch. "It's almost visiting hours. Just time for a bite of breakfast."

Julian heaved a sigh. All he wanted to do was collapse into bed but he couldn't delay seeing his mum any longer. They went to the kitchen. Julian wolfed down cereal and toast as if he hadn't eaten in days, but there was a void inside of him that no amount of food could fill.

CHAPTER 32

Robert phoned for a taxi to take them to the hospital. They sat at opposite ends of the backseat. The space between them was almost palpable enough to touch. And yet, when they exchanged a glance upon arriving at the hospital, that thrill of connection tingled through Julian again. Something even deeper than blood bound them together now.

They made their way up to the ward. "You ready for this?" asked Robert.

Arranging his lips into a bland smile, Julian nodded. They entered the room. Christine was sat up in bed, slurping tea through a straw. Julian was faintly surprised to find that she looked the same as always. He'd somehow expected her to look different. Sunlight was streaming through the window, lending a deceptive glow to her lopsided face.

With obvious effort, she lifted a corner of her lips into a smile. "Hello you two."

Robert stooped to kiss her. "Morning my love. How are you feeling?"

"Much better."

"Good."

Christine held out her hand to Julian. He hesitated to take it. *She must be itching to know how I found Phoebe and Susan,* he thought. But he saw no such question in her eyes. She merely looked delighted to see him.

"She's not infectious," Robert said with a little faux-laugh.

Julian took his mum's hand and bent to kiss her. Her cheek felt cold and dry beneath his lips. He had a sudden urge, almost a compulsion to murmur, *Murderer,* in her ear. Clamping his teeth together, he drew away from her more quickly than he'd intended to.

"Are you OK?" Christine asked.

Barely trusting himself to speak, he replied, "Fine."

"What happened to your forehead?"

Julian touched the plaster. "It's nothing. I walked into a branch when I was out with Henry." The lie came with ease. After all, what did one more lie matter?

Christine tutted. "Julian, when will you learn to be more careful?"

He smiled thinly. "Probably not until it's too late."

"I missed you yesterday."

"I had to talk to the police again."

"Oh."

'Oh', is that all you've got to say? Julian bit down on the urge to retort. Christine and he stared silently at each other. *Murderer, murderer...* The word echoed in the darkness of his mind.

"There's nothing to worry about," Robert assured Christine. "In fact, quite the opposite. Tom wants to nominate Julian for an Outstanding Citizen Award."

Julian couldn't help but stiffen slightly as, resting a hand on his shoulder, his dad said proudly, "Our son's a hero."

Julian cast him a sceptical glance. "No I'm not."

"Well I think you are."

"It makes no difference what you think." There was an edge to Julian's voice that made Robert remove his hand. "Phoebe's brother, Dylan is the hero. We wouldn't have found her if not for him." Watching for his mum's reaction, he added, "By the way, Phoebe's going to be OK."

"I know," said Christine. "The nurses have been keeping me updated." She closed her eyes, drawing in a small breath as if the conversation had tired her.

Robert swiftly changed the subject. "Hey, you'll never guess what happened last night. I hit a deer on the way home. Made a right mess. Blood and fur everywhere."

Christine pulled a pained face. "Poor thing. Did it die?"

Robert nodded. "Lily's car needs a new headlight and bumper. On the upside, at least we won't run out of venison steaks anytime soon." He gave another forced-sounding laugh at his joke.

Christine prodded him. "That's not funny, Robert."

He caught her hand and kissed it.

An angry nausea welled up in Julian as he watched the happy charade. "Something else happened last night," he couldn't resist but say. His anger turned to satisfaction at the flash of panic in his dad's eyes. He let his words hang in the air for a few taunting seconds, before suggesting, "Why don't you tell her, Dad?"

"Tell her about what?"

"You know. The factory. Your plans."

Now it was Robert's turn to hesitate. Lines gathering on his brow, he gave Julian a look that verged on pleading.

"Go on," Julian urged mercilessly.

"I don't think now's the time."

"There couldn't be a better time."

Julian stared unwaveringly at his dad. Robert's eyes flashed with resentment, but the light died as quickly as it had appeared. Turning to Christine, he spoke through a rictus smile. "Julian and I have been talking and…" His words snagged like fishhooks in his throat. He cleared it and continued, "And, well, this latest health scare has forced me to re-evaluate." He took Christine's hand as if about to propose. "None of us know how long we have left, but however long that may be, I want to spend every hour of it with you."

Christine's good eye widened. "Are you saying what I think you're saying?"

"Yes. I've given over twenty years to the factory. It's time to hand the reins over to someone else."

"Oh Robert that's… wonderful."

Does she mean that? wondered Julian, catching the slight hesitation in her reply. *Does she really want to spend every remaining hour of her life with the man who drove her to murder?* Maybe she did. After all, no one would ever know her better than her darling liar of a husband. And if she didn't, so what? They deserved each other.

"But what will happen to the factory?" asked Christine.

Robert motioned to Julian. "Our little hero has offered to take up the challenge."

Even Christine's drooping eye widened a fraction as she turned to Julian. "I thought you hated the factory."

"I never said that," he replied. "I always knew I'd take over from Dad one day. I just didn't think that day would come so soon."

She eyed him with tender curiosity. "You're not doing this out of some misguided sense of duty, are you? Because the most important thing to me isn't the factory, it's your happiness."

Is that why you killed Susan? Julian asked with his eyes. *For the sake of my happiness?* "Dad's not the only one who's done some re-evaluating. Being back in town has made me realise what I want. And what I want is not just to take over the factory. I want to diversify, expand."

"Let's just get you familiar with the fundamentals first, shall we?" said Robert. "Learn to walk before you run and all that."

Julian responded with a dismissive flick of his hand. "No one cares about the fundamentals anymore. All you need nowadays is ambition, vision, the willingness to do whatever it takes to succeed. You know a bit about that, don't you? Doing whatever it takes?"

Robert gave a nervous laugh. "All the will in the world means nothing without capital."

"Oh I'll get the money. One, two, ten million. Like I said, whatever it takes. I want our brand to be on every shelf in every shoe shop." Julian reached for his parents' hands. "I want to take Harris Shoes global."

Stunned silence followed this pronouncement. Robert and Christine stared at Julian as if unsure how to respond. He squeezed their hands. "I can't wait to get started. In fact, I'm going to head over to the factory right now."

"There's no need for–" Robert started to say.

"Keys," cut in Julian.

Robert's fingers gave a spasmodic little contraction against Julian's. Then he let go to reach into his pocket. Very slowly, as if he was handing over some priceless object, he stretched out his hand and placed the keys in Julian's palm.

Julian smiled. "Thanks, Dad." He turned his too-wide smile on his mum. "Fingers crossed you can go home today."

"Fingers crossed," Christine echoed a touch bemusedly.

Julian turned to leave. As if an afterthought had hit him, he looked at his mum again and said matter-of-factly, "You should get in contact with Grandma. She's not a fraud." Before she could reply, he left the room, muttering under his breath, "Unlike the rest of us."

CHAPTER 33

Wading through waves of exhaustion, Julian made his way to Phoebe's room. The strip lights overhead seemed dazzlingly bright. Tears welled into his eyes. Wiping them away, he peered through the observation window. Phoebe appeared to be asleep. The wrinkles of tension were absent from her forehead. A halo of blonde hair was spread over the pillows around her head. A hint of a rosy glow had found its way into her cheeks.

God, she was beautiful. Not conventionally like Eleanor. Phoebe's was the beauty of the broken, something flawed and ephemeral, which made it all the more heart-rending.

Julian eased the door open and padded to the bedside chair. His phone rang. He snatched it out and, seeing Eleanor's name, hit the red 'Decline' icon. He tapped in a text message 'Please don't call me again. I'm sorry.' He stared at his phone for a long moment, his face clouded with uncertainty, before deleting 'I'm sorry' and touching send.

As he pocketed his phone, he saw that Phoebe was watching him with her usual knowing expression. He gave her a guilty little smile as if he'd been caught doing something wrong. "Sorry for waking you. You look a lot better."

"You look like shit. What's up with the plaster?"

Julian opened his mouth to feed her the same line as his mum, but the words wouldn't come. His lips trembled. From somewhere deep within, rose an irresistible swell of emotion. It burst from him in a flood of tears. "I'm a liar," he sobbed, thrusting his face into the mattress. "That's all I am. Just a pathetic fucking liar. I… I'm the worst thing in the world."

He felt a soft touch on the back of his head. He shuddered as Phoebe pushed her fingers through his hair. "We're all liars, Julian. If we weren't, the entire world would be fucked."

He looked at her, his eyes swimming. "It's not like that with you. You're the only one I can be myself with."

Arching an eyebrow, Phoebe pointed at Julian's forehead. "I bet there's stuff in there you wouldn't tell me."

Julian's thoughts returned to the previous night – the knife 'falling' into Ginger's belly; the car crushing Bear's skull… A breath heaved out of him. "I'm so tired."

"Then go to sleep."

Julian's eyebrows bunched. "What? Here?"

"Yeah, why not?" Phoebe patted the bed for him to lie down beside her.

He remained seated. "I don't know if that's a good idea."

"Then kip on the floor. It's not much harder than this frigging bed."

"That's not what I meant."

Phoebe arched her eyebrow again as if to say sarcastically, *Really? I wouldn't have known.* "Don't worry. If you look like you're having one of your nightmares, I'll just wake you up."

Still Julian hesitated, but his body was screaming for sleep. More than that, the thought of curling up next to Phoebe was too much to resist. Slowly, awkwardly, he got onto the bed. He tensed as she rolled onto her side, hooking a hand across his chest.

"Close your eyes," she murmured.

He half-closed his eyes, but then opened them wide and looked at her with a sort of puppyish fear. "You're not going to leave me, are you?"

Phoebe frowned. "What makes you say that?"

"How much is enough?"

Her face smoothed in understanding. "I didn't write that or do the drawing of Mr Ugly. Chloe did. We always used to talk about getting enough cash together to leave town. Chloe didn't care how many pricks she had to fuck or suck to get away from this shithole."

She's a whore through and through.

"What about you?" Julian asked as Ginger's taunt rang in his mind. "Do you care?"

Phoebe was silent for what seemed an agonisingly long moment, then she said again, "Close your eyes."

There was a firmness in her voice that Julian couldn't refuse. Drawing in a deep breath through his nostrils, he closed his eyes. The room's antiseptic aroma wasn't enough to block out the musky scent of Phoebe's hair. As he exhaled, the tension drained from him. His body felt so heavy it seemed to be sinking into the mattress. Anxiety fluttered through his stomach as he silently pleaded, *Please don't let me dream. Just this once. Please, please...*

As if reading his mind, Phoebe said, "It doesn't matter if you dream. Fuck the dreams. Say it."

"Fuck the dreams."

"Say it again."

"Fuck the dreams. Fuck the dreams." Julian's voice slowed and dropped lower with every repetition.

Phoebe's arm tightened across his chest, pressing him downwards, deeper and deeper into the mattress.

"Fuck the... dreams... Fuck... the..." Julian trailed off into the embrace of sleep...

...He squinted at the night sky. The crater-scarred disc of the moon seemed brighter than the midday sun. Its rays licked his skin as tenderly as a lover's tongue. He bowed his head as if in reverence, his gaze coming to land on a figure at his feet. His lips twisted with contempt as he looked into the young woman's fear-swollen eyes. These bitches laughed in your face. But they weren't laughing anymore. Now it was his turn.

The woman futilely tried to squirm away from him as he bent to crush his lips against hers. His tongue forced its way into her mouth, tasting her saliva. The kiss felt so good. So right. A heady sense of elation surged through him. He wanted more. He wanted everything she had.

His hands darted to her throat. As his fingers dug into the flesh around her windpipe, a hoarse scream tore from her. Her blue eyes pulsed with pain. He could feel the strength leaving her body and passing into his. It crackled up his arms like electricity, swelling his muscles, supercharging his heart. And still it wasn't enough.

The woman's struggles subsided, but her carotid artery continued to pulse. That was good. His mouth gaping, he ducked towards her neck. His teeth clamped onto her flesh, pierced it. Hot blood seeped into his mouth. The taste was sickeningly irresistible. His throat contracted into a retch as he greedily sucked and swallowed.

He bit deeper, gnawing like a starved rat through tough muscles and ligaments. His teeth found their target. Blood spurted from the artery so forcefully that he choked on it. A warm red spray decorated his face as he reared up. He yanked off his clothes and massaged the blood into himself. When his entire body was painted red, he threw back his head and a banshee howl that was both triumph and agony echoed through the forest. He didn't care if anyone heard. He was Mr Moonlight. He was–

An ear-splitting scream interrupted his ecstasy. The bitch was still alive! Well, he'd soon deal with that little problem. He looked down. His forehead furrowed in confusion. He was no longer in the forest. He was on a bed. Where the hell was he?

The bed was a tangle of blood-soaked sheets. A hank of blonde hair was poking out from under them. The seemingly never-ending scream continued to assault his eardrums as he pulled back the sheets, revealing more hair, a gauze bandage, then lifelessly blank blue eyes.

A name rang out in his head – *Phoebe!*

He drew the sheets lower, exposing a ragged tear in her throat. Weakening spurts of blood issued from the mess of chewed-up flesh. His gaze falling to his own body, he saw that he was naked. There was blood on his legs, his arms, his stomach... Everywhere. It was as if he'd bathed in it for some sort of sacrificial rite.

He reeled backwards, falling with a wet slap to the tiled floor. He saw where the scream was coming from – a nurse was in the doorway, mouth and eyes agape, feet seemingly rooted to the spot. As their eyes met, though, she whirled and fled, still screaming.

He hugged his arms across his chest, lungs heaving as if he was fighting for his last breath. "Wake up," he pleaded with himself. "Wake up." But there was nothing to wake up from.

CHAPTER 34

'Anyone damaging or defacing these cells will be prosecuted' was stencilled in black on the stark white wall. Above the warning, a metal-encased CCTV camera lurked in a corner of the high ceiling. Dingy light seeped through a lattice of thick glass squares. Beneath the window, a thin blue-plastic mattress overlaid a low-lying concrete bed. At one end of the bed were an equally thin plastic pillow and a grey blanket. At the other end was a bible. A stainless steel toilet and sink were attached to the wall at the side of the bed. The small cell reeked of disinfectant with an underlying sour tang of bodily fluids.

Head hanging, Julian plodded into the cell. A shapeless grey sweatshirt and tracksuit bottoms had replaced his blood-splattered clothes. His hands were cuffed behind his back.

Tom Henson and a constable followed him into the cell. The constable warily removed the handcuffs, then stepped back, hand on the Taser at his hip. Julian slumped onto the bed and sat staring at the floor.

Tom motioned for the constable to leave them alone.

"Are you sure, sir?" the constable asked.

The chief inspector nodded. He watched Julian intently, his forehead furrowed as if he was studying some strange new lifeform.

Julian's face was as white as the walls. His glazed eyes seemed to look without seeing.

"Why?" asked Tom, sounding more bemused than anything else.

Fifteen or twenty seconds of silence passed.

"Why?" repeated Tom. "Why save her life, then do…" he searched for the right word, "*that* to her?"

Once again, the question received no reply.

"If you don't speak to me, I can't help you, Julian," persisted Tom.

Julian's eyes remained fixed the floor.

Sighing heavily and shaking his head, Tom turned to leave. The thick metal door clunked shut. The lock clicked into place with an ominous finality.

From the neighbouring cells came the relentless banging and shouting of other prisoners. Julian's gaze slid along the mattress to the bible. As if not wanting to dirty his hand, he nudged it off the bed with a fingernail.

Moving like someone in a trance, he lay down and spread the blanket over himself. His eyelids dropped shut.

In the cracked mirror of his mind, a jowly, heavy-featured face confronted him. A monobrow snaked over close-spaced eyes and a snoutish nose. Lips like slugs were drawn up into a taunting smile that seemed to whisper to Julian, *You never had the power. It was always mine. Always mine. Always…*

Julian's nostrils flared as a new smell – the sweet fragrance of roses in full bloom – enveloped the cell. He opened his eyes slowly as if afraid what he might see, but there was nothing there.

The smell seemed to fill his lungs, his head, his entire body. As if obeying a silent command, he closed his eyes again. This time, there was no face waiting for him and nothing, not the banging and shouting, not even the agony in his heart, could keep him from falling into a dark, dreamless sleep.

ABOUT THE AUTHOR

Ben is an award winning writer and Pushcart Prize nominee with a passion for gritty crime fiction. His short stories have been widely published in the UK, US and Australia. In 2011 he self-published Blood Guilt. The novel went on to reach no.2 in the national e-book download chart, selling well over 150000 copies. In 2012 it was picked up for publication by Head of Zeus. Since then, Head of Zeus has published three more of Ben's novels – Angel of Death, Justice for the Damned and Spider's Web. In 2016 his novel The Lost Ones was published by Thomas & Mercer.

Ben lives in Sheffield, England, where – when he's not chasing around after his son, Alex – he spends most of his time shut away in his study racking his brain for the next paragraph, the next sentence, the next word...

You can find out more about Ben and his books at www.bencheetham.com

OTHER BOOKS BY THE AUTHOR

Now She's Dead

(Jack Anderson Book 1)

What happens when the watcher becomes the watched?

Jack has it all – a beautiful wife and daughter, a home, a career. Then his wife, Rebecca, plunges to her death from the Sussex coast cliffs. Was it an accident or did she jump? He moves to Manchester with his daughter, Naomi, to start afresh, but things don't go as planned. He didn't think life could get any worse...

Jack sees a woman in a window who is the image of Rebecca. Attraction turns into obsession as he returns to the window night after night. But he isn't the only one watching her...

Jack is about to be drawn into a deadly game. The woman lies dead. The latest victim in a series of savage murders. Someone is going to go down for the crimes. If Jack doesn't find out who the killer is, that 'someone' may well be him.

Who Is She?

(Jack Anderson Book 2)

A woman with no memory.
A question no one seems able to answer.

Her eyes pop open like someone surfacing from a nightmare. Shreds of moonlight glimmer through a woodland canopy. How did she get here? A thousand bells seem to be clanging in her ears. There is a strange, terrible smell. Both sweet and bitter. Like burnt meat. Her senses scream that something is very, very wrong. Then she sees it. A hole in the ground. Deep and rectangular. Like a grave...

After the death of his wife, Jack is starting to get his life back on track. But things are about to get complicated.

A woman lies in a hospital bed, clinging to life after being shot in the head. She remembers nothing, not even her own name. Who is she? That is the question Jack must answer. All he has to go on is a mysterious facial tattoo.

Damaged kindred spirits, Jack and the nameless woman quickly form a bond. But he can't afford to fall for someone who might put his family at risk. People are dying. Their deaths appear to be connected to the woman. What if she isn't really the victim? What if she's just as bad as the 'Unspeakable Monsters' who put her in hospital?

She Is Gone

(Jack Anderson Book 3)

**First she lost her family. Then she lost her memory
Now she wants justice.**

On a summer's day in 1998, a savage crime at an isolated Lakeland beauty spot leaves three dead. The case has gone unsolved ever since. The only witness is an amnesiac with a bullet lodged in her brain.

The bullet is a ticking time bomb that could kill Butterfly at any moment. Jack is afraid for her. But should he be afraid *of* her? She's been suffering from violent mood swings. Sometimes she acts like a completely different person.

Butterfly is obsessed with the case. But how can she hope to succeed where the police have failed? The answer might be locked within the darkest recesses of her damaged mind. Or maybe the driver of the car that's been following her holds the key to the mystery.

Either way, the truth may well cost Butterfly her family, her sanity and her life.

Don't Look Back

What really haunts Fenton House?

Adam's eyes swelled in horror at the sight that confronted him. Henry was standing with his back against the front door, pale and rigid, his left hand pressed to his neck. Blood was seeping between his fingers, running down his wrist and dripping from his elbow onto the back of Jacob's head. Jacob was facedown on the tiled floor, arms outstretched to either side with blood pooling around his wrists. There was a faintly metallic butcher's shop smell in the air...

After the tragic death of their eleven-year-old son, Adam and Ella are fighting to keep their family from falling apart. Then comes an opportunity that seems too good to be true. They win a competition to live for free in a breathtakingly beautiful mansion on the Cornish Lizard Peninsula. There's just one catch – the house is supposedly haunted.

Mystery has always swirled around Fenton House. In 1920 the house's original owner, reclusive industrialist Walter Lewarne, hanged himself from its highest turret. In 1996, the then inhabitants, George Trehearne, his wife Sofia and their young daughter Heloise disappeared without a trace. Neither mystery was ever solved.

Adam is not the type to believe in ghosts. As far as he's concerned, ghosts are simply memories. Everywhere he looks in their cramped London home he sees his dead son. Despite misgivings, the chance to start afresh is too tempting to pass up. Adam, Ella and their surviving son Henry move into Fenton House. At first, the change of scenery gives them all a new lease of life. But as the house starts to reveal its secrets, they come to suspect that they may not be alone after all…

The Lost Ones

The truth can be more dangerous than lies...

July 1972

The Ingham household. Upstairs, sisters Rachel and Mary are sleeping peacefully. Downstairs, blood is pooling around the shattered skull of their mother, Joanna, and a figure is creeping up behind their father, Elijah. A hammer comes crashing down again and again...

July 2016

The Jackson household. This is going to be the day when Tom Jackson's hard work finally pays off. He kisses his wife Amanda and their children, Jake and Erin, goodbye and heads out dreaming of a better life for them all. But just hours later he finds himself plunged into a nightmare...

Erin is missing. She was hiking with her mum in Harwood Forest. Amanda turned her back for a moment. That was all it took for Erin to vanish. Has she simply wandered off? Or does the blood-stained rock found where she was last seen point to something sinister? The police and volunteers who set out to search the sprawling forest are determined to find out. Meanwhile, Jake launches an investigation of his own – one that will expose past secrets and present betrayals.

Is Erin's disappearance somehow connected to the unsolved murders of Elijah and Joanna Ingham? Does it have something to do with the ragtag army of eco-warriors besieging Tom's controversial quarry development? Or is it related to the fraught phone call that distracted Amanda at the time of Erin's disappearance?

So many questions. No one seems to have the answers and time is running out. Tom, Amanda and Jake must get to the truth to save Erin, though in doing so they may well end up destroying themselves.

Blood Guilt

(Steel City Thrillers Book 1)

Can you ever really atone for killing someone?

After the death of his son in a freak accident, DI Harlan Miller's life is spiralling out of control. He's drinking too much. His marriage and career are on the rocks. But things are about to get even worse. A booze-soaked night out and a single wild punch leave a man dead and Harlan facing a manslaughter charge.

Fast-forward four years. Harlan's prison term is up, but life on the outside holds little promise. Divorced, alone, consumed by guilt, he thinks of nothing beyond atoning for the death he caused. But how do you make up for depriving a wife of her husband and two young boys of their father?

Then something happens, something terrible, yet something that holds out a twisted kind of hope for Harlan – the dead man's youngest son is abducted.

From that moment Harlan's life has only one purpose – finding the boy. So begins a frantic race against time that leads him to a place darker than anything he experienced as a detective and a stark moral choice that compels him to question the law he once enforced.

Angel Of Death

(Steel City Thrillers Book 2)

They thought she was dead. They were wrong.

Grace Kirby kisses her mum and heads off to school. It's a day like any other day, except that Grace will never return home.

Fifteen years have passed since Grace went missing. In that time, Stephen Baxley has made millions. And now he's lost millions. Suicide seems like the only option. But Stephen has no intention of leaving behind his wife, son and daughter. He wants them all to be together forever, in this world or the next.

Angel is on the brink of suicide too. Then she hears a name on the news that transports her back to a windowless basement. Something terrible happened in that basement. Something Angel has been running from most of her life. But the time for running is over. Now is the time to start fighting back.

At the scene of a fatal shooting, DI Jim Monahan finds evidence of a sickening crime linked to a missing girl. Then more people start turning up dead. Who is the killer? Are the victims also linked to the girl? Who will be next to die? The answers will test to breaking-point Jim's faith in the law he's spent his life upholding.

Justice For The Damned

(Steel City Thrillers Book 3)

They said there was no serial killer. They lied.

Melinda has been missing for weeks. The police would normally be all over it, but Melinda is a prostitute. Women in that line of work change addresses like they change lipstick. She probably just moved on.

Staci is determined not to let Melinda become just another statistic added to the long list of girls who've gone missing over the years. Staci is also a prostitute – although not for much longer if DI Reece Geary has anything to do with it. Reece will do anything to win Staci's love. If that means putting his job on the line by launching an unofficial investigation, then so be it.

DI Jim Monahan is driven by his own dangerous obsession. He's on the trail of a psychopath hiding behind a facade of respectability. Jim's investigation has already taken him down a rabbit hole of corruption and depravity. He's about to discover that the hole goes deeper still. Much, much deeper..

Spider's Web

(Steel City Thrillers Book 4)

'So he wove a subtle web, in a little corner sly...
And merrily did sing, "Come hither, hither, pretty fly..."'

A trip to the cinema turns into a nightmare for Anna and her little sister Jessica, when two men throw thirteen-year-old Jessica into the back of a van and speed away.

The years tick by... Tick, tick... The police fail to find Jessica and her name fades from the public consciousness... Tick, tick... But every time Anna closes her eyes she's back in that terrible moment, lurching towards Jessica, grabbing for her. So close. So agonisingly close... Tick, tick... Now in her thirties, Anna has no career, no relationship, no children. She's consumed by one purpose – finding Jessica, dead or alive.

DI Jim Monahan has a little black book with forty-two names in it. Jim's determined to put every one of those names behind bars, but his

Printed in Great Britain
by Amazon